Colin Youngm

SAND DANCER

Colin Youngman

Sand Dancer

The Works of Colin Youngman:

The Ryan Jarrod Series:

Sand Dancer (Book 10)
The Graveyard Shift (Book 9)
Bones of Callaley (Book 8)
The Tower (Book 7)
Low Light (Book 6)
Operation Sage (Book 5)
High Level (Book 4)
The Lighthouse Keeper (Book 3)
The Girl On The Quay (Book 2)
The Angel Falls (Book 1)

**

Other Standalone Novels:

The Doom Brae Witch

Alley Rat

DEAD Heat

**

Anthology:
Twists*

**Incorporates the novelettes: DEAD Lines, Brittle Justice, The Refugee and A Fall Before Pride (all available separately), plus a BONUS READ: Vicious Circle.*

Colin Youngman

This is a work of fiction.

All characters and events are products of the author's imagination.

Whilst most locations are real, some liberties have been taken with architectural design, precise geographic features, and timelines.

Seaward Inc.

Copyright 2024 © Colin Youngman

All rights reserved.

No part of this publication, hardback, paperback or e-book, may be reproduced, stored in a retrieval system, or transmitted, in any form or in any means – by written, electronic, mechanical, photocopying, recording or otherwise – without prior written permission of the author.

Cover design incorporates an original image courtesy of Sam Leighton.

ISBN: 979-8-32841-029-8

Sand Dancer

Colin Youngman

DEDICATION

FOR:

THOSE WE HAVE

LOVED

AND

LOST

**

'And those who were seen dancing were thought to be insane by those who could not hear the music.'

Friedrich Nietzsche

Colin Youngman

'Ballerina.
You must've seen her
dancing in the sand.
Now she's in me,
always with me:
tiny dancer in my hand.'

Bernie Taupin

ONE

Shivers ran up his spine. Even though he'd planned and researched it for weeks, the claustrophobic confines of the dark, dank tunnels and corridors never failed to unnerve him.

Bare lightbulbs hung above his head, suspended by random lengths of tangled wire. The temptation to use them was overwhelming yet he resisted. He had to replicate the conditions he'd be working in.

He counted out his paces, from one to twenty-two. A sharp left turn, and another eight paces. He reached out with his hands and touched the doorframe. His measurements were correct. A smile.

The door creaked open. He smelt fresh air. Distant, but clearly present against the stale corridor. Another twelve paces, a right turn, and a rectangular glimmer of light showed itself.

He walked towards the light. Touched the handrail of the fire door. Although he'd disabled the alarm several days ago, he still held his breath as he pressed down on the bar.

The door gave and he opened it, blinking against daylight. He stepped back inside and pulled the door shut.

Another smile.

The web was spun. All it needed now was the fly.

**

'Ten minutes, Miss Rachman.'

'Mmh-hh,' she mumbled in reply to the voice behind the closed door.

Her eyes never left the magnifying mirror as she applied lipliner to add definition to her ruby lips.

Violet wiped sweaty palms on the ruffles of her pink tutu and tried to forget about the audience. Instead, a buzz of nervous energy flooded through her little body. Today, in only a few minutes, she'd be on stage performing alongside her heroine, the great Semilla Rachman.

Excitement turned to panic. She needed a wee. DESPERATELY needed one. She tried to attract Madame Sophia's attention. The instructor's eyes continued to assess the performance of those on stage.

'Can I help you?'

Violet jumped and took a pace back. She looked up at a slim man, dark hair, green eyes, flawless complexion, and a gleaming smile.

'I need the toilet,' Violet whispered.

The man's smile faded. 'I don't think there's time. You're on stage any minute.'

'Plee-ease,' she begged.

The stagehand tisked. 'I'm not allowed. You'll need one of the lady chaperones.'

'But why?'

'Well,' the young man stuttered, 'You know…' He stopped. Of course she didn't know. She was far too young.

'I need to go. Right now.' Violet stamped a foot, but the man was right - there really wasn't time.

When Violet looked up, the man was gone, the performance on stage had drawn to a close, and Madame Sophia was moving from the wings to centre stage.

A warm trickle meandered its way down Violet's inner thigh.

**

'I really ought to take it seriously,' Semilla thought to herself.

It might be a pokey theatre to her, but she recognised it was still the best her hometown had to offer. She owed it something.

Semilla continued her warmup routine as if it were the Marinsky Theatre. Once finished, she closed her eyes, breathed deeply through her nose, and composed herself.

Through the floorboards, Semilla heard the exuberant and classless whoops and hollers of over-enthusiastic or pushy parents as the dance school concert reached its finale. She recognised the sound so well: her parents were both enthusiastic AND pushy.

Semilla gave a slight sneer at the memory but she didn't have time to dwell on the past.

'They're ready for you now, Miss Rachman,' the deferential voice said from behind the door.

**

Madame Sophia took centre stage to warm applause.

She looked up at the packed auditorium, barely an empty seat, and gulped. It was only now she realised how daunting a task it must have been for her little ones, standing before such an audience. Her pupils had done her proud.

The cooing of two hundred mothers distracted her and pulled her eyes towards the tiny tot waddling to her in full make up, princess dress, and ballet shoes. Tina Straughan – at four, the youngest of her troupe – thrust a bouquet of flowers into Sophia's hands before dashing off stage to a collective *'Ahhh,'* from the audience.

Sophia cleared her throat and stared up to the Grand Circle.

'Thank you, Tina,' she began, 'And thank YOU all for coming to the Sophia's Stars annual concert'. She flourished a gesture meant to represent her thanks but it came out more like a Nazi salute. 'I'm sure you'll agree it's been one of the best our talented troupe have ever put on.'

She said the same every year, and every year the same set of parents murmured their agreement.

'Now, before we come to the moment you've all been waiting for - our very special guest appearance - I have a quick announcement to make.'

Still clutching the flowers in one hand, she shook out a sheet of paper held in the other.

'As you know, our annual concert is usually held at the Westovian Theatre but, quite simply, it wasn't big enough for all those who wanted to attend this evening's event, which is why we've transferred to this wonderful venue. I know this has meant a number of you have had to travel across town, and parking has been a problem.'

She looked at the notepaper. 'So, if anyone has used the parking facilities at The Word library and literature centre, I should warn you I've been advised the barriers are about to close for the night.'

She glanced at the audience. She could barely see them for the stage lighting but she sensed no movement in the gallery.

Madame Sophia decided to be more specific.

'I've been told there's a blue VW Golf, a grey Fiesta, a white campervan, and a silver Audi about to be locked in,' she continued. 'If they belong to anyone in the audience, please move your car immediately.'

A woman in a middle seat seven rows back closed her eyes and swore to herself. Her row was packed solid – apart from the seat next to her but, deep down, she'd known that one wouldn't be occupied.

Stooping low, she shuffled past a line of tutting parents. 'Sorry.' 'Excuse me.' 'Watch your feet.' 'Excuse me.' 'I'm so sorry,' she muttered to them all.

Once she reached the aisle, she took the stairs two at a time.

**

Madame Sophia addressed the audience once more.

'Now, we come to the moment you've all been waiting for.' A frisson of anticipation ran through those in the gallery. 'As you know, we have had a number of successes here with

Sophia's Stars over the years. Melanie Darke, who left our school in 2019, has since performed on the West End in, among other productions, The Lion King. Before her, Wendy Allison regularly appeared on our TV screens, and Amy Cook currently travels the world choreographing cruise ship performances.'

Sophia paused to take in a ripple of applause.

'But, undoubtedly, the ex-student who has had the biggest impact is this evening's very special guest. Very few British women have achieved what she has. In fact, barely a handful – and the one before was also a Tynesider, from Gateshead. There must be something in the water up here…'

Sophia became aware of the audience's bored shuffles. Time to get a move on.

'Without further ado, please welcome little Violet Ridley who has the great honour of performing alongside the young woman who was a member of our school right up until the age of seventeen. Of course, she went onto achieve even greater things. Even I think our school comes second to the world-famous Bolshoi Ballet.'

Applause and cheers drowned out Sophia's final words as she walked backwards to the wings.

'Ladies and gentlemen, boys and girls, please welcome to the stage one of our own: the great Miss Semilla Rachman!'

**

The woman gasped for breath after the short but uphill dash to the car park. She hurried past the man in a black puffer jacket speaking into a walkie-talkie held in front of his face, no doubt eager to close the barriers and head to the Alum Ale House.

The silver Audi's indicators flashed as she depressed the key fob button and jumped inside the car. With a bit of luck, she'd still catch most of the performance.

The tyres squealed as she hurriedly reversed out of the parking bay. Without stopping, she thrust the car into gear and raced towards the exit, ignoring the attendant and his walkie-talkie.

Such was her haste, she also didn't notice the sign at the exit. It read: *'Car Park Now Open 24 hours.'*

The Audi sped down Harton Quay before it screeched to a halt when she saw the road ahead blocked by people. The driver abandoned her car on double-yellows near the 1865 Monument and fought her way through the crowd.

She caught snatches of conversation.

'What a rip-off.'

'The little girl must be so disappointed.'

'I divvent think it was ever gonna happen. I reckon it was all a big con.'

The woman didn't join the dots at first. Not until she reached Dalton's Lane where she realised where the people were coming from: the Customs House.

'I can't have missed her performance. Surely it wouldn't be over so quickly,' she thought.

Then the snippets of conversation began to resonate.

'Sneaky way of making money, I say.'

'I'm going to make a complaint.'

The woman noticed children crying. They asked questions no-one could answer.

'I think she's got too big for her boots.'

'Aye, fame's turned her head, for sure.'

She was at the Customs House door now. A tearful Madame Sophia stood in the entrance, furious and broken at the same time.

Madame Sophia saw the woman approaching and strode towards her.

'You've made a fool out of me,' she said.

'Pardon?' the woman replied, genuinely confused.

'Where's she gone?'

'I don't know what you mean.'

'Semilla, is what I mean. She didn't show. Left poor Violet standing on that big stage all by herself, hundreds of people disappointed. My reputation shot.'

The woman ran a hand through hair damp with sweat. 'I haven't a clue what you're talking about.'

Madame Sophia jabbed a finger at the woman. 'After everything I've done for her, for your family, and she didn't even have the decency to let me know.'

The woman's brow remained furrowed.

'Don't give me that look,' Madame Sophia continued. 'She's disappeared into thin air without so much as a by-your-leave.'

She spat out her closing words.

'I have no time for Prima Donas. Fame has obviously turned your daughter's head. You've created a monster, Mrs Rachman, and I want nothing more to do with her.'

TWO

Ryan Jarrod stared blankly at the screen in front of him.

He'd typed in the URL, input the unique username and password he'd received in an earlier e-mail, clicked on the first tab labelled *'Evidence and Procedure'* and, from the sub-menu, chose *'PACE Code 3: Detention and Treatment of Persons.'*

Ten minutes later, he'd progressed no further.

If technical problems hadn't delayed the start of the on-line DI exam, he'd be sailing through it. As it were, he'd received the text message just as he was about to switch off his phone.

He glared at the monitor screen, shook his head, and blinked. Instead of the multiple-choice questions, all he saw was the message he'd read on his phone from his DCI, Stephen Danskin.

'Hope the exam went well. I know you won't see this until you're done so, when you do read it, get your arse into gear. Hannah's in labour.'

Ryan pushed back his chair.

'Sod this for a game of soldiers.'

He left the conference room and headed towards a different future to the one he'd envisaged less than half an hour ago.

**

The maternity unit at the Royal Victoria Infirmary is amongst the largest in Britain. Set directly opposite the original Newcastle University building, the hospital lies in the shadow of Ryan's beloved St. James' Park football stadium.

Football was the last thing on Ryan's mind as he discovered a new one-way system in operation in the nearby streets.

'Not more bloody cycle lanes going in,' he cursed, hammering the horn of his little Peugeot in the hope traffic would part like the Red Sea.

When it didn't, he abandoned his vehicle in a side street and ran towards the hospital.

He speed-read the signage, followed the wrong-coloured line on the floor, retraced his steps, and finally found the maternity unit on Level Four of the Leazes Wing.

'Hannah Graves,' he heavy-breathed to the nurse at the desk.

She gave him directions which he didn't listen to, got lost again, and stumbled across Ward Forty-One by accident, five minutes later.

He dashed through the door and stopped dead in his tracks.

'What the…?'

Hannah Graves sat on a high-backed chair next to her bed, fully clothed, with nothing but her overnight bag cradled in her arms.

Stephen Danskin perched on the edge of his stepdaughter's bed. He saw Ryan first and gave him a sheepish smile.

'What's wrong with the baby? Where is he?' Ryan stuttered.

'Relax, Ry,' Hannah said. She patted her tummy. 'He's in here.'

'Shouldn't you be in bed?'

'I've been in. Now, I'm out again.'

'Well you need get back in, then. That's an order, DS Graves.'

Danskin spoke next. 'She's aal reet where she is, bonny lad. Nothing's going to happen. Not today, anyway.'

'Oh aye? Since when did you become a gynaecologist, like?'

'He's not,' a voice said over his shoulder. 'I'm Moussa Khalife. I'm Hannah's midwife.'

Ryan took the offered hand. 'You're a man.'

'Last time I looked, yes,' Khalife chuckled. 'Don't worry - they all say that.'

'What's going on, doctor? Or nurse. Or whatever. I'm confused.'

Hannah rolled her eyes at Ryan's stuttered efforts. 'False labour, Ry. I've had a false alarm, that's all.'

'How do you know?' He addressed his next question to Khalife. 'Surely she must know whether she's in labour or not?'

'Mr Jarrod, a false labour doesn't mean Hannah's imagining things. The contractions are very real. They're quite common. So common, in fact, they have a name: they're called Braxton-Hicks contractions.'

'Isn't that what the Large Hadron Collider's for?'

'That's Higgs-Bosun, Mr Jarrod.'

'I know, man. I'm just taking the piss.'

'Ryan!' Hannah scolded.

Khalife gave her a warm smile. 'Don't worry, Hannah. I've heard a lot worse, believe me. It's okay, Mr Jarrod. I know this is a stressful time for you but I assure you baby just isn't ready yet.'

'How do you know? I mean, apart from being a midhusband, and all that?'

'Mainly, because Miss Graves' cervix isn't dilated to six centimetres.'

Ryan's eyes screwed up at the thought. 'Okay. Might it not grow, or whatever the technical term is?'

'Of course it will. But only when Mum and baby are ready. Which isn't yet.'

Ryan puffed out his cheeks. 'How long will she be in for?' he asked Khalife.

'I am here you know, Ryan,' Hannah chided.

'About another hour should do it,' Khalife said.

'An hour? You mean you're sending her home?'

'Hello? I said, *'I'm still here'*, Hannah complained.

Khalife smiled. 'It may be days or perhaps a couple of weeks before we see her here again.'

Ryan shook his head. 'Jeez.'

Stephen Danskin raised himself from the bed and slapped Ryan on the back. 'We've got work to do, Jarrod. Or should I be saying Detective Inspector Jarrod?'

Ryan's eyelids slid shut. 'Nah. The exam was delayed, which means I saw your message before it started. I bailed oot.'

'You what?' Hannah and Danskin said together.

'What was I supposed to do, man? Pretend nowt was happening? I had to be here.'

Danskin looked at Hannah. Gave a slight nod. '*He's right,*' it said.

'Of course you had,' Hannah reassured, her voice soft. 'And I love you for it.'

Ryan smiled. 'And I love you, too.' He shifted his gaze towards Danskin. 'And there'll be other exams. Just means you're stuck with me for a bit longer, sir.'

Danskin squeezed his protégé's shoulder. 'Suits me just fine, Jarrod; suits me just fine. I'll see you at the station once you've got Hannah settled back in at home.'

**

The Executive Mayor of Tyne South Bank fiddled with his cufflinks as the reconvened joint committee on Planning and Climate dragged on. The Mayor's attendance wasn't mandatory but, such was the rarity of a joint committee and the strength of opposition to the plan, he believed his presence might be enough to ensure the decision swayed towards his preference.

More importantly, last night's session provided the perfect excuse to switch off his phone and silence the torrent of vexatious calls of his ex-wife. Anything, even a second day of circuitous discussions around the detoxing of derelict dockland, was better than that.

His Samsung remained in blissful hibernation, silent in his jacket pocket. Not so the committee. A red-faced man was in full flow at the far end of the table, pointing a finger towards an opposition councillor sat beneath a portrait of Catherine Cookson.

'This project,' the man shouted, 'Will entirely transform the disused graving docks. While dock four will be infilled, the refurbishment of the other three enable them to be put to public and commercial use.'

The woman opposite shook her head. 'You need to remember the river is a marine wildlife habitat. Any development works must consider the ecological sensitivities. I don't see any evidence which shows conservation matters have been taken into account.'

'Hah! I'd expect such nonsense from a Green candidate, not you. Listen, you need remember the contamination legacy from the ground's industrial past. Preliminary work already shows the site has high levels of metals and hydrocarbons. It also sits inside an area badly hit by chemical discharge. This plan will improve, not damage, the environment. Unless, of course, you like the idea of three-headed newts or man-eating seagulls.'

Cue both raucous laughter of support and vociferous opposition.

'Mr Mayor,' the woman councillor pleaded, 'I implore you to ensure the suspension of the works remains in place until a full ecological impact analysis has been undertaken.'

'It's the joint committee's decision, not the Mayor's,' the red-faced man insisted.

The Mayor rolled his eyes. 'I think we need a time-out to let emotions die down. I suggest fifteen minutes. No fisticuffs in the coffee bar, please.'

He meant it as a joke but, by the look on the faces around the table, the reprimand was well-timed.

Although tensions remained high, the prospect of caffeine and pastries calmed tempers. There was even a hint of reconciliation as councillors mingled together in the queue, sharing small talk; although the Mayor hung around at the back of the line, keen to appear neutral.

'Mr Mayor…'

He turned to find his personal assistant at his elbow. Intelligent and pretty with the hint of a French accent, Charlotte Spencer had the added bonus of being damn good at her job. Never shy of long hours, papers and agendas always prepared, briefing papers spot-on and relevant, Charlotte also had the uncanny knack of keeping the Mayor's ex at arm's length from him.

Until now.

'She's not going to give up,' Charlotte said. 'Third time this morning, and six last night.'

The Mayor puffed out his cheeks. 'I thought she might have calmed down by now. She's the only person I know who can put someone in the doghouse when they prefer being a stray.'

'I think you should call her.'

'Charlotte, I've sat through hours of this damn meeting. I'm not going to leave it now.'

'I think you should.'

The Mayor's brow wrinkled. 'That's not like you. Everything okay?'

'She says she's called the police.'

He groaned. 'What's she made up about me this time?'

Charlotte smiled. 'There's only one way to find out - call her.'

'Jeez,' he whistled. Before he slipped away, he asked Charlotte to order a double espresso.

In a corner of the seated area, he switched on his phone, saw more than a dozen missed calls, and rang his wife. *Ex*-wife, he reminded himself.

She answered almost before he heard the ringtone.

'Bastard!'

'You've met my parents. You know I'm not.' It only served to irritate her more.

'Don't play silly buggers with me! You'll be getting visitors soon. I just thought you should know.'

'Ah yes: Charlotte said. What have I done now?'

'As if you don't know. You've finally done what you threatened all those years ago.'

The Mayor rolled his eyes. 'Remind me what that was, again? I've been accused of so much...'

'You've taken my daughter from me.'

'Elizabeth, I have absolutely zero idea what you're talking about.'

'Yes. You. Do,' she hissed. 'You made up the car park shit to get me out the way, didn't you?'

He shook his head. 'I think you need help; I really do.'

'Damn fucking right I need help. That's why I called the police. They'll be with you any minute. Don't think you'll get away with this. I'll get my Semilla back and you'll never see her again.'

'Semilla isn't a kid. She'll see me whenever she wants.' A chord struck in the recesses of his mind. 'Wait: what do you mean by you'll '*Get her back*'? She's already with you, right?'

'You think you're so clever, don't you? Well, you can't fool me. I know that's why you weren't in the audience with me last night, and I *know* you snatched her. You'll pay for it, I promise you.'

**

Ryan's drive back to the Forth Street station from Hannah's Jesmond apartment was conducted on autopilot, his mind lost in a world of umbilicals, placenta, and six-centimetre dilations.

Today may have been a false alarm but soon, possibly tomorrow or the next day or the day after, he'd be a father. Just as he feared becoming overwhelmed by the thought, his mobile jarred him into the real world.

'Jarrod,' he answered on hands-free.

'Ah good.' The voice of Stephen Danskin. 'Sounds like you're on the move.'

'Aye, sir. Hannah's safely home. I'm on my way in.'

'Great timing. There's a new case landed on me desk. Not sure how significant it is but the Super specifically asked for us two to oversee it.'

'What about DI Parker?'

'Lyall's cool with it. He knows what happened today with the exam and he's as keen as I am to see you progress. He'll be on hand to assist but no more.'

Ryan joined the traffic queuing for the Central Motorway. 'Where's the crime scene?'

'South Shields. Customs House theatre.'

'I've seen it, sir. It was the butler.'

'Very funny. How far from HQ are you?'

'Just a couple of minutes, traffic permitting.'

'Good. There's a few things we need to discuss about the case first.'

'Like I said, it's the butler. End of discussion.'

Danskin laughed. 'It's not a murder. It's a possible abduction. A lass.'

'Christ.' Ryan hated child abduction cases at the best of times. With fatherhood so close, this one chilled him to the bone. He shifted the car into gear and crawled forward a few yards. 'How old?'

'Well, when I say lass, she's early twenties.'

'When did she go missing?'

'Last night.'

'What? So, why are we on the case? She's probably just copped off with somebody and stayed at his.' Ryan entered the motorway and came off at the next exit, no more than a hundred yards after joining, and made his way down towards the river via Broad Chare. 'Surely it's a uniform job at this stage until they find hard evidence she's been taken?'

'This is a bit different,' the DCI said. 'The missing girl is Semilla Rachman.'

Ryan ran the name through his head and came up with nothing. 'Should I have heard of her?'

'Apparently, yes. Divvent worry, though. I don't know her, either. She's a ballet dancer, it seems.'

Ryan drove along the Quayside. 'That'll be why I've never heard of her.'

'Aye, but not only is she famous, her dad's the Mayor of Tyne South Bank.'

'Now I get it. I'll be no more than a couple of minutes.'

Ryan heard Danskin's tongue click against the roof of his mouth.

'I don't think you do get it, Jarrod. You see, the girl's mother is convinced the Mayor's behind it all.'

THREE

Superintendent Maynard perched on Stephen Danskin's desk, so close the DCI's nostrils flared at the scent of her perfume. Lyall Parker was in the room, too, when Ryan entered.

'Stephen, fill us in on the details we have,' Sam Maynard instructed.

'The alleged missing person is Semilla Rachman. She's a member of the Bolshoi Ballet. Even I've heard of them so she must be canny good at what she does.'

'What else do we know about her?' Ryan asked, more to ensure the others were as up-to-speed as he was.

'Born in South Shields, she's the daughter of Elizabeth and Stephen Rachman. Parents are divorced: mother lives in Cleadon Village, father is Executive Mayor of Tyne South Bank.'

'I know she was last seen at the Customs House theatre. Why was she there?' Ryan asked.

Sam Maynard filled in the blanks. 'Seemingly, she is an ex-pupil of the Sophia's Stars School of Dancing. It was their annual concert last night and Miss Rachman was due to perform as a special guest.'

'She came back from the Bolshoi just to perform in her hometown?'

'Not exactly,' Danskin explained. The way things are with Ukraine, the Bolshoi are *taking a break*.' Miss Rachman's been home for a few months now.'

'Right,' Ryan said. 'So I presume this appearance was well-advertised? Folk would know she was due to attend?'

'Oh aye,' Danskin confirmed. 'Place was packed to the rafters.'

'Do we know how she was taken? I mean, it's pretty hard to make someone vanish in front of a capacity audience unless you're Dynamo or David Blaine or summat.'

'That's the thing, Jarrod. Whoever took her – if she's been taken at all – managed to grab her in front of hundreds of mothers and fathers and squealing kids.'

Maynard eased herself off the desk and smoothed down her skirt. 'We wouldn't normally be involved this early in the investigation unless the victim was a child or classed as vulnerable but there's a certain degree of,' she picked her words carefully, 'Pressure, because of who she and her father are.'

Through the office's glass wall, Ryan watched the rest of the squad go about their routine business, unaware of the gathering storm. 'I believe we have a suspect, sir.'

'No. Not a suspect as such,' Danskin warned.

Maynard jumped in. 'And I'd caution against using such a phrase. What we have is an allegation, made by the Mayor's ex, against him.'

'Why does she think the Mayor took his own daughter? I mean, the girl's old enough and capable enough of making her own decisions.'

'There's a lot of bad blood between them,' DCI Danskin explained. 'When they split, the father wanted custody, he didn't get it, and Stephen Rachman swore in front of the Family Court he'd get her in the end.'

'That must have been donkey's years ago, man. Pretty flimsy grounds if you ask me,' Ryan observed.

'I agree, Ryan,' Maynard said. 'But we have to consider the threat as part of our investigation into Miss Rachman's disappearance.'

Ryan shook his head. 'I'm still not convinced she has been taken, like.'

'The missing girl's phone has been switched off since before the show, according to her mother,' Maynard explained. 'It's not unusual for her to go off grid in the build up to a performance, apparently, to allow her to get in the zone. But it's most unlike her to remain silent afterwards – in fact, Mrs Rachman says it's never happened before.'

'Ha'e the press no got wind of this, yet?' Lyall Parker asked.

'We'd know if they had,' Danskin said. 'They'd be all over it like flies on a dog turd.'

'Indeed,' Sam Maynard confirmed, 'But the news Semilla didn't show for her performance is already out there and that's a story in itself. We've persuaded Elizabeth Rachman to keep quiet about Semilla's actual disappearance for now but, from what we know about her, she'll be quick to throw said dog turd in our face if she thinks we aren't treating her allegation seriously.'

**

'Mrs Rachman might be more comfortable with a female officer present,' Ryan argued.

Superintendent Maynard, keen to do what she could to prevent possible leaks reaching the press, at first disagreed but finally relented. Ryan could take DC Lucy Dexter – and only Dexter at this stage - into confidence.

Ryan used the journey to the Rachman property to update the diminutive Lucy Dexter.

'I went to dance school as a kid,' Dexter lisped as Ryan drove through the Tyne Tunnel.

'So you've heard of this Semilla, then, have you?'

'Nah. I did modern. You know, show dancing. Glitzy costumes and all that.'

'Right.'

'It's an odd name,' she said. 'Semilla.'

The name came out as *Themilla* but Ryan was used to Lucy's speech pattern by now. 'Aye. I've never heard of it before,' he said. 'Could be worse, I reckon. She might have been named Semolina.'

Dexter laughed. 'You always manage to look on the bright side.'

He looked sideways at her. 'Me? I divvent think so.'

He sighed as they exited the tunnel south-side of the Tyne. He screwed up his eyes, not just against the sudden exposure to sunlight. 'I've been to the village where the Rachman's live. Lovely place but terrible memories.'

'Operation Sage,' Dexter nodded. 'My first case.'

Ryan blinked slowly. 'Of course.' It had been the City and County force's first encounter with Benny Yu, the drug lord who changed Ryan's outlook on life and the man responsible for Lucy Dexter's scars and lisp. 'Sorry, Luce. Didn't mean to bring it all back.'

'It's okay. I'm cool with it.'

They both knew neither were.

Ryan and Lucy drove into Cleadon Village's West Park Road in silence.

When the Satnav ordered them onto a gravel driveway leading to a double-fronted mansion, Lucy let out a low whistle.

'Nice. Do you think the daughter's money paid for this?'

'Dunno. I guess Mr Mayor won't be short of a bob or two himself. If his ex rinsed him in the divorce, could all be hers.'

The time approached four p.m. as Ryan crunched to a halt alongside a silver Audi and a lavender-coloured Bentley GT. The grille of another luxury car peered out from the side of the property.

'Not sure she'll be happy with a Peugeot 107 stuck on her drive,' Lucy commented.

'Tough titties,' Ryan said. 'Right, it's been a helluva day already. Let's howay oot and see what she's got to say for herself.'

**

Ryan was surprised to find the door answered by a grey-haired man in pale blue suit and shirt and royal blue tie. Ryan thought he looked like a summer sky. The man led Jarrod and Dexter down a broad corridor.

Ryan leant towards Lucy as they followed him. 'I told Danskin the butler did it. That's our man right there,' he whispered with a smile.

At the end of the corridor, the detectives saw a spacious lounge waiting for them through a glass door. The back of a woman's head showed from above a green Chesterfield.

Ryan took a deep breath in preparation as the man opened the door.

'Elizabeth – the police are here.'

The woman rose unsteadily and turned to face them. Behind their puffy lids, her eyes were a fierce emerald green, laser-like and piercing.

'About fucking time,' Elizabeth Rachman spat, as Ryan's preparation fell apart. He looked her up and down and, for a split-second, thought she held a decapitated head in her hand. It was nothing more than an ash-blonde wig.

'Mrs Rachman,' he said more calmly than he felt. 'I'm DS Ryan Jarrod and this is my colleague, DC Lucy Dexter.'

The woman seemed to look beyond them, her eyes darting left and right. She played with her natural hair, mousy-brown and thinning.

'You're going to find my daughter?'

'We'll do everything we can…'

'Where's the rest of them?'

'Sorry, the rest of who?' Ryan asked.

'Police. Detectives. Sniffer dogs. The rest of you who are going to find my daughter.'

'Mrs Rachman...'

'Two. Is that all I'm going to get? We've a world-famous performer missing and the City and County finest send out two frigging kids. Seriously?'

Lucy decided to try. 'There will be more of us – a lot more – once we have some evidence...'

'Talk to HIM. That's how you'll find her. He's got her. You should have gone to him first; not me. Go talk to him.'

The blue man walked towards Elizabeth and put his arm around her waist.

'I'm sorry – you are?' Ryan asked.

The man left Mrs Rachman and extended his hand. 'Kennedy. Keith Kennedy. I should have introduced myself. I'm sorry. It's just, you know, with everything...' He let the sentence hang.

'Mr Kennedy is a good friend,' Elizabeth explained.

Ryan, somehow, hid a smile. 'As DC Dexter explained, we will recruit plenty more officers to the enquiry once we've established the facts. However, it's best we keep this low-key for now. We don't want to spook whoever has Semilla, do we?'

Mrs Rachman didn't reply.

'It's your daughter, though, so it's your call.'

Fresh tears brimmed in Elizabeth's eyes. 'Do you have children, Detective Sergeant?'

'No; not yet, anyways. My first's on its way,' he said, casually.

She dipped her head. 'You'll soon understand.' She took a deep breath. 'Are you sure low-key is the best approach?'

'I think it is,' Lucy confirmed.

Elizabeth Rachman gave a succession of short sharp nods before breaking into a series of sobs. 'I've been stupid,' she cried, covering her face with her hands.

'Why do you say that, Mrs Rachman?' Lucy asked.

'I should have stayed. I should never have gone,' she gasped between tears.

'I think Semilla would want you to be there,' Lucy said.

Ryan looked around the room. Every wall, every nook and cranny, held photographs and portraits of Semilla at various ages, always in ballet dress, usually holding a trophy. Above an open fireplace, an oil painting of an adult Semilla on stage and in arabesque pose dominated the wall.

'I WAS there. That's the problem – I shouldn't have left.'

Lucy shot Ryan a puzzled look. 'Tell us what happened.'

Kennedy took hold of Elizabeth's fingers as she began her explanation.

'I sat through two hours of mindless kids performing mindless routines in front of mindless parents. All so I could Semilla dance. It's been four years since I last saw her perform, what with the pandemic and visa issues and then the war. I was minutes away from seeing her, then I had to leave.'

'Why did you have to leave?'

'There was an announcement. They asked me to go and move my car. It was parked where it shouldn't have been.'

'Who do you mean by '*they*'?'

'Madame Sophia. The woman who runs the school. She taught my Semilla from her being knee-high.'

'And she specifically asked for you?'

'No, not really. I think there were three or four cars she asked to move.'

Ryan finished updating his notes before speaking again. 'What happened next?'

'What do you think? I moved my car, that's what happened.'

'Did you spot anything unusual?

Elizabeth studied the floor while she thought. 'No, nothing at all. Just the car park attendant waiting to lock up. Wait, yes – there is something. I never thought of it before but the car park was full yet Madame Sophia only mentioned four or five. Why'd she do that?'

Ryan said nothing. He'd been formulating his own theory and this revelation jarred with it.

'What happened next?' he asked in time.

'I went back to the Customs House. By the time I got there, everybody was leaving. I heard them bad-mouthing Semilla, then I saw Madame Sophia and she had a right go at me.'

She convulsed with tears at the memory. Kennedy handed her a tissue and she blew her nose noisily. 'If I hadn't gone to move the car, I'd have known straight away something was wrong. I could have done something about it.'

Ryan waited until the woman had calmed herself. 'How has Semilla been since she returned from the Bolshoi?'

Elizabeth almost smiled. 'Her usual feisty self.'

'Feisty?'

'Yes. It's a tough business, detective sergeant. She knows how to look after herself.'

'Any boyfriends?'

She shook her head. 'She hasn't time. Too busy touring.'

'Does she enjoy what she does?'

Elizabeth's eyebrows raised. 'Of course. She's doing what she loves, travels the world, stays in luxurious hotels. Yes, the regime is tough – training, rehearsing, having her every move scrutinised – but all of that comes with the territory. The perks and prestige far outweigh the downsides.'

'Okay,' he said, gathering his thoughts. 'What about her social media presence? Does anyone monitor her accounts?'

'There aren't any.'

Kennedy saw Ryan's look of disbelief. 'She's a member of the Bolshoi. Let's just say Russia doesn't approve of social media,' he explained.

Ryan tapped a pen against his teeth. Time for a change of tactic. 'Why do you think your husband is involved in this?'

'My *ex*-husband,' she corrected. 'Because he's a bastard.'

Ryan pursed his lips. 'If you could give us a bit more than that?'

'For years he's been saying he'd take Semilla from me, that's why. Plus, he specifically asked me to get him a ticket for her performance. Of course, he didn't show, did he? At least, not in the theatre. He didn't show because he was backstage, orchestrating the snatch.'

'You know that for a fact?'

'YES!!'

Lucy sensed the woman's growing anger and stepped in. 'It would really help if you had some evidence for us.'

'I don't need any.'

Lucy gave a sympathetic smile. 'I know but, unfortunately, we do.'

Elizabeth Rachman turned away from them. 'Speak to him. You'll know straight away what I mean.'

Ryan nodded towards Lucy. 'Thank you, Mrs Rachman. We'll do that straight away. We also need to talk to this Madame Sophia. Do you have her full name?'

'Yes. It's Ridley. Sophia Ridley. Her niece was supposed to be performing with Semilla.'

FOUR

'I think it's the wrong call,' Lucy Dexter said as they approached the Customs House.

Ryan disagreed. 'Look, the Mayor's in his office, according to his PA. If we burst in there, the investigation's hardly going to be kept low key. Besides, this way, we kill two birds with one stone. We get Sophia Ridley's take on events plus we get to check out the scene.'

'I suppose,' Lucy conceded, 'Although I suspect you'd already decided to speak to Ridley before we even heard she was collecting her props from the theatre.'

Ryan flicked on his headlights as dusk gathered. 'You could be right,' was all he said.

In the courtyard of the Customs House, Ryan was pleased to note minimal uniform presence. One car, two PCs. *'Suitably discreet,'* he thought.

He drew to a halt and flashed his warrant at the elder of the PCs. 'Anything new?' he asked the cop.

'Nowt that's not already on record.'

'Where's Ridley?'

'Inside, somewhere.'

'Alone?'

The cop shrugged. 'Couple of blokes helping her tidy up.'

Ryan led Lucy into the theatre. A middle-aged woman, hair held back by a rainbow band and dressed in dungarees, was loading costumes into a large cardboard box.

'Mrs Ridley?' Ryan called, warrant still open in his hand.

'Yes. That's me.' She stood and wiped her hands on her dungarees.

'DS Jarrod and DC Dexter.'

'Ah, right. About last night's shambles, I presume. I want you to know I knew nothing about it so, if someone's calling me out for fraud, you can forget it.'

Ryan was non-committal. 'Who else is here?'

'Noel Gowland and Edwin Trove.'

'Were they present last night?'

'They were. Noel is our technician, in charge of lights and sound. Edwin is a patron of the theatre. He facilitated the agreement to lease the property to us for the night.'

Ryan looked up to see a man disconnecting cables from a gantry high above the stage. 'Is that Mr Gowland?'

'Yes, it is.'

'Who else was here last night?'

Sophia laughed. 'Who wasn't? Five hundred in the audience, twenty-eight young performers, seven chaperones, and two on front of house. Catherine Nunn - my assistant, choreographer Myshka, and my stage manager, Patrick. Edwin and Noel, also, of course. In fact, just about everyone except the precious Semilla.'

'I see,' Ryan said, still looking up to the Gods. 'I understand you made an announcement before Semilla was due to appear on stage.'

'Did I?'

'Yes. Something about a car park closing and a request for folk to move their vehicles.'

The woman stared out over the rows of empty seats. 'Yes, I remember. Sorry, it was organised chaos last night. I'd forgotten. Someone handed me a sheet of paper and said, *'We've been asked to read this out'* just before I went on stage.'

'Who handed you the note?'

'I'm sorry. I really don't know. There was so much going on.'

'Can you remember anything at all? Was it a man or a woman?'

Before she could answer, a warning shout came from above. 'Below!!'

Ryan looked up just as a wrench tumbled inches from his head, bounced on the edge of the stage, and clattered into the orchestra pit.

'Sorry,' Noel Gowland called. 'Everyone okay?'

'Can you come down for a moment, sir? Just while I finish talking to Mrs Ridley.'

'Nee bother. I'll stop work. Don't want any more accidents. Is it okay if I hang aboot up here, though? It'll save me climbing down and back up again,' he called, sitting astride a beam like one of the Empire State constructors in the infamous photograph.

Ryan nodded his consent before his attention returned to Sophia Ridley. 'Just a couple more questions then we'll leave you to it. How long have you known Semilla?'

'Oh, more than a dozen years, for sure; probably closer to fifteen. I taught her almost from infancy.'

'Would you say what happened last night was out of character?'

Madame Sophia considered the question. 'For the younger Semilla, most definitely but I couldn't say for sure what she's like now. We've kept in touch only occasionally since she joined the Bolshoi. I never had her down as a Diva but,' she shrugged, 'You never know, do you? People change and she was rather, how shall I put it, standoffish last night. Aloof, almost. I assumed it was nerves but would she really be nervous about performing here?' She gestured at the banks of chocolate-brown seats. 'Somehow, I doubt it.'

Careful not to divulge too much, Ryan casually asked, 'Semilla didn't go home last night. Do you know where she might have gone?'

'Why would I? Probably too ashamed to face her mother. Possibly went to her father's. No, I really don't know and, frankly, I don't care. Now, if there's nothing else…'

'I'd like the names of everyone here last night.'

Sophia snickered. 'Don't ask for much, do you?'

'Well, let's forget about the audience and children for now. How quickly could you get us a list of your assistants and the chaperones?'

'Tomorrow morning. I've a lot to get through tonight,' she said, gesturing at the littered backstage area, 'But I can get the names to you by lunchtime.'

Ryan thanked Mrs Ridley, signalled his permission for Noel Gowland to resume his tasks, and exited the theatre with Lucy in tow.

Once outside, Lucy yawned and stretched in the darkness. 'Just the Mayor to see now. Thank God for that. I'm done in.'

'Get yourself home, Luce. There's no hurry to see the Mayor.'

'But what about Mrs Rachman's accusation?'

'That's all it is: an accusation. We'll talk to him tomorrow.'

Lucy whistled. 'Talk about livin' on a prayer. Still, you're the boss.'

Ryan opened the door of his Peugeot. 'Get in. I'll drop you off on my way, then I'll update the DCI and see if he's uncovered any juicy secrets about Semilla Rachman. After that, I'm off to stop at Hannah's. Don't want her dropping wor kid on the bathroom floor.'

Lucy joined him. 'Thanks,' she said, buckling the seatbelt. 'I still think you're taking a helluva risk waiting to speak to Rachman. If the Mayor's involved…'

'It's cool, man. I'm sure he's not.' He drove out of the Customs House courtyard.

Lucy shook her head. 'If it's not him, I don't know who else would want to snatch Semilla.'

Ryan smirked. 'Nor me.'

'So, what's your plan for finding out who did take her?'

'Plan? I don't think we need one.'

She turned to look at him, mouth wide, as the Peugeot made its way onto Laygate.

'I divvent think we need a plan cos I don't believe there's been a crime,' Jarrod concluded.

'I think she's made a conscious decision to disappear. If you ask me, I reckon she's done a runner.'

**

From the air, the four graving docks, the cause of so much consternation in the council chambers, looked like the spread blades of a Swiss Army knife slicing into the Tyne bank.

The easternmost and largest dock had been drained, the loch gates shut, waiting for its development. The remaining three lay in suspended animation, their future subject to the whims of the planning committee. Although largely non-tidal, the dock pumping mechanisms were no longer operative so the inlets remained flooded with stagnant, grey-foamed river water.

A scruffy wooden craft floated unseen in a wall crevice of Dock One. Holed above the waterline and with sun-bleached and flaked paintwork, anyone stumbling across it would assume it an abandoned wreck.

It wasn't.

On the deck, a man stood with feet apart, knees slightly bent to counteract the gentle swell born from the wake of a river cruiser returning from its trip to the mouth of the Tyne. The sound of laughter and loud chatter from the revellers on board drowned out the man's voice.

'How much did she have, for Chrissakes?' the man asked.

'I dunno,' his colleague shrugged. 'Bottle of wine. Mebbe a couple of miniatures on top. Not much.'

'Not much? Micky, man - she's been flat out, virtually comatose, all day.'

'She asked for it. She said she hadn't had a drink for yonks.'

'All the more reason to be careful.'

'Looker, she said she wanted to get pissed. I probably would an' all, in her shoes.'

The first man lowered his voice as the party noise subsided. 'When did you last check on her?'

'About an hour ago.'

The first man plucked at his eyebrow with perfectly manicured nails. 'Let's check again.'

The stepladder down to the tiny cabin consisted of six splintered wooden stairs, yet the man clung grimly to them. Micky, on the other hand, simply launched himself through the cabin hatch and braced his knees on landing.

'Beat you. Na-na-ne-naaah-naah.'

'Piss off and grow up,' ordered the other man; the man clearly in charge.

Micky unzipped his padded black jacket as he hunkered down next to a scruffy bunk bed barely bigger than a cot.

'She's so beautiful,' he cooed. A lock of hair had come undone from the girl's bun and Micky gently teased it away from the girl's eyes. 'She's like sleeping beauty in that dress.'

The other man placed the sole of his shoe against Micky's shoulder and sent him sprawling to the cabin floor. 'Don't go getting any ideas. That's not in the remit.'

'Ah, spoilsport,' Micky leered.

It was pitch black down below and the man could barely see Micky just a couple of paces away. 'I mean it. I've got to go ashore cos the cops are bound to come sniffing. I need to trust you. If I find you've touched her…'

'I won't. Cross my heart and hope to die,' Micky sung.

'Good. You wouldn't like me angry.'

Micky laughed. 'Okay, pretty boy. I get the message. I won't touch her.' He paused. 'Mind, if she decided to touch me...'

'Don't even joke about it.'

Micky didn't. Instead, he spat out the remnants of an Airwaves. 'I'll look after her, man. When she wakes up, she can even munch on my sausage roll.' He winked, realised his pal wouldn't be able to see it, so Micky held up the Cooplands bag to ensure the other man knew he was joking. 'All the way from King Street's finest.'

The man in charge brought his wristwatch millimetres from his eye so he could read it in the oily blackness.

'How long since you called him?'

'A few minutes before I last checked on the princess, here.'

'And his reaction?'

'Just as you'd expect. He'll be putty in wor hands,' Micky assured him.

The man took a last look at the girl curled up on the bunk, as if checking she really was still breathing. 'Leave her for now. Let's get back up top.'

Outside the rancid confines of the cabin, the pungent smell of the Tyne Docks seemed almost pleasant. Across the river, the lights of North Shields twinkled like fuzzy stars. The night was moonless and, out at sea, a barrier of distant mist blotted out the horizon.

The sound of rock music came from somewhere above their heads, ramped up louder even as they listened.

'Sounds like the set's coming to an end. It'll be hoying oot time at The Trimmers soon. We need to get going in case somebody decides to come down this way for a shag.'

'I can think of better places. They'll get brick dust and broken glass up their arse, for starters,' Micky observed. 'So, plan's still the same?'

'It is. I go home to my warm comfortable bed waiting for PC Plod to arrive, assuming he does. You sail this ramshackle thing out of the dock and lay up where we agreed.'

'If she'll make it that far.'

'You'd better make sure she does, Sailor Jerry. Just remember to keep away from the shipping channels and as close to the dock walls and coastline as you can. We don't want to attract the harbourmaster's attention.'

'Aye, aye, cap'n,' Micky saluted.

'And don't forget - keep your hands off her.'

'Just my hands?' He raised his own as the man in charge moved towards him. 'Joke, for fuck's sake; it's a joke,' Micky said.

'Not a funny one.'

Micky spat into the thick, still waters beneath the bow. 'Reet, once I've anchored up, what do we do?'

'We do what The Boss said, that's what. You transfer her to the launch and scupper this useless pile of junk while it's still dark.'

Micky rubbed his jaw. 'When will you be back?'

'As soon as the cops have been and gone. Forty-eight hours at the most, I'd say. Then, the fun begins.'

He smiled at Micky for the first time.

'We send the ransom note.'

FIVE

Ryan never slept well when not in his own bed, though rarely was his night as bad as the one he'd just experienced.

Evert twitch of Hannah's foot, every snore or somnolent moan or deep breath, each time she turned, Ryan sat bolt upright in bed expecting an imminent arrival. When a lovesick tomcat wept and wailed outside Hannah's window shortly after four, he was convinced baby Jarrod had slipped out unnoticed.

Once satisfied the bed wasn't occupied by a third party, he slid out from beneath the covers, stumbled through the dark, and snuck into the kitchen.

He poured himself a glass of milk and buttered a slice of bread before smoothing a thick layer of jam over it. Perched on a stool alongside the breakfast bar, he contemplated life, the universe, and everything.

The more he thought about his unborn son, the more he wondered about Mayor Rachman. He began to doubt his own belief in the Mayor's innocence.

What would Ryan do in the same position? Deprived of his son, what lengths might he go to gain access? He wiped jam from the edge of his mouth as he considered the question. The conclusion he reached furthered his doubts: he'd do anything.

And yet, would he wait until his son was in his twenties? He answered himself. 'Not bloody likely.' He hoped to God he was right.

He'd persuaded Stephen Danskin that his decision to delay interviewing the Mayor was the right one. But, what if he was wrong? What if his prevarication hampered the search for Semilla?

He cursed as the ifs and buts circulated in his brain. Finally, he shrugged. What was done was done. Besides, he'd be speaking to the Mayor first thing, with Danskin alongside him.

Ryan had shared the little he and Lucy had unearthed about Semilla Rachman's disappearance to the DCI last night, and Danskin backed Ryan's judgement.

They'd soon find out if he was right to do so.

**

DC Todd Robson was scheduled to provide early morning cover for Danskin's squad in the Forth Street HQ. This was never a good thing and, if Ryan needed a reminder, it came in the form of Todd's greeting.

'Gan get us a bacon sarnie man, will you?'

'And a very good morning to you, too, Todd.'

'Aye, that an' all. Now, do what your telt and bugger off to the caff.'

'Get it yourself. Last time I looked, I was the senior officer.'

Todd grunted and settled for a coffee and Mars bar from the vending suite. 'Take it the sprog hasn't dropped yet, then?' he said over his shoulder.

Ryan shook his head, realised Todd couldn't see him, so added a simple, 'Nah.'

'Doubt you'll be so cheerful early morning once it comes.'

'*He* comes, Todd; when *he* comes.'

'Whatever,' Todd replied through a slurp of coffee. He made a face like a bag of smashed crabs. 'Yuggh. This stuff's piss poor first thing.'

'Did the DCI say what time he'd be in?' Ryan asked. 'I've got a couple of things to run by him.'

'I divvent knaa, Ry. Not sure if…'

'Morning, men,' Stephen Danskin said from the doorway. 'By, you're looking very chipper this morning, Robson.'

'I don't feel it.'

'Of course; I forgot you don't do irony, do you?' Before Todd could come up with a reply, Danskin signalled for Ryan to step into his office.

'How's Hannah doing?' Danskin asked, business-like and already in work mode.

'Canny. Better than me I reckon, to be honest.'

Reassured, the DCI dove straight in. 'Reet, plan for today. I get your reasons for leaving the Mayor out of things yesterday, but we bite the bullet today. There's nothing to indicate he has any involvement but we always look at family first.'

'Sir,' Ryan agreed.

'You're still confident he's out the picture, though, aren't you?'

Ryan hid the doubts which surfaced overnight. 'There's nowt to show he's got anything to do with it but I suppose we won't know for sure until we've had a word. Like I said yesterday, though, I'm not entirely convinced Semilla Rachman hasn't just buggered off hersel', to be honest.'

'Aye, but we can't risk it. Besides, we owe it to the girl's mother to check him out.'

Ryan shrugged. 'I guess it'll keep her away from the press, if nowt else.'

Danskin opened a filing cabinet and brought out a thin sheaf of papers. 'See this? I spent yesterday finding out everything I could about Semilla Rachman and this is all I came up with.' He waived the file in the air. 'For someone allegedly so famous, there's not a lot out there about her.'

'That's the Ruskies for you, sir. More than a tad secretive.'

'Aye, I get that, lad, but to have no social media presence, no agent, no press officer, no management behind her – it just doesn't gel.'

Ryan sucked on his bottom lip. 'She could just be shy and reticent, yet from what I was told yesterday she was quite feisty. I agree it doesn't add up.'

'Which is why we spend the day talking to the Mayor, seeing her mother again, pay another visit to the dance-wifey, Sophia. Basically, we find oot all we can about the lass. What's in this file tells us nowt.'

'Seems sensible to me. What do we tell the others?'

'We tell them sod all, Jarrod. They've got enough to be getting on with as it is. After today, we'll know if this Rachman lass is taking the piss or really has gone missing. Then's the time we rope in the others.'

**

Stephen Danskin had learnt from a source on Tyne South Bank council that Mayor Rachman was working from home that morning. He'd asked if that was part of his usual routine. The contact had told him it wasn't normal but neither was it particularly unusual, which Danskin found a fat lot of help.

Rachman lived in Hebburn, a town on the banks of the river, west of South Shields. Danskin opted to drive and used the Tyne Tunnel rather than risk the early-rush hour bottleneck caused by the Tyne Bridge refurbishment works.

He and Ryan followed the B1297 through Jarrow before turning right at the Caledonian Hotel into Ellison Street. The new housing to their left answered Ryan's growing bemusement at the Mayor choosing to live in such an area.

Indeed, at the bottom of Ellison Street, almost on the riverbank itself, they entered the upmarket housing of The Riverside.

'Nice place,' Danskin observed, looking up at the large, modern house of Mayor Rachman. 'Nice views, too,' he added, looking out across the Tyne.

'Are you serious?' Ryan said, following the DCI's gaze. All Ryan saw was grey water, grey skies, the industrial dockland of Willington Quay, the Shepherd Offshore facilities plant, and tall rusting cranes bent over the Tyne like giant, observant heron.

Stephen Danskin reconsidered his opinion. 'When the fog rolls in it'll be alright. Anyway, the house is impressive.'

'Aye, but it's nowt compared to his ex-missuses, though.'

They wandered up a flagstone path which bisected a modest but immaculate lawn. Danskin checked his watch. 'Hope he's up,' he said as he rang the doorbell.

'Should be, if he's working.'

They were both right, in their own way. Rachman was up but he wasn't working.

He answered the door dressed in a navy-blue robe and with a steaming mug of tea in one hand. Ryan noticed a fuzz of grey-tangled chest hair protruding from above the dressing gown. Worse, he saw the Mayor wore flipflops and long black socks.

'Mr Rachman?' Danskin presumed. 'DCI Stephen Danskin and DS Ryan Jarrod, if you could spare us a moment.'

Stephen Rachman studied the warrant card for longer than necessary before saying, 'I wondered when you'd get here.'

'May we?' Danskin asked, gesturing towards the hallway.

'Be my guest.' The Mayor led them into a lounge smaller than either had expected, yet tastefully furnished. 'Please, take a seat.'

Ryan carefully placed a cushion on the floor and sat on the spot it had previously occupied. Danskin joined him.

'It'll be about Semilla, I guess.'

'It is. I wonder, sir, when did you last see your daughter?'

'She's talking out her arse again, you know.' The Mayor fiddled with the tie of his robe. 'I've nothing to do with Semilla not showing last night. She's a grown woman, is Semilla. She's stood on her own two feet for as long as I can remember. It's a competitive world she lives in, and she thrives. Semilla hasn't gone missing, I'm sure.'

Danskin noticed the Mayor made only sporadic eye-contact. 'At this stage, we're only here to do some background checks, Mr Rachman. We've no hard evidence anything untoward's happened to...'

'And you won't. She's just off enjoying a little downtime, I'm sure. Letting her hair down away from the regime she's normally forced to adhere to.'

Danskin smiled. 'Of course, sir. But you must understand we are taking this matter seriously.'

Rachman spat a laugh. 'Oh, yeah. I bet she made sure you did just that.'

'Semilla?'

The Mayor pulled the neck of his robe closer together in a gesture Ryan thought effeminate. 'No. The mad bitch: you know, my ex. Elizabeth, if you insist I use her name.'

'Mr Rachman, do you know why your wife might accuse you of taking Semilla?'

'Have you met Elizabeth?' Rachman asked.

'The DCI hasn't, but I have,' Ryan confirmed.

'In which case, you'll know she's as loopy as a tin of spaghetti hoops. Off her rocker. Mad. Anyway else you'd like me to put it?'

Danskin touched Ryan elbow in a *'leave this to me'* gesture. 'Thank you, Mr Rachman. Just before we begin to put together a picture of the sort of girl your daughter is, can I just ask if there's any other reason your wife might accuse you? Apart from her being a little eccentric.'

'Hah! That's a new adjective for her.'

'Could she be jealous of your position, perhaps?'

'You haven't seen her house, I take it. She's nothing to be jealous of.'

Before Danskin could speak again, the lounge door opened.

'Oh. Sorry,' a voice said. 'I didn't realise you had company. I'll leave you to it.' The woman, striking rather than beautiful, finished buckling the belt of her short cream skirt and was gone as quickly as she'd appeared, leaving behind a puff of Frapin Parfums and a lingering French accent.

'She's as good a reason as any for his ex to be jealous,' Ryan thought.

**

Despite the gentle rocking of the boat, a profound sense of stillness and peace settled over the man in the unzipped puffer jacket - until the shrill cries of seagulls circling overhead broke the tranquillity.

Micky returned below deck and crouched down next to the bed. 'This is better than the heap of shite you were in last night, isn't it?'

The girl rubbed her eyes, stretched, then massaged her stiff neck. 'What do you mean? Where am I now?'

'Don't worry,' Micky smiled, ruffling a pleat in the dress the girl still wore. 'We're still at sea. Just anchored offshore in a different boat, that's all.'

'What happened to the first one?'

'You really were out of it, weren't you? Once I got you on board this little beaut, I pulled the plug on the owld wreck. Quite literally. It's down below us, somewhere.'

The girl tried to sit up, but the pain in her head forced her back down. 'Can I have a glass of water, please?'

Micky's brow creased. 'Water? Surely you fancy something a bit stronger?'

'No. Not after the last lot. Christ, never again, actually.'

Micky left the cabin. 'It's not a very nice day oot there. A bit grey and mizzley,' he shouted from the galley. 'You're lucky the sea's calm. You'd be chucking up aal ower the place otherwise.' He stooped back into the cabin. 'Here – get your lips round that,' he smiled, passing her a full tumbler.

The girl squirmed herself upright and took a gulp.

She spat it back out like a spouting whale.

'What the fuck…' she coughed.

'Sorry. I didn't think you meant it when you asked for water. I thought you'd be used to vodka by now.'

'Fuck off. It's vile stuff.'

Micky's eyes took on a faraway look. 'Say that again.'

'Say what?'

'What you told me to do.'

'Fuck off, you mean?'

Micky hunkered down beside her once more. He ran his fingers down the inside of the girl's arm. 'You're such a contrast, you know. Beautiful make up, gorgeous dress, those doe-like eyes - and the filthy language. I like it. Say it again.'

She shrunk away from him. 'Fuck off, you creep.' She said it without thinking.

'That's ma girl,' he smirked.

'Where's the other one? When will he be back?'

Micky smiled through thin lips. 'He'll be a while yet. Until then, there's just me and you.'

The craft lurched with the ebb of the tide. The scent of the sea, a heady blend of brine and seaweed, filtered through the cabin door as it swung open. Micky stumbled as the swell receded. He landed on top of her on the bed.

Micky reached out and pulled the door closed, more interested in the unmistakeable scent of the young woman beneath him.

SIX

Stephen Danskin and Ryan were back in the DCI's office by eleven. Danskin called Lucy Dexter in and, as he closed the blinds on the office window, Sam Maynard joined them.

'You got through your 'to-do' list quickly today, Stephen. Do I assume from the early return you're satisfied we're not looking at a crime?'

'Jarrod and I are back because I want to run a few things by you and Dexter, see what you think.'

'Very cryptic,' Maynard said. 'Go on: I'm all ears.'

Danskin wheeled a small whiteboard from the back to the front of his office. In the centre, he wrote the name of Semilla Rachman. To the left, he wrote *Stephen Rachman* and, beneath it, *Charlotte Spencer*. At the right of the board, he scrawled *Elizabeth Rachman* above a name familiar to Lucy Dexter – Keith Kennedy.

As an afterthought, he added Sophia Ridley to the foot of the board.

Maynard sucked on a pen as she waited for Danskin to continue.

'Now,' the DCI said, 'Jarrod and me had planned to talk to the Mayor, his ex, and the dance teacher today. More to discover as much as we could about the missing girl than anything.'

Still nibbling the pen, Superintendent Maynard mumbled, 'I'm presuming you didn't get very far.'

'Correctimundo. We didn't press the Mayor too hard because it turned out he wasn't alone.' He tapped the whiteboard. 'He was with his PA, Charlotte Spencer.'

'A bit early in the morning for him to be hard at it,' Lucy contributed.

'I think he'd been hard at it all night, Luce,' Ryan replied. 'The relationship seemed a bit more – well, a lot more – than a working one.'

Lucy nodded. 'And Ryan and I suspected the same about Mrs Rachman and the Kennedy fella.'

'Okay,' Maynard threw up her hands, 'But they're entitled to a life. They've been apart, like, forever. I'm not sure why the Mayor's philandering prevented you from questioning the others.'

Danskin looked at Ryan. 'The DCI and I both thought the Mayor's behaviour a bit off. He seemed edgy, fidgety, ma'am,' Ryan explained.

'His daughter's missing. He's been caught in the act, as it were, with his secretary. No wonder he's on edge.'

'That's just it, ma'am,' Danskin went on to explain, 'The Rachman's daughter is missing, yet the Mayor spends the night with a lass half his age. Doesn't it seem a bit off?'

'Not if he thinks his daughter's just having a bit of fun and not been snatched, it doesn't. He is still maintaining that's the case, isn't he?'

'He is,' Danskin conceded, 'But Ryan and I both sense there's something he's not telling us.'

'And you didn't press him, why?' Maynard argued.

'Because if we did, our questioning would be along the lines of a suspect interview rather than information-gathering.'

Sam Maynard nodded, slowly. 'And, because he's the Mayor, the shit would hit the fan.'

'Precisely, ma'am. I wanted to get your approval first before we all got covered in it.'

The Super began pacing the room, fingers drumming against her leg. 'We need more about the girl, first. Any known associates, friends, colleagues...'

'The colleagues are nearly all in Russia,' Ryan reminded her. 'And the DCI found nothing on her yesterday. You come up with anything new today, Lucy?'

'Nope. Not a thing.' She hesitated. 'I did come across something which could be relevant. Like, literally just before I came in here.'

'Yes?' Danskin encouraged, irritated he hadn't been informed.

'The car park Mrs Rachman was told to move her car from – it doesn't close. It's open twenty-four hours.'

Ryan swore under his breath. He was beginning to realise Semilla may have been abducted, after all.

'That does put a different perspective on things,' the Super conceded, 'Though I still agree we don't alert the parents to our suspicions. At least, definitely not the Mayor.' She gnawed on a knuckle. 'Is there no other family we could approach for more background on Miss Rachman?'

'Negative, ma'am,' Danskin said.

Ryan clicked his fingers. 'There is someone else.'

They looked at him, then followed his eyes to the whiteboard.

'Of course! Sophia Ridley. She's known the lass since she was a nipper,' Danskin realised. 'She'll be able to give us a more rounded and objective picture than either of the Rachman's.'

'Aye,' Ryan concurred, 'Plus, she was the one who told the mother to shift her car from somewhere it didn't need shifting.'

'Well, you missed your chance to talk to her earlier. Don't waste another one.' Maynard raised her eyebrows questioningly. 'What are you waiting for? Go. Now.'

She shooed them to the door.

'Out, damned spot!'

**

Six miles south of South Shields dry dock, between the beaches of Marsden and Whitburn, the replacement launch sat moored seaward side of Elephant Rock.

Despite a watery sun, the windchill factor kept temperatures down. Huddled on deck, Micky wore his North Face jacket zipped to his chin. The North Sea was a cold, inhospitable place at the best of times and, while sheltered from the view of those on shore, the mooring point left him exposed to the brutal whims of the elements.

He felt as isolated and desolate as the rugged coastline, despite the 'company' of the girl below deck.

She stayed locked in the cabin while Micky nursed a newfound respect for her – and a dull ache in his groin.

The moment he'd tumbled onto her and flicked shut the door; the girl's instincts kicked in. She brought her knee up and caught him square between the legs. As he recoiled, she squirmed from beneath him and gave Micky's balls three swift kicks, tendu-style.

Until then, he'd never given a thought as to how ballerinas remained on their toes for so long. Now, he knew. The strength of the dancer's leg muscles was etched in Micky's memory while the reinforced, multi-layered, toecap of her ballet shoe was engrained in his nether regions.

He'd sat doubled-over, winded and retching, for a good five minutes before finally whispering, 'It was a bliddy accident, man. Nee need for that. Jesus.'

Semilla was the one standing over the bed, now. 'Don't even think of trying a stunt like that again.'

'It wasn't a stunt. I fell on you. That's all,' he spluttered.

Both parties stared at each other for a long time, neither sure of the truth, before Micky promised to leave Semilla alone.

She demanded the key, and it was Semilla herself who locked the cabin door. From the inside.

An hour later, Micky sat on deck, his arms wrapped around himself. His eyes caught sight of the walkie-talkie tucked into an underseat cargo net. It was useless to him now, being far out of range. He pulled out his phone. He knew he shouldn't, but he did: he dialled.

'What the hell do you think you're doing, calling me like this?' his accomplice screamed at the other end. 'I said I'd be in touch when we were good to go. What do you think would have happened if the cops were here?'

'Are they?'

'No.'

'Then there's nee harm done, is there?'

Micky heard his accomplice suck in a breath. 'Everything okay your end?' the man said.

'Oh, aye. Freezing me nuts off, expecting a police launch to come a'calling at any moment, a psychopathic ballet dancer held captive below deck – everything's just cushtie, mate.'

'Sarcasm gets you nowhere, dear Michael. So, how is our little ballerina? You'd better be looking after her.'

Micky snorted a laugh. 'I think I'm the one who needs looking after. She's a feisty bitch, but she's locked up in the cabin, safely sober, at last. Look, when are you coming back? I'm feeling a bit vulnerable stuck oot here with no escape route.'

'It'll keep you on your toes,' the man said, unsympathetically. 'I'll be there soon. It's reassuring that the cops haven't come sniffing to any real extent. Means they aren't onto anything. I'll give it another day, then the plan gathers pace.'

'Okay. I suppose.'

'And remember – keep your dirty mitts of the lass.'

'Don't worry about that. It's the last thing on me mind.'

The man ended the call and Micky checked he still had his full quota of balls.

**

There were protocols to follow. Sophia Ridley, owner of Semilla's old dance school and the best hope of discovering whether Semilla Rachman had any skeletons lurking in her closet, lived in an area under the jurisdiction of the neighbouring Prince Bishops police force.

The investigation into the girl's disappearance lay wholly with Sam Maynard's City and County force but courtesy dictated the Bishops were informed, especially as any uniform presence would be supplied by them.

While Danskin did the necessary, Ryan took the opportunity to check on Hannah. She didn't answer his call. He tried again. Nothing.

Just as panic welled, Hannah called him.

'What's up? Everything okay? Why didn't you answer?' he gabbled into the mic.

'Whoa. Had on, man. All's good.'

'You sound out of breath. You sure you're okay?'

'Yes.'

Ryan remained unconvinced. 'So, why not answer straight away?'

He heard Hannah sigh. 'I hope you're not gannin' to be like this all the time.'

'Like what?'

'Panicking, that's what.'

'I was worried something was wrong when you didn't pick up.'

'Ry, man, I'm about three years pregnant. It's like I'm carrying a big sack of tatties around inside us. My phone was charging beside the telly. I can't just hop up like I did. It takes a while.'

Ryan checked Danskin's office. Through the glass wall, he saw the DCI still on the phone. 'Aye, I guess. Sorry, like.'

'Accepted – but I can't have you faffing on like this all the time. Anyway, how's things with you?'

'Aal reet, I guess. Having second thoughts about the missing dancer, though. I think the odds are still favour her doing a runner on her own accord but there's a few things putting doubts in my head.' In the office, Danskin was slipping his arms into a jacket. 'Listen, I've got to go. Let me know if owt happens, won't you?'

'I'm aal reet but, if it keeps you happy, yes: of course I'll let you know.'

'Jarrod,' Danskin called, 'We're off *'darn Sarf'.*'

**

'Darn Sarf' turned out to be the County Durham seaside town of Seaham. Or, at least, near as dammit.

Had they taken the coastal route, they'd have drove right by Elephant Rock and the boat housing Semilla Rachman. Instead, they took the quickest route, straight down the A19, bypassing Sunderland.

They also bypassed the turn-off they should have taken and so were forced to backtrack along Stockton Road, through the hamlet of Cold Hesledon, and into Dalton-le-Dale village. Sophia Ridley's house lay on Weymouth Drive and had a pleasant outlook over a well-maintained area of grassland.

'Bet that land will be built on in next few years,' Ryan commented. Danskin grunted in reply, his focus on Madame Sophia's property.

'Canny house,' he said.

The property was large and detached. It appeared to have plenty of land to the rear while, at the front, a small lawn and driveway led to a white-framed red door with opaque glazing.

'Aye,' Ryan agreed. 'Everybody connected to this case does. I think we're in the wrong job, sir.'

They walked to the door and, while they waited for Mrs Ridley to answer the doorbell, Ryan peered through the glass into the hallway. It was bereft of furniture and was decorated with plain white walls and a plush red carpet.

He pulled back from the glass when Sophia's shadow darkened the hall.

'Hello again,' she smiled at Ryan.

'Hello, Mrs Ridley. This is Detective Chief Inspector Stephen Danskin. As I said on the phone, we'd just like to pick your brains on Miss Rachman. You know, paint a picture of her. We thought we'd get a more rounded opinion from someone, well, someone perhaps a little more objective than her parents.'

Sophia offered a thin smile. 'I'll do my best but I'm not sure how much help I'll be. Anyway, please come in. I've a coffee percolating if you'd like one.'

They both did.

'Good. The living room is just on your right, there. I'll join you with the coffee in a few moments.

Ryan and Danskin thanked her and made their way to Sophia's lounge. The sight which greeted them was not what Ryan had expected. He knew he'd have to leave the questioning to Danskin.

At least, he would until he'd recalled every module of unconscious bias training he'd ever taken.

SEVEN

Sophia Ridley's lounge was decorated in much the same vein as the rest of the house: white walls, red carpets. At the window, heavy coal-black curtains were tied back by an ornate red and white tie.

Ryan and Danskin sat on a black sofa, Jarrod's eyes glued to a mural painted on the wall facing them. It depicted a scene far too old for him to remember in person but one he'd witnessed many times in photographs and TV re-runs.

Sophia Ridley chose that moment to enter the room with coffee and biscuits. She set down the tray and smiled at Ryan.

'Ah, I see you're admiring my mural. What do you think?'

Ryan knew what he thought but didn't know what to say. 'Not exactly a Banksy, is it?' he settled on.

His eyes scanned the mural again. A middle-aged man in a beige raincoat and trilby hat sprinted across the lush green turf of Wembley stadium, his arms outstretched.

Sophia saw his look of disdain. She narrowed one eye and raised the brow of the other. 'Hmm. You're a barcode, aren't you?' she presumed, using the derogatory term directed at Newcastle United fans.

'Yes, and a proud one, at that.'

Sophia shook her head. 'Must be awful, having all that blood money and not being able to spend a penny of it.'

Ryan wasn't going down that road. 'I'm surprised. Didn't have you down as a footie fan.'

Sophia gave the mural a wistful look. 'Fifth of May, nineteen-seventy-three, that was. The day I was born. My father had a ticket for the final. He had to give it away because I was overdue. Mind, he still missed the birth. He hired a colour telly from Rediffusion and was so engrossed in the match he forgot all about me. I guess I caught the bug from him. Never missed a Saturday home match since I was seventeen. Seen us beat your lot plenty of times recently.'

Danskin coughed. 'This is all very pleasant but can we get on, please? DS Jarrod and I wish to know as much as you can tell us about Semilla Rachman. Anything at all in her background which might help us discover what happened to her.'

Ridley looked up to the ceiling. 'Well, where to begin? Semilla first came to my school when she was, what, five or six, at most. She was a shy little thing initially but performing seemed to give her something. Call it confidence, a sense of finding herself, knowing she was better than her peers. Possibly a bit of them all.' She looked at Danskin. 'Semilla was an amazing little girl, and not just in terms of her talent.'

'Go on, please.'

'She was such a quick learner. Whenever a new piece was introduced to her, she seemed to know what was required. Remember, we're talking about a girl in her first year or two at school. Above all else, she was determined, resilient, and, if I'm honest, a tad arrogant. She knew she was bloody good.'

'And in her later years?'

Sophia shook her head. 'I didn't get to see much of her once she *'made it'*, though we did keep in touch occasionally. I got the sense she'd hardened. Can't put my finger on it, but she'd changed. There again, don't we all?'

'And you knew her parents?'

'Only through the dance school. We didn't socialise.'

'How old was Semilla when her parents split?'

Sophia vibrated her lips. 'Now you're asking. I don't know – probably around ten, I'd say.'

'Did she seem affected by the separation?'

She nodded before qualifying, 'No more than you'd expect, though. She still came to every class and, if anything, seemed to focus on her dancing more than ever.'

Despite Danskin's wish to lead, Ryan intervened. 'Which parent brought her to your lessons?'

'Mrs Rachman.'

'Always?'

Sophia nodded. 'She was the one with custody.'

'Stephen Rachman never brought her?'

'No. He did take an interest, though.'

Ryan and Danskin shared a glance. 'In what way?'

Sophia topped up her mug with coffee. Ryan put his hand over the top of his cup, declining the offer. Danskin refused a top-up, too. 'Well,' Sophia went on, 'He'd turn up at our annual shows. Most of them, anyway. And he'd watch her.'

'I'm not surprised. Why else would he attend her performances if he wasn't there to watch?'

'I'm sorry. I haven't made myself clear. I meant he used to watch her in other ways.'

Ryan's forehead creased. 'I'm not sure what you mean. What other ways are there?'

Sophia looked to the floor, as if she'd said too much. 'As Semilla became more independent, in the Summer months Elizabeth would bring her to class but she'd walk home afterwards. Semilla and her mother lived in Shields at that point, in a house overlooking Littlehaven Beach. I used to drive home that way, and that's when I'd see them.'

Danskin leant forward. 'Semilla and Stephen Rachman – together?'

'Not exactly, no.'

'Mrs Ridley, this is important. Please explain what you mean.'

Sophia took time to think how best to explain it. 'As I indicated earlier, Semilla was self-motivated, always striving to better herself. When she walked home, she'd detour onto the beach itself. Once there, she'd dance. No music, other than the music in her head.'

'Did she say why?'

Sophia Ridley smiled. 'Yes. I asked her one day and she said dancing on the beach increased her strength. Have you ever tried running on sand, Detective Chief Inspector? Much harder than on grass or tarmac, isn't it? Semilla also said it improved her balance. The dry sand shifts underfoot yet she ensured she held her relevés. From what I saw, without fail.' She smiled again. 'Yes, she was as dedicated as they come.'

'Where does Mr Rachman come into the equation?', Danskin asked.

'I'd see him standing on the prom, watching Semilla dance on the sand. On a couple of occasions, I'd park up, just to watch her. Mr Rachman would follow his daughter at a distance then, as she neared home, he'd turn tail and head off.'

Danskin spoke to Ryan. 'Stalking his own daughter. That's a bit off, isn't it?'

Ryan was about to agree when a thought struck. 'Aye, except…'

'Except what, Jarrod?'

'Except, if he'd really wanted to take his daughter, it means he had ample opportunity to do it when she was in her early teens. It doesn't make sense for him to do it now.'

The DCI scratched his forehead. Ryan was right – the Mayor wasn't their man. Time for a change of tactics.

'Did Semilla have any boyfriends?'

'Not that I know of. Oh, I believe she was seeing a lad but it didn't last long.'

'Do you know his name?'

'No. I never met him. I heard Semilla talking to one of the other girls about him. She'd have been about sixteen or so at the time. I remember thinking I hope she doesn't stop dancing for him. I needn't have worried. She knew where her priorities lay.'

Ryan pulled his eyes away from the mural. 'Are all your students female?'

'Mostly. I can count on my fingers the number of lads I've taught over all the years I've been doing this. It's not seen as the most macho of interests. That's one thing Billy Elliott got right.'

'Just a couple more questions, Mrs Ridley,' Danskin assured her. 'Do you know a Charlotte Spencer?'

'I know a lot of people. I don't recall the name. In what context?'

'In the context of Stephen Rachman.'

'Ah. No. I know little about the Mayor or his associates.'

'What about a Keith Kennedy?'

A light went on behind Madame Sophia's eyes. 'Mrs Rachman's friend. Yes, I know him.'

'Anything strike you as different about him? Anything unusual?'

Sophia pursed her lips.

'Mrs Ridley?' Danskin prompted.

'It's probably nothing.'

'But it may be something. So, please, tell us.'

She exhaled through her nose. 'A few years back, a long time after Semilla left to join the Bolshoi, he and Mrs Rachman turned up at my annual concert. It was at the Westovian Theatre, our usual venue. Seemingly, he needed the loo but he took a wrong turn and got lost.'

Danskin waited for Sophia to continue.

'One of the chaperones discovered him as he was about to enter the backstage area where the girls were changing. Of course, I'm sure it was an accident but, well...it can make you wonder, can't it?'

'It certainly can,' Ryan thought as he made a note.

'I've one last favour to ask of you,' Danskin said to Sophia. 'I know my uniformed colleagues and DS Jarrod have been to the Customs House but it would really help if I could see it, too. Do you think you could arrange it for me?'

'Mmm. I'd have to speak to Edwin about that.'

'Edwin?'

'Edwin Trove, sir. He organised the venue for the performance,' Ryan explained.

Sophia raised an eyebrow. 'Well remembered, Detective Sergeant. I'm impressed. A Mag with brains. How very unusual.'

'Howay, let's not start all that again,' Danskin said with a smile. 'If you could call this Edwin straight away, I'd appreciate it.'

'Of course. I'll do it now.'

As Sophia made for the hallway, Ryan shouted. 'And it'd be good if you could get me the list you promised. You know – the list of the adults who were on duty at the time Miss Rachman went missing.'

'Thank you for reminding me. I'd completely forgotten,' Sophia said from the corridor as she made her call to Edwin Trove.

'What do you make of things?' Danskin whispered.

'Jury's out, sir. Like I said, I can't see Stephen Rachman being involved. He's had ample opportunity to take the lass in the past if what Ridley says is true.'

'What about this Kennedy bloke?'

Ryan snorted a laugh of disdain. 'Not sure I buy his *getting lost* story. It's definitely worth having another word with him.'

'I agree. You do that whilst I have a neb around the theatre with Mrs Ridley.'

Ryan's phone vibrated. A shiver ran through him.

'Hannah,' he said to Danskin as he clicked to accept the call.

'What's up? Is baby on his way, love? I'll get there as soon as I can.'

'No, Ry. He's still safely tucked away.'

He didn't pick up on her downbeat tone of voice as he chastised her. 'Man, don't do that. Me and Stephen are out on a case. You shouldn't be bothering us if nowt's wrong.'

'I didn't say nowt was wrong.'

'You did…'

'I said, there's nothing wrong with the pregnancy.'

'Then, what is it?' There was a long silence. 'Hannah?'

'Ryan, you need to get home. Like, right now. It's your Gran.'

EIGHT

'Let us in, man. I'm desperate for a slash.'

'Piss over the side,' Semilla responded. 'There's probably worse than that in the sea, anyway.'

'I'm starving an' all. All the scran's inside.'

Micky heard her groan before the sound of a lock turning. 'Remember last time,' she cautioned.

'How could I forget?' He closed the door to the tiny chemical toilet and let loose. 'Make us a sarnie, can you?'

'What? I'm a hostage and a skivvy now, am I? Make it yourself.' The toilet door opened. 'And wash your hands, scruff bag.'

The door closed again.

When Micky emerged, he saw the larder door stood ajar. On its shelves, three blackened bananas, half a jar of pickled onions, a tin of tuna, and a pack of Oreos.

He settled on the biscuits.

'We need more food,' Semilla commented.

'Hadaway. You don't say.'

She fingered the ballet dress she still wore. 'And I need a change of clothes.'

The sound of dogs barking on the nearby clifftop provided Micky with a reminder of how close to civilization they were.

Micky stuffed a whole Oreo into his mouth. 'He'll bring both when he gets here. Then, we'll move somewhere safer,' he mumbled through a spray of crumbs.

Semilla raised a finger. 'One: how long will he be?' Another finger shot up. 'Two: where is *'safe?'* and, three, safe for who?'

Micky swallowed down his biscuit. *'She's pretty cool about all this,'* he thought. *'Probably summat to do with the Ruskie mentality.'*

'Are you going to answer or just sit there like a cabbage?'

Micky decided he needed to reimpose his authority. 'Safe for all of us because, if someone does happen to find us here, you'll be first overboard, I promise you. So, shut the fuck up and remember who's in charge, yeah?'

She snorted a laugh. 'Somehow, I don't think you're the one in charge.'

Micky opened his mouth to speak then realised he felt more prey than predator. He settled for perching on the single stool screwed to the cabin floor. 'So, how did you start this dancing lark?'

'It's not a lark. It's a career. You know, like yours is following orders.'

Micky clung to his stool for support as a large wave rocked the vessel. 'Y'know what I meant.'

She shot him a contemptuous look. 'I do. Ask your mate. He seems to know a bit more about what's going on. If he ever decides to come back, that is.'

'Divvent worry about that. He'll be here soon enough,' Micky said.

'Will he, though?' he wondered. *'What if the cops took him in? Or, what if he's had second thoughts?'*

An overhead gull released its sorrowful squawk as Micky looked into Semilla's steely eyes.

'I'm up shit creek, that's what.'

**

Danskin immediately ordered Ryan home. 'I'll take it from here,' he said. 'You get off and see what's up.'

'Thanks, sir. If you're sure…'

'Aye, I'm sure. Besides, it'll give me an excuse to ask the same questions you did. If I get a different set of answers, I'll know summat's up.'

Once he'd dismissed Ryan, Danskin climbed into the passenger seat of Sophia Ridley's car for the journey to the Customs House. It took longer than expected. She drove as if she had a pallet of fresh eggs on the back seat.

Danskin valiantly hid his frustration. He comforted himself in the knowledge at least the Trove fella would be ready and waiting for them.

Once they left the coast behind and began navigating the streets of South Shields, Danskin caught the occasional glimpse of the broody Tyne between buildings. Soon, they were on the approach to the Customs House, its distinctive architecture and imposing sandstone exterior evoking a sense of timeless stoicism.

Sophia checked her phone as she drew to a halt. 'Edwin's here,' she said. 'Ah, good. He's roped in Patrick, as well.'

'Patrick?'

'Sorry. He's my Stage Manager. Patrick Wheatley. If you want a tour, between them they'll be able to tell you everything you need to know.'

'Yeah, I might have a shufty while I'm here. They were both present when Miss Rachman disappeared?'

Sophia seemed to nod as she clambered out the car. Danskin followed.

'Better lock that, Mrs Ridley.'

Without turning, she pressed the key fob twice and they heard the door lock engage. They weren't the only doors locked. The Customs House was also locked down. Eventually, a shadow darkened the glass in the door. A jangle of keys preceded its opening.

'Mrs Ridley,' the man said. 'Good to see you. How are you, after everything?'

They exchanged air kisses.

'Still processing things, if I'm honest.' She broke free from the embrace. 'Edwin, this is Detective Chief Inspector Danskin. Mr Danskin – meet Edwin Trove.'

Trove had a ruddy, pock marked complexion. Danskin thought it made him look as if he'd been for a jog behind a road gritter. Stephen locked eyes with the theatre patron as they shook hands.

Trove's grip belied his slight frame. He smiled at Danskin, a hint of wariness in his eyes, before he gestured them inside. 'Please, step into my parlour.'

Danskin looked around the foyer. Empty chairs stood stacked in a corner. Others lay close to the bar, its shutters down. The walls were covered in posters advertising upcoming events. One, he noticed, advertised the Sophia's Stars concert, an image of Semilla Rachman the focus. Two sets of double doors stood either side of an unmanned ticket booth with darkened windows and unlit interior.

Although never a theatregoer, the DCI still felt the lack of activity and energy sad, somehow. He found the interior, deserted as it was, drab and had difficulty imagining what it must have been like, crowded and throbbing with excitement on the night of Semilla's disappearance.

'You have security cameras, I see,' Danskin said, glancing upwards.

Trove's suit was slightly too large for him. He shrugged his shoulders to keep the fit. 'We have. Your colleagues have already been through it.'

'I'm sure they have but I'd like a copy, please. As our enquiries continue, we may find something which requires us to review the footage.' He smiled. 'It would be awful if we found it had been wiped, wouldn't it?'

Edwin Trove shrugged. 'It would. Yes, I'm sure I could arrange it for you.'

'Have you more than one camera?'

'In the lobby here, no. That's it. It covers the whole foyer, though.'

'Elsewhere?'

'We have two external cameras monitoring folk approaching and leaving.'

'I'll need footage from those, an' all.'

Trove nodded. 'I'll see you get it. And we've one above the curtain inside the auditorium, facing the audience. Don't worry, you'll get access to that.'

Danskin scrutinised the man's face. It seemed to redden even more under the DCI's stare. 'I'm not worried,' he said.

Sophia Ridley broke the awkward exchange. 'Has Patrick arrived yet?' she asked Edwin.

'He has. He's still got a couple of backstage matters to wind up following the show. I'll ask him up, should I?' Without waiting for an answer, he unclipped a communication device from his belt and pressed a couple of buttons before reattaching it. 'He'll be here soon, I'm sure.'

Stephen Danskin had turned his back on Edwin and Sophia and was studying the theatre entrance. 'Is this the only way in-and-out?'

'It's the main one, yes.'

Danskin rolled his eyes. 'You sound like you're answering to the Post Office scandal enquiry. I'll try again – is there another door?'

Trove bristled. 'Sorry. I didn't mean to be evasive. There's no other point of entry but there's one exit point at the back of the auditorium. I can show you if you want.'

'Mebbe later. Is it covered by CCTV?'

'Externally, no. There's no need because it's not an access point. You can see those leaving through it from the curtain camera records but you need to zoom in to get a clear view. It's a bit of a fish-eye lens.' Trove shrugged his shoulders and his jacket shifted up. 'Your colleagues have already accessed it.'

'So you said but I'd prefer it if my digital analyst took a look, as I mentioned earlier. Email the footage to DC Ravi Sangar.' He handed a card to Trove. 'I presume it's a digital recording, not a VCR or owt?'

'It's digital. I'll have it compressed and sent as a ZIP file.'

'Cheers. I'll make sure he knows to expect it.'

Their attention was drawn to the auditorium doors which opened with a shudder. A young man stepped through, rubbing dusty hands against the sides of his scuffed jeans. 'Sorry I took a while, Ed. You caught me dismantling the last of the sets from the performance.' He smiled towards Sophia. 'How are you, Mrs Ridley?'

'I'm not too bad, thank you, given everything.'

She introduced Danskin to Patrick Wheatley. They shook hands before Danskin turned back to Edwin Trove.

'Don't forget to send the CCTV images to DC Sangar. Just before I let you go, can you just confirm the only doors are the main ones at the front and the one to the rear of the auditorium?'

'Yes.'

Wheatley opened his mouth to speak then closed it again.

'Not even a stage door?' Danskin pressed.

Trove sniggered and hitched up his jacket. 'This isn't the Empire, you know. It might be the bigger of the two theatres in Shields but everybody comes in that way,' he said, gesturing towards the main entrance. 'There's no other way in.'

'Okay. I think I'll take that look inside now,' Danskin said.

Trove glanced at his watch.

'I'll take it from here, if you need to get off,' Patrick Wheatley offered.

'I do, and I need to get the video stuff to…' he glanced at the card Danskin had given him, 'DC Sangar first. Are you okay to go with Patrick, Detective Chief Inspector?'

'Aye. You can leave as well, Mrs Ridley. I'll get a squad car to take me back to the station. I'm sure we'll be in touch with you but, please, call me or DS Jarrod if you think of anything.'

Once they'd left, Wheatley led Danskin into the theatre. It was smaller inside than Danskin had imagined, he counted around twenty rows, each of twenty seats. A small upper gallery added to the capacity. In front of him, the stage hid behind a safety curtain illuminated by a shaft of sunlight from the open door. Specks of dust circulated like food in a fishtank.

'Can I show you anything in particular?' Wheatley, a tall man in his early twenties, asked.

'Whatever you think might be relevant.'

'Well, for starters, I think I'll show you the other doors.'

'What other doors?'

'Oh, you know…the two Ed forgot to mention.'

Danskin set his jaw. 'Did he, now. Any idea why?'

'No idea. Probably because they're only emergency exits.'

Danskin nodded, slowly. 'Are they covered by the security cameras?'

'Nah. They're alarmed, though, so we'd know if anyone opened them. Here, I'll show you.'

Wheatley led Stephen down a staircase of polished oak at the left of the auditorium, fringing the rows of seats. At the front, they stepped up half a dozen narrow stairs at the side of the stage before squeezing behind the safety curtain into the wings.

At the rear, a double-door fire exit was partly-hidden behind a row of baffle boards.

'Should I demonstrate?' Wheatley asked. Danskin nodded, and Sophia Ridley's stage manager depressed the handrail.

The moment the doorlatch released, the theatre filled with the sound of a shrill, repetitive siren. Strobe lights picked out the route towards the emergency exit, visible to all in the backstage area.

Wheatley closed the door, pressed a code, and the cacophony ceased despite lingering as an echo in Danskin's ears.

'Aye, I'd say that was canny noticeable, like,' the DCI agreed. 'You said there's another?'

Wheatley gave a smile. 'Follow me,' he said, 'And watch your step. It's a bit of a trip hazard.'

Patrick's words were an understatement. They disappeared beneath the stage into a realm of secret labyrinths.

'Bloody hell. Is there nee lights down here?'

'Yes. Bear with me.' Wheatley's fingers felt for a light switch, and a bare bulb illuminated the passageways.

'What the hell's this place used for?' Danskin mused, looking around.

Wheatley raised an eyebrow. 'God knows. I don't work here regularly. I do a bit of stagehand work now-and-again but I was mainly here because I help Madame Sophia with her classes and shows, usually at the Westovian.'

Danskin ducked his head in the confines of the low corridor. 'Have you helped her for long?'

'Long enough to know she's a saint when it comes to her students.'

As they navigated the winding passageway, the air became cold and musty. Danskin swiped at a cobweb. 'Does anybody work down here? Odd place for a fire exit.'

'Oh aye. I know the dressing rooms were housed down here years ago. Now, it's mainly a storage area for stage props and generic background sets. Sometimes, the sound and lighting gear and emergency generators are kept down here. I suppose that's why it still has a fire exit.'

'Makes sense. Mind, I think getting to the exit's more of a danger than a bloody fire,' Danskin said as he stepped over the thick disconnected cables which snaked the length of the corridor like veins on the back of a hand.

Wheatley laughed. 'I did warn you.' He found another switch which spread a blanket of light as far as a bend in the tunnel up ahead. 'Nearly there,' Patrick assured Stephen.

They turned the corner and were met with a fire door, paintwork faded with age and damp, and metal guard plates which bore the first hint of rust.

'It's alarmed, you said.'

'Aye.' Patrick reached for the handrail. 'You might want to cover your ears. This is seriously loud in the corridors down here.'

'I'm sure it is,' Danskin said, complying with the young man's advice. 'Reet, I'm ready. Go ahead.'

Patrick depressed the handrail.

Nothing happened.

The eerie silence swallowed them.

'Blow me,' Wheatley whispered.

NINE

Ryan made a quick call to his father before setting off from Sophia Ridley's. Norman Jarrod's response – that his Gran was 'Still with us but get here as soon as you can' – provided him with little reassurance, especially as Norman refused to say anything more until Ryan got there.

The journey passed in a blur. Deep down, he knew he had supported Doris Jarrod through her time in the Care Home, yet he couldn't help but wonder if he should have done more.

He'd devoted his energy over the previous six months to Hannah, the baby, and work. He'd visited Doris less often. Ryan knew she was deteriorating. When she didn't nod off in front of him, the visits often ended up in nonsensical conversations which he went along with simply so he didn't confuse his grandmother even more. But – should he have seen this coming; whatever *'this'* was?

He only came off automatic pilot once he realised he'd turned onto Whickham Highway. In less than five minutes, he'd know what had happened. The village streets were quiet, yet he hit every traffic light on red. Temporary three-way lights at the top of Whickham Bank delayed him further.

The fact he could see the home from where he sat in queuing traffic made him more impatient. The moment the lights turned green, he set off at like Max Verstappen and swung into the car park with a screech of tyres.

He buzzed the door, told the intercom who he was, and waited for the lock to disengage. An ashen-faced Norman Jarrod met him inside the doorway.

'Is she okay?' Ryan asked.

Norman put an arm on his shoulder. 'They'll explain it better than me. Howay into the office.'

'But is she okay?'

Ryan's father made a noise. 'Not really, son. Not really, at all.'

Angela Doyle, the manager, offered him a sympathetic smile which only rendered matters even worse. 'Sit down, Ryan,' she said, patting a chair next to her.

'I'm alright here, ta. Just tell me what's happened.'

'Your grandmother's had another fall.'

'How? Wait. Had on – what do you mean by *another* fall?'

Norman stepped in. 'It's her third. I didn't tell you about the others because she was fine afterwards. Well, y'know; no different to normal.'

'Which I take it means this one's more serious.'

Mrs. Doyle said, 'Yes, I'm afraid it is. The doctor's been out to see her and says there's no lasting damage from the fall itself.'

'Why do I feel a *'but'* coming?'

'Dr Trewick believes the falls are the result of TIAs. That's a transient…'

'Aye, I know what they are. Mini-strokes.' He glanced towards his father. 'Wor James on his way?'

'No.'

Ryan tisked. 'Bloody typical.'

'Not this time. Your brother's got a job interview. I'll tell you more later. For now, let's just listen to what Mrs Doyle's got to say.'

Angela gave Ryan her sympathetic smile again. 'To answer your question, I'm afraid there is a 'but'. At Doris's age and with her rapid deterioration…'

'Hang on again. What rapid deterioration?'

Angela looked at Norman who lowered his head. 'You haven't seen her for three weeks, son. She's not been great.'

Ryan scratched his head and puffed out his cheeks. 'Just tell us, man.'

'Your Gran's had trouble eating. In fact, she hasn't been. They've put her on a blended diet. You know, softened stuff. A bit like baby food, it is.' Ryan winced as Norman continued. 'You already know she's been sleeping most of the day. Well, she's not been out of bed for more than a week now, apart from accompanied trips to the toilet and things.'

Jarrod looked at Angela Doyle. 'If she hasn't been out of bed, how'd she fall?'

'I'm sorry, Ryan,' she said. 'We do our best but we can't be with her twenty-four hours a day. Doris forgot to ring the assistance bell. She tried to go to the loo by herself. That's when it happened. Because she hasn't been up unsupported for a while, we assumed her blood pressure had just dropped suddenly which caused the fall. Dr Trewick's run some tests and, although he can't be certain, he thinks she been having TIAs.'

Ryan pinched the bridge of his nose. 'So what treatment is she on?'

'None, I'm afraid. She's already on warfarin.'

Ryan shook his head. 'We're just expected to wait for the big one to hit, are we? Nah, that's not good enough.'

'Ry,' his dad said, 'They know what's best.'

For the first time since entering the office, Ryan sat. With his head in his hands, he said, 'Can I see her?'

'Of course. But I should warn you she's got a lot of facial bruising and swellings. She's a lot more confused and incoherent, too.'

'Shit.'

'And,' Angela Doyle continued, 'I think there's something we should discuss before you see her.'

'Oh aye? What's that, then?'

Neither Ryan nor Norman expected to hear what followed.

'I think it's time to think about Doris's dignity and what comes next.'

She lowered her voice.

'It's time to consider end-of-life care.'

**

The loud rumblings of Micky's stomach rolled around the cabin's interior.

'He's not coming back, is he?' Semilla said. 'You might as well sod off before the cops arrive and cart you away.'

'Don't you just wish? Nah, I'm going nowhere.' His nostrils twitched. 'Bloody hell. I'm fantasising now. I can smell fish and chips.' Just to emphasise the point, his guts gave another growl so thunderous it masked the sound of footsteps on the deck.

The door flung open. Micky jumped. Semilla cowered.

'Get your laughing tackle round that,' the man said, lowering a carrier bag of assorted goodies from a nearby chippie onto the small Formica-topped table. He hauled an overstuffed rucksack off his shoulder and dumped it on the floor.

'Bloody hard work rowing out here with that thing. Weighs a ton. Tide against us, too.'

The man started offloading its contents. Tins of food, bread, cheese, a large water carrier, and a few cans of beer emerged first. Next, three or four T-shirts, a couple of pairs of joggers, socks, and underwear. All menswear.

'What about me?' Semilla complained.

The man's head disappeared into the bag. 'Here,' he said, tossing a pack towards her.

She caught it one-handed. 'I meant clothes, not sanitary wear.' She looked at the pack. 'They're not even the right size.'

He looked at her, bemused. 'Size? You mean they come in different sizes? Bloody hell. Who knew?'

'Anyway, how long do you expect to hold me? I mightn't need any.'

The man looked directly at her. 'True. But you might. You'll be here as long as it takes, and I don't want things getting messy in any shape or form.'

Despite herself, she laughed. 'You seriously don't expect to keep me hidden away for long, surely? Come on, where's my change of clothing?'

He shook his head. 'There isn't any. You can wear men's stuff or walk about naked. It's your call.'

Micky's eyes sparkled but he refrained from comment, self-consciously guarding his nuts with his hands.

'I think if anyone spots me, you're going to be in deep shit,' Semilla said. 'I'll stand out wearing this garb.'

The man stretched his back until it clicked. 'Has she been this arsey with you while I've been away?' he asked Micky. Without waiting for a reply, he continued speaking to Semilla. 'Anyway, no-one will spot you where we're going.'

'You think?'

'I *know*, not '*think*'. Micky, start the motor up. We're heading out to sea. Nobody will find us out there. Or, if they do, we'll see them coming from miles off.'

'You think you're so clever, don't you?' Semilla taunted.

'Yes. Probably because I am clever. So clever, in fact, that if you don't behave you'll be taking a long walk off a short plank and I doubt your body will ever be found.'

The colour drained from her face.

Micky didn't bat an eyelid as he asked the man if he'd seen off the cops.

'They'd have taken me in by now if they suspected anything,' he replied.

'Good.' Micky began making preparations to set sail. 'Hang on. How do we send the ransom note if we're out there?' he asked, tilting his head towards the open water. 'I don't think a postie's likely to call by.'

'We won't be sending a ransom note.'

Micky stopped what he was doing. 'Waddyamean? There's no point doing all this if there's nowt in it for us.'

The man smiled. 'We won't be sending one because it's already been sent. It's on its way now. That's why we need to get out of here, straight away, before all hell breaks loose. So, you'd better get a bloody shift on, Micky.'

**

Ryan's day had been long and traumatic. He felt drained, hungry and, more than anything, flat as a fart. After dropping his dad off at home, he fully intended going to his own house – until he realised it wasn't a good idea. The property had previously belonged to Doris Jarrod and, haunted as he was by the frailty of his grandmother, it was the last place he felt able to relax.

Instead, he made a quick call to Hannah before heading to the City and County's HQ in Forth Street. He grabbed a pre-packed sandwich from the petrol station at the foot of Broom Lane for sustenance and, by the time he pulled into the police station's compound, he felt less troubled.

Ryan reached the office after most his colleagues had shut up shop for the night. Lucy Dexter, on late cover, was at her desk. He made towards his own workstation with a plan to run through the Semilla Rachman case file until he noticed Superintendent Maynard's office bathed in lighting. He headed towards the door and entered after a polite knock.

He'd interrupted Maynard and Danskin arguing and counter arguing the case.

Danskin made a plea for more resources, which Maynard declined due to other pressing cases. Then, they reversed their positions. The DCI commented that they still had no certainty a crime had been committed whilst Sam Maynard countered that they couldn't risk a potential diplomatic incident if a member of the Bolshoi had been snatched on her watch.

Ryan politely suggested they run through what they knew to better inform their decision.

Danskin took a deep breath and kicked off the session. He began by recapping known facts. Elizabeth and Stephen Rachman were divorced. She had been a senior independent consultant at a major financial institution based in Sunderland. She remained adamant her husband is behind Semilla's disappearance. Danskin said they now knew it was highly unlikely.

'Have you more info on the Mayor, then?' Ryan asked, anxious to catch up on developments.

'Aye. Historically, the Mayoral role has been mainly ceremonial. You know, opening new businesses, attending Armistice parades, poncing around to show off his bling and chains of office and other such bollocks. Stephen Rachman, though, is more hands on. He attends more council sittings than any of his predecessors and plays a lead role in some. We've confirmed that's where he was on the evening of Semilla Rachman's disappearance. A debate on the redevelopment of Shields' graving docks overran and the Mayor was particularly keen to ensure the issue was resolved.'

'Okay,' Ryan said. 'And we know Mrs Rachman was at the theatre at the time the lass went missing but she was sent out to move her car. Someone distracted her, using Sophia Ridley as the conduit, but we still don't know who.'

Sam Maynard spoke next. 'We have the CCTV footage from the foyer, the main entrance, and a stage camera which covers the rear auditorium door. DC Sangar has only just begun trawling through it but the reports from uniform indicate he'll find nothing of material interest.'

Ryan tugged an earlobe. 'I need to do some digging on Mrs Rachman's friend.'

'Lyall's already done it while you were away. Keith Kennedy's not known to us. Turns out he's the 'Kennedy' part of Bloor Kennedy Smythe; the leading accountancy firm in Durham city. He first met Elizabeth Rachman through their work. They've been friends for several years and he's accompanied her to some of Sophia Ridley's previous annual shows.'

'But not this one. Interesting,' Ryan mused.

'DI Parker is given to understand Kennedy didn't go because Stephen Rachman was due to watch his daughter. He didn't want risk a ruckus.'

'Can he vouch for his whereabouts?' Ryan asked.

'He says he was at Elizabeth Rachman's but, obviously, Mrs Rachman wasn't there.'

'Kennedy's still in the frame, then.'

Sam Maynard poured water on the premise. 'There's no motive.'

'None that we know off, you mean, Ma'am.'

'True.'

Danskin persuaded Maynard to keep Kennedy as a person of interest.

'I guess the same goes for the Mayor's bit-on-the-side.'

'Careful, Ryan,' Maynard cautioned. 'We don't know that's what she is.'

Ryan sneered while Danskin added, 'Charlotte Spencer was at the same council meeting as Rachman. On the bit-on-the-side front, though, Spencer was headhunted by Rachman himself so there's probably summat in it but that doesn't mean she'd be involved in a kidnap.'

They sat in silence for a moment, contemplating if the case really was a case, at all. Ryan said as much but the Super offered a convincing argument.

'Semilla has no money with her, her mobile's switched off, her credit card hasn't been used, and I'm sure she's well enough known for someone to post a selfie with her on social media if they'd come across her.'

'Really, we've got sod all, haven't we?' an exasperated Ryan exclaimed.

'Not quite,' Danskin said.

Ryan encouraged him to continue.

'Firstly, Sophia Ridley's finally sent through the list of people on theatre duty that night. Dexter is following up on them. Secondly, Jarrod, do you remember the name Edwin Trove?'

'Aye, he's a theatre patron, isn't he?'

'Correct. Well, he talked me through the theatre set-up and conveniently forgot to highlight two other exits from the theatre. Both were alarmed or, rather, should have been. One had been disarmed. If the security footage gives us nowt to go off, I'll bet my arse that's how the Rachman lass was taken out.'

Maynard and Ryan both nodded.

'That's where I'll be starting tomorrow. A less-than-quiet word in Trove's shell-like seems in order,' Danskin concluded.

'What should I do?' Ryan asked.

'You should go home and rest. You've got enough to contend with for now. A good night's sleep is what you need.'

Ryan couldn't disagree with a word of it.

'Okay, sir.' He paused. 'Tomorrow, though, I'll pay another visit to Stephen Rachman.'

'To what end?' Maynard queried. 'His whereabouts on the night of his daughter's disappearance are already accounted for.'

'True, but I still smell a rat.'

'On what grounds?'

'On the grounds I still don't get why he was stalking his daughter when she was a teenager. Summat doesn't seem right.'

Maynard looked towards Danskin for advice.

'It can't do any harm, I suppose,' Stephen said.

They were soon to learn how true the DCI's words were.

TEN

The boat was motionless; the sea, a millpond. The two men lay on deck, soaking up the early morning sun. Micky had even removed his puffer jacket which he used to swat away a gull perched on the gunnel. It flew off with an angry squawk.

'Bloody things had me awake at four,' he scowled.

'Blame the fishing boats. The birds think everything out here is a Just Eat delivery.'

Micky sighed. 'So you've no idea how long we'll be staying out here?'

'Nope. We wait for as long as The Boss tells us to wait.'

'We'll need more food before long. Can't stay here forever.'

'If we need more food, you'll sail this thing back to Elephant Rock and one of us will row ashore. Simples.'

Micky sighed again.

'Micky, man. Lighten up. It's all good.'

'I don't trust her.'

'Rachman?'

'No. Mary-fucking-Poppins. Yes, of course I mean Rachman – who else?'

From his position prone on the deck, the man held one arm aloft, a set of keys hanging from his fingers. 'She's locked inside. We're the best part of a mile from shore. What damage can she do?'

Micky conceded he had a point. 'True. There's summat about her, though. She's too calm. I mean, the first night her head was all over the place. She worked her ticket plenty but she didn't seem scared, even then. She still doesn't.'

His companion propped himself up on his elbows. 'I bet she's seen it all with the Bolshoi. Probably been threatened with the salt mines if she didn't conform, and all that.'

'D'ya think?'

The man shook his head. 'I honestly don't know. What I do know is that The Boss will have everything covered.'

Micky shielded his eyes from the sun's glare. 'Do you think they'll pay up?'

'Probably.'

'Do you think they'll involve the cops?'

'Probably.'

'Shit, man. What have we done?'

The man lowered himself back onto the deck. 'We're doing what The Boss asked us to do. And, we're getting well paid for it.' They heard the loo flush. 'She's up and about. Better go inside and keep an eye on her.'

Micky stiffened. 'I thought you said she couldn't do any harm.'

'Not in the way you mean but remember the state she was in the first night.'

'Drunk, you mean?'

'Yep.'

'And?'

'And all our beer's in there with her. If this weather keeps up, I'm gonna need a can or two before she downs the lot.'

Micky grabbed the keys off the man and bolted for the cabin door.

**

The morning dawned bright and sunny for Ryan, too. The TV forecast promised the hottest day of the year so far and, as he set off for the Mayor's, he already needed a car window down.

He'd surprised himself by sleeping well. No dreams, no negative thoughts about Doris Jarrod, no worries about Hannah and the baby, and no stressing over the Rachman case which mightn't be a case. He'd soon know.

It took Ryan less than half an hour to reach Hebburn. The only downside was the fact that the warmth of the day meant the Tyne, although for once reflecting blue rather than her usual sludge-brown, was on full hotch mode. His first whiff of it came as he passed the Banks of the Tyne Motor Company. By the time he reached Stephen Rachman's residence, it was overpowering.

Across the river, the sun danced on the white metallic rooftops of the Bridon Ropes factory and its neighbouring industrial units, spinning a dazzling spotlight directly onto the Mayor's front door.

Ryan followed the trail and rang the doorbell.

'Working from home again, is he?' Ryan sniffed as Charlotte Spencer opened the door. 'You're here early,' he said, the implication clear.

'The Mayor is working, as it happens. He's a busy man and doesn't need the extra worry of his daughter going missing.'

'I thought the Mayor wasn't worried. He said she'd gone for a jaunt by hersel'.'

'Well, yes but… I mean, it's bound to be on his mind, isn't it?'

'I'd ask him if you'd let me in.'

'I'll tell him you're here.'

Once her back was turned, Ryan stepped over the threshold, uninvited.

Charlotte Spencer returned a couple of minutes later.

'He'll see you now.'

'You'd think he was the bloody Pope, the way she gans on,' Ryan thought.

She led him into a plainly furnished room which clearly doubled as an office.

'Please, sit,' Rachman said without looking up from the papers on his desk. It was at least a minute before the Mayor raised his head, the faintest of smiles on his face.

'You have news?' he asked, emotionless.

'Not yet. Just a few more questions, if you don't mind.'

With an exaggerated sigh, Stephen Rachman set down a pile of unopened mail. 'Sure. Go ahead.'

'Again, I'm just trying to paint a picture of Semilla. Did you see her often after your divorce?'

Stephen snickered a bitter laugh. 'Three times a year, perhaps. Always with the Mad Cow present.' He saw Ryan's face. 'Sorry. I shouldn't call her that. Always with Elizabeth present.'

'I understand Mrs Rachman had custody but surely you had parental rights?' The question was relevant to the case but Ryan asked it with half a mind on his own circumstances should things go tits-up with Hannah.

The Mayor opened an envelope with a paper knife, studied the contents, then placed it on one of three piles on the desk in front of him.

'It wasn't worth the hassle,' Rachman said. 'I knew, one day, Semilla would want to see me, when she was old enough. If I was awkward with Mad Cow – Elizabeth – she'd just poison Semilla against me. Poison her against me even more, I should say.'

The Mayor reached for another envelope as Ryan considered Rachman's response.

'Why did you stalk her?'

The letter knife clattered to the desktop. 'I beg your pardon?'

'Mr Rachman, I understand you would follow your daughter home from her dance lessons.'

Rachman glanced at the letter in his hand before setting it on the smallest of the piles. Finally, he answered Ryan's question. 'Yes. I did. Sometimes.'

'Why?'

'Semilla's my daughter, for Christ's sake. Wouldn't you want to see your child if the mother put all sorts of obstacles in your way?'

Aye. I would,' Ryan thought. 'What did you get out of it? I mean, you're a busy man and to take time out just to watch her and not speak to her...'

'Look, Detective Sergeant, if you had children, you'd understand. I wanted to see Semilla develop. Watch her grow. She used to dance on her way home, you know. Apart from an annual concert when Elizabeth deigned me permission to attend, it was the only opportunity I got to see her dance.'

The Mayor set down his work again before meeting Ryan's gaze. 'I'm proud of her, you know. More proud than you'd ever imagine.'

Ryan paused for thought. He'd been right all along. If Semilla had been snatched, the Mayor wasn't behind it.

'Do you know a Keith Kennedy?'

Stephen Rachman smirked. 'Not as well as someone else I could name.'

'What's your opinion of him?'

The Mayor shrugged. 'I don't really have an opinion,' he said, opening another envelope. 'More charity shit,' he muttered, putting it on the largest pile in front of him.

'What's Mr Kennedy's relationship with Semilla?'

The Mayor's mouth opened although it was several seconds before any sound emerged.

'What are you suggesting?'

Ryan blushed. 'Sorry. I didn't mean to insinuate anything, you know... Anyway, I meant do they get on; Kennedy and Semilla?'

'You'd be better off asking Elizabeth. I really wouldn't know.'

Ryan turned to face Charlotte Spencer, still hovering behind him. 'And what about you, Ms Spencer? What do you make of Semilla?'

'I've never met her,' she said in an accent straight out of *'Allo 'Allo.'*

Stephen Rachman jumped in. 'I don't know why you might think Charlotte would know my daughter when I barely know her myself.'

Ryan ignored him. 'Are you French, Ms Spencer?'

She shook her head. 'My grandmother is, not me or my parents. I lived with her for most of my childhood. People do say I have the accent. It's not significant, surely? To Semilla going missing, I mean.'

Ryan turned his attention back to the Mayor who had resumed sorting his mail. 'Your daughter has an unusual name.'

Without looking up, the Mayor asked, 'Semilla or Rachman?'

'Semilla. French, is it?'

Stephen Rachman smiled. 'I see where you're coming from, but you're off-track. Semilla isn't a French name. It's Spanish. It means seed. We – Elizabeth and I – thought it appropriate. Semilla was our little seed.'

For the first time, Ryan thought he heard Rachman's voice break with emotion. Either way, Charlotte Spencer and her *'French-ness'* no longer seemed relevant.

'I was told Semilla didn't have many boyfriends but I understand there was one.'

Rachman looked up. 'Really?'

'So I gather. I believe it was when she was, perhaps, sixteen?'

The Mayor thought for a long time. 'Yes. Now you mention it, she did say something about one boy.'

Ryan's brow furrowed. 'I thought you didn't see Semilla more than a couple of times a year.'

The missing girl's father sighed. 'Give it a rest, will you? I still spoke to her, fairly regularly as it happens. There is such a thing as mobile phones, you know,' he said, holding his aloft to make the point.

'This boy. What do you know about him?'

'Very little, actually. I know she didn't want her mother to know about him. He was a couple of years older than her. More keen on Semilla than she was on him. If I remember correctly, he was all set to go to Uni. Electrical engineering, I believe. He must have been keen because he turned down his place so he could be around Semilla. Then, a couple of months later, she buggered off to London to the Royal Ballet before the Bolshoi headhunted her after her first performance.' The Mayor shook his head and smiled at the same time. 'He wasn't best pleased, poor sod.'

Ryan brightened. They had another possible suspect. 'What happened to the boyfriend?'

Stephen Rachman twisted his mouth. 'I think I heard he became an apprentice sparky but can't be sure.'

'Mr Rachman, did Semilla ever mention his name, or where he lives?'

'It was years ago, man. Wait – I think he was called Neil. No idea what his second name was.'

The Mayor opened another letter.

'I can see you're busy, Mr Rachman. I'll leave you to it. If you remember any more about the boyfriend, please get in touch.'

Ryan's hand drifted to his pocket for a card with his contact details. When he handed it to the Mayor, Rachman wasn't looking. He was staring at the contents of an envelope, all colour drained from his face.

'Stephen?' Charlotte Spencer asked in a concerned tone.

The Mayor said nothing. His eyes shimmered as he closed his eyelids.

'What is it, Mr Rachman?' Ryan asked.

'Nothing.' He crumpled the letter into a tight ball. 'I'll do what I can to remember more about the boyfriend.' He swallowed noisily.

'Can I see what's in your hand?'

The Mayor thought for a moment, then relented. He had no choice, really. He handed the note to Jarrod.

Ryan carefully unfolded the paper.

In stylised capitals, as if using a child's stencil as a template, were the words:

'WE HAVE YOUR DAUGHTER.

TELL YOUR EX-WIFE TO STAY BY HER PHONE.

WE'LL BE IN TOUCH.

DO **NOT** INVOLVE ANYONE.

DO **NOT** TELL ANYONE.

IF YOU DO, YOUR DAUGHTER HAS HAD HER LAST DANCE.'

ELEVEN

Ryan called it straight in. Sam Maynard ordered him to bring the Mayor to the station until Jarrod reminded her of the note's contents.

'Ma'am, if there's a watch on the Mayor, bringing him into the station will only alert suspicions. Whoever's behind this are bound to know we're looking into Semilla's disappearance so if we make the odd appearance at either of the Rachman residences we won't raise eyebrows. Hauling Stephen Rachman in is another matter.'

The Super agreed. She told Ryan to bring the note with him before diverting Danskin back to Forth Street for a briefing. If Edwin Trove was involved, Danskin needed to know before speaking to him.

By ten o'clock, all the key players were assembled in her office.

Ryan passed the note, sealed in a transparent evidence bag, around the room. 'We don't need a calligraphy expert to know that's not natural handwriting. It's a stencil,' he said.

Danskin, Parker, and Dexter agreed.

'Prints?' Maynard suggested.

'Possibly but it'll have the Mayor's and mine aal ower it, as well.'

'In that case, we need the envelope.'

Ryan swore. 'I didn't bring it, ma'am. If there's any DNA on it, it'll be in the bin by now.'

Sam Maynard recognised the pressures on an investigating officer. Mistakes happen. Her ice-blue eyes showed understanding, not chastisement.

'At least we now know we're looking at an abduction,' she said. 'Stephen – you've got all the resources you need on this one.'

He nodded his appreciation. 'Cheers. We still need to keep things discrete, though, given the threatening tone of the note.'

'Agreed. Okay, we need a word with Edwin Trove. Stephen – that's back with you. Sorry I brought you back when you were already on your way to him but I thought we all needed to know we're walking on eggshells now.' Maynard looked at the makeshift board. 'Lyall, can you update the rest of the team and draw up an official crime board for us? I'd like you to co-ordinate activity for me.'

'Aye, ma'am. Nae problem.'

'And I'd also like you to see if Todd can find anything about the ex-boyfriend. I think he's a rank outsider but I want no stone unturned.'

The Super fingered a list of names on an A4 sheet of paper. 'We've still got the cast of characters Sophia Ridley provided from the night of the show. Lucy, get Trebilcock and O'Hara to help you chase some of them up. No cats out the bag, though. Tread carefully.'

'I'm assuming it's too early for Ravi to come up with owt from the CCTV, is it?' Ryan said.

'It is. It's a good point, though. That gives us a problem.'

'In what way, ma'am?'

She drummed her fingers on her desktop. 'It's okay. I'll get DCI Kinnear's team to trawl through the footage. They're experienced enough to spot anything untoward.'

'So, what's Ravi going to do?'

Maynard smiled for the first time. 'He's going with you.'

'Where to?'

'You saw the note. *'TELL YOUR EX-WIFE TO STAY BY HER PHONE,'* it said. Which means the kidnapper will contact Mrs Rachman, not the Mayor. Ravi's going to set up bugging and tracking equipment. When that call comes in, I want us to be all over it like a cat on a car bonnet.'

**

Ryan kept his radio tuned in as he took his previous route to Elizabeth Rachman's home in Cleadon Village. Ravi Sangar set off from Forth Street ten minutes later. He drove a nondescript unmarked van and was wearing clothing he hoped would pass as a plumber's dress-code.

Both kept in touch with DI Parker via their radios, and with Danskin's efforts to locate Edwin Trove.

Ryan's nose twitched as a strong smell of garlic drifted through the open car window from the Bistro Romano. 'Nearing Elizabeth Rachman's now. What's your ETA, Ravi?' Ryan asked over the radio.

'I'm on the John Reid Road. Satnav says around fourteen minutes.'

'Sounds a reasonable time gap. Wait 'til I give the all-clear before approaching, though.'

Lyall Parker was following their progress on Google Maps. 'If you arrive before Jarrod says the word, there's a One Stop store off Front Street. Park oot o' sight there. It's nae more than a minute or two away from Rachman's.'

'Got that,' Ravi confirmed.

Ryan's voice came next. 'Turning into West Park Road now. Aw bollocks, man!'

'What's up, Ryan?' Parker asked.

Ryan was parked up on the driveway. The same three cars he encountered on his first trip sat outside the house.

'Looks like Kennedy's here again. He remains a person of interest. We have to play this carefully. If he's involved, Ravi can't set up his kit while he's there.'

Danskin had been listening in. 'Too bloody true, he can't,' the DCI's voice crackled. 'It'll alert Kennedy to the fact we've seen the note. Get him out of there, Jarrod. Sangar, divvent gan anywhere near the place until we know it's safe.'

'Copy,' Ravi said.

All parties heard Ryan suck in a breath. 'I'm going in now.' Jarrod felt faintly ridiculous at using a contrived phrase but this wasn't the time for semantics. He switched off the radio and grabbed his mobile from its cradle.

Elizabeth Rachman opened the door before he rang the bell. Sunlight illuminated the hallway, casting Ryan's elongated shadow along its length.

'Have you found her?' She was back in her blonde wig, trying to make herself feel normal, Ryan assumed.

'Not yet,' Ryan answered, 'But we will. May I come in?'

She stood aside. Ryan remembered the layout and walked straight to the lounge. Kennedy wasn't there.

'Have you questioned my ex yet? Did he admit to anything?'

'Aye, we've spoken to him. Mrs Rachman, we have strong grounds for believing the Mayor isn't involved.'

'I hope you're not taking his word for it.'

Ryan didn't answer directly. Instead, he asked, 'Is Mr Kennedy here?'

'Keith? No, he's not. Why?'

'His car's outside.'

'I wanted some time alone to process things. He's gone to Coulthard Park for a walk. I can ring him if you need him.'

'I don't need him but you can ring him for me. Tell him to stay away for at least another hour.'

Elizabeth pursed her lips. 'Why would I do that?'

'Because I need to speak to you alone.'

The mask dropped and her face crumpled. 'You *have* found her, haven't you? My baby's dead. I just know it.'

Ryan gave her a comforting smile. 'We haven't found her and we're as sure as we can be that Semilla's alive. Please, if you could ring Mr Kennedy, I'll explain everything. Don't mention I'm here, though.'

Elizabeth pulled a puzzled expression but said nothing. She made the call, gave a plausible excuse to Kennedy, and turned back to Ryan. 'Now, tell me what the bloody hell is going on.'

Ryan called Ravi Sangar and asked he give them ten minutes. 'We have some new information,' Ryan explained to Mrs Rachman. 'We believe Semilla has been taken by someone. We don't, though, know by who or why.'

Mrs Rachman's hand covered her open mouth. Eventually, her eyes focused again on Ryan. 'But you're certain it's not Stephen?'

Ryan nodded.

'Then, who would do it?'

'That's what I intend to find out, Mrs Rachman.'

Elizabeth nodded but continued with her silent cry. 'Tell me what's happened. Please. I need to know.'

Ryan contemplated showing Elizabeth the photocopied note. He weighed the options, then reached inside his pocket.

'This was sent to your ex-husband this morning.'

The woman's eyes studied the note. Read it five times, each time she pressed her fist further inside her mouth.

'My baby. Oh my God. Why would anybody…?' She could say nothing more. Her chest heaved, tears flowed, and her cry was no longer silent.

Ryan waited until Elizabeth gathered herself. It was a long wait.

'It's not all bad news…'

'..the fuck? What's not bad about this?' she waved the note in the air like a flag of surrender.

'They won't harm Semilla until they get what they want.'

'I don't have anything to give them!'

Ryan thought about the house and its contents and concluded she had more than enough to give them. Assuming they wanted money, which most kidnappers did.

'I'm sorry I had to make sure Mr Kennedy stayed away, but I hope you'll understand. The note says nobody must know.'

'No. No, I don't understand. Keith wouldn't say a word to anybody...' Elizabeth stopped mid-sentence. Realised what Ryan was implying. 'Keith wouldn't do that. He wouldn't.'

Ryan tried to reassure her. 'We just want to keep Semilla safe. You wouldn't want to jeopardise her safety, I'm sure.'

Elizabeth's face hardened. 'No. Of course not. Somebody has, though.'

'I'm sorry?'

'That bastard Stephen. He's involved you. The note says not to tell anyone, but he did. He told you.'

'Mrs Rachman, he didn't. I was there when he received the letter. He couldn't *'not'* tell me.'

Elizabeth stood. 'I need a drink.' She strode to a cabinet, picked up a crystal decanter, and began pouring herself a large measure.

The doorbell rang.

Elizabeth's brandy plummeted to the carpet.

'That'll be my colleague. Sorry he startled you.'

She sat down with a thud.

'You're joking me,' she said as Ryan accompanied Ravi Sangar into the room.

Ravi was anointed in sweat, dressed in a threadbare lumberjack shirt, and racing green corduroy trousers. He carried a heavy, scuffed metal box in one hand while the other bore a long-handed plunger over his shoulder.

'Please tell me this isn't the best the City and County can offer.'

'Appearances can be deceptive,' Ryan smiled before giving a long list of Ravi's credentials. 'He's only dressed the way he is so neebody will guess he's one of us.'

'Well, I think you're right about that,' Elizabeth said, half-smiling. 'What's he here for?'

Ravi spoke for himself. 'The note says the kidnappers will contact you by telephone. I'm here to fit trackers, listening devices, bugs, and things you could never imagine to all your telephony, both mobile and fixed. Trust me, I'll make sure everything's covered. Are you okay if I get on with it by myself?'

He had already clicked open the case and was offloading his equipment. Elizabeth's 'Be my guest' was largely unnecessary.

While Ravi busied himself, Ryan gently questioned Elizabeth. 'The most obvious reason why someone took Semilla is because of her fame. They will assume she – and, by default, her family – are loaded. This house, and Mayor Rachman's status, would serve to back up that thinking.'

'God. To think I pushed her into her career. If she was Semilla Rachman the medical receptionist, none of this would have happened. It's my fault. Mine, and Stephen's.'

Ryan gently touched her arm. 'Don't blame yourself. There could be another motive.'

'Such as?' Elizabeth said, her tone disbelieving.

Ryan shrugged. 'Revenge is one of the most common reasons.'

Her eyes widened. 'Revenge for what?

'That's what we need to discover.'

'Have you asked *'him'* if he's upset anyone? Stephen, I mean.'

'I knew who you meant. No; not yet, but we will.'

Elizabeth poured another drink, successfully this time. 'I need Keith here. I can't do this by myself.'

'I'm afraid that's not possible. Not yet. I promise we'll do what we can to rule out Mr Kennedy as a priority but, until then, he can't know about what's happened this morning. Now, has Semilla any enemies?'

'Jeez. I don't know. Not that I can think of. Mind, there's bound to be jealousies amongst dancers. It's that kind of environment but, surely, they wouldn't go to those lengths.'

Ryan tended to agree but didn't voice an opinion. 'What about boyfriends?'

Elizabeth shook her head. 'None in this country. Can't vouch for what she got up to in Russia or on tour. I don't kid myself she's a virgin but I'm not aware of any serious commitments.'

'She doesn't know about this Neil kidda, for sure,' Ryan thought.

'I have to ask: what about girlfriends?'

'She's not that way inclined.' Elizabeth stopped for a moment. 'I don't think.'

'Was she popular at school?'

'Oh, Detective Sergeant, I think you're stretching things a bit far. That's ages ago.'

'It is, but if she's been out the country for years, this may be the first opportunity someone would have.'

Elizabeth gave the matter a moment's consideration. 'No. She did get the Mick taken out of her because of her dancing but nothing serious.'

Ravi popped his head round the door. 'That's the landline done. Could I borrow your mobile for a sec, please?'

Elizabeth handed him her iPhone and Ravi began weaving his sorcery on it.

'Which leaves us with you, Mrs Rachman. Have you any enemies?'

'Apart from the bastard, you mean?'

Ravi raised his eyebrows but Ryan pressed on. 'I gather you were a financial advisor. Did you ever make a bad investment on someone's behalf? Cost anyone shedloads of cash? Upset the applecart with a competitor?'

Elizabeth considered the question carefully. 'In my line of work, everything was a gamble. You win some, you lose some. With a bit of luck, you win more than you lose. I certainly did.'

Ryan fixed her with a stare. 'What about those you didn't win?'

'None that springs to mind. None for individuals, anyway.'

'Meaning?'

Elizabeth nodded her head almost imperceptibly. 'There was a company who I did some consultancy work with. They went bust.'

'Because of your advice?'

'Not directly, no. I gave them a range of investment options, pros and cons for each, and they chose from that list. They didn't select the one I recommended so I wouldn't have thought they'd hold a grudge against me.'

Ryan glanced at Ravi who had stopped what he was doing.

'What was the name of the company?' Ryan asked.

Elizabeth didn't answer. She raised her glass to her lips. Ryan noticed her hand was trembling as she drained it.

'I don't think it's anyone in the company.'

'Why not?'

'They sought further advice before investing. Someone else suggested one of my other alternatives. They took that advice, came a cropper, and ended up suing the other party for megabucks.' Her eyes sang a sorrowful lament.

'Do you know who the third party was, the one who was sued?'

Elizabeth Rachman closed her eyes. Made a noise like a deflating bagpipe.

'It was their accountants.'

Sand Dancer

'Their name?'
Her voice was a whisper.
'Bloor Kennedy Smythe.'

TWELVE

They brought Semilla Rachman out of the cabin with a word of caution. The men knew sound carried far over open water so they warned her that there'd be consequences if she raised her voice. Severe ones.

She saw in their eyes they meant it.

The air inside had been stuffy and fetid. On deck, the sun created a pleasantly Mediterranean air. Micky donned a pair of AirPods and pulled at the tab of a beer can. It opened with an appetising swoosh.

The other man handed Semilla a can. She popped it on the deck floor while she knotted the oversize T-shirt above her navel and turned up the legs of her jeans until they were knee-high.

She took a slug of lager. 'I'm scadding hot in this,' she said, pulling at the neck of the T-shirt.

'Scadding?' the man scoffed.

Semilla giggled, too. 'I haven't forgot the old accent, you know.' She tipped her can towards the man. 'Nostrovia,' she added.

'Cheers,' the man replied.

'You understand Russian. I'm impressed.'

'It's the only word I know. Apart from *Pravda* and *Yuri Gagarin*. I guess you speak it a bit better than me.'

'I'm multi-lingual, me. Fluent in Russian, Spanish, and Geordie. *Whey aye, man.*'

They sunk into a silence broken only by the loud and tinny music which squeezed from Micky's AirPods.

'He'll be deaf as a post before he's forty,' the man said.

Semilla moved closer to him. 'Can we get rid of him for a while?' she said softly, looking into the man's eyes.

He glanced at Micky then back to Semilla. 'Not a chance. I'm not falling for that,' he said, loud enough for Micky to hear above the electronic beat of eighties retro music.

Micky smiled before he resumed bobbing his head in time with the beat.

Semilla sat on the deck, knees pulled up, arms wrapped around them. 'I'm too famous. Somebody will recognise me. The plan won't work.'

He wasn't falling for that one, either. 'It will. Trust me.'

'Ha! Why should I trust you?'

He raised a hand against the sun. 'You haven't come to any harm yet, have you?'

'Apart from getting pissed out my head and left alone with Pervy Pete there, no.'

The man laughed. 'Micky's alright, really. Not the sharpest of tools…'

'Maybe not, but a tool he is, right enough.'

More laughter. He'd have to remember to keep his distance from Semilla. He couldn't afford to get too pally.

They sat in silence, the boat barely rocking in the still tide. Out at sea, a BG freight liner on route to Rotterdam appeared little bigger than a child's bath toy. A couple of fishing trawlers, nets cast deep, edged lazily southwards.

Micky had piloted their vessel a few miles north of Elephant Rock. It lay off the coast of South Shields, far enough offshore to remain invisible to the naked eye.

Semilla tilted her head to the sun and let out a sigh.

'I want to go home.'

'No way, Jose. Not until I get my payday.'

She sighed again. Stretched cat-like. Her shirt rode up. She tugged it down, self-consciously.

The sun's rays landed on something ashore, a pin-prick reflection which sparkled like a bright star.

'Know what that is?' Semilla said, pointing to the light. It was a rhetorical question. 'That's Ocean Beach funfair. I loved it there when I was a kid. Until they made me dance. Once they committed me to that, the only chance I had to go was on a Saturday. Sophia never had a class on a Saturday. Even then, it was *'Semilla do your homework, Semilla do this, Semilla do that'* yada-yada-yada.'

She teased with her hair, long-since freed from its bun, over one shoulder.

'There again, you already know all that, don't you?'

**

'This is an outrage!'

'You're nae under caution.' Lyall Parker said, attempting to quell Keith Kennedy's protestations. 'I've just got a few wee questions for you.'

'Fair enough but why not ask me them in the park, where your PCs picked me up? Bringing me all the way here, it's an infringement on my civil liberties. Not to mention a waste of police resources.'

'Thanks for your feedback. I'll be sure tae pass it on.'

Behind the darkened glass of the adjacent observation room, Superintendent Sam Maynard chortled. DI Lyall Parker was one of the best interrogators in her command. Cool, sharp, and observant, it was a shame DCI Danskin relied on him more for meticulous report-writing and top-notch administration work than his interviewing techniques.

'How long have you been living with Elizabeth Rachman?'

'What?' Kennedy spluttered. I don't *'live'* with her. I've been staying with her, that's all. In one of the spare rooms, if you must know.'

Parker made a point of noting everything down, more to stress Kennedy than anything.

'I'll rephrase it. How long have you been staying with Mrs Rachman?'

'I don't know. Three weeks, maybe?'

Parker scribbled more notes. 'Why choose to stay with her now?'

'Because I had time off work. I knew Elizabeth wouldn't want to go anywhere because Semilla was home.'

'Ah yes: work. We'll come onto that in a wee while.'

'What are you getting at?'

Lyall Parker ignored him. 'Did you nae think she'd appreciate some time alone with her daughter? It's not often she gets to see her. Did you feel you were intruding?'

Kennedy appeared genuinely nonplussed. 'I never thought of that. Neither of them seemed put out by me being there, though. I mean, I've known Semilla for a good few years now…'

'Yet, you didnae' have a ticket to see her perform at the Customs House. Why was that?'

Kennedy rolled his eyes. Sweat dripped into them and he rubbed away the saltiness. 'I've already told you lot why. Semilla's father was supposed to attend. I didn't want to cause a scene. Why don't you ask him why he wasn't there? It's his daughter, for God's sake.'

Lyall's hands pressed on the desktop as he stared at Kennedy. 'We have done. And we know where he was at the time of Semilla's disappearance.' He help the silence. 'Where were you, Mr Kennedy?'

Kennedy sat back and raised his eyes to the ceiling. 'I was at Elizabeth's.'

'Can you prove it?'

Kennedy smirked. 'I believe the burden of proof is on you.'

**

Sam Maynard strolled to the opposite wall of the observation suite and began listening in to the interview in the next room.

'Why did you lie to me?' Stephen Danskin asked.

Edwin Trove's ruddy face glowed like a beacon under questioning. He fidgeted with his fingers.

'I didn't lie to you.'

'Mebbe not but you didn't tell the truth.'

'I have no idea what you mean.'

Danskin stood and paced the floor, carefully studying Trove as he moved. 'How long have you worked at the Customs House?'

'I don't really work there. I'm a patron. It's more fund raising. Organising publicity, that sort of thing.'

'I'll rephrase me question. How long have you been *involved* with the Customs House?'

Trove sucked in air. 'Six years, give or take.'

Danskin nodded as he continued walking.

'Yet, you conveniently didn't know aboot the two fire exits backstage.'

'Who says I didn't know about them?'

'If you did, why didn't you mention them?'

'You didn't ask about exits. You asked about entrances and CCTV.'

Danskin walked towards Trove, who cowered away from him.

'Don't. Be. A. Clever. Shit. It doesn't wash with me, pal.'

Trove scratched the pockmarks on his cheek.

'Okay, then. If you're suggesting I had something to do with Semilla's disappearance, why would I go to the lengths of sending you all the CCTV footage we had? I mean, you saw how much there was, know I got onto it straight away, and sent them to what's-his-face in a matter of hours. If I was involved, why'd I do all that?'

'Why indeed,' thought Sam Maynard, invisible behind the one-way glass.

**

'How did you first meet Elizabeth Rachman?'

'Through work. We were both in finance.' Kennedy unbuttoned the top button of his shirt.

'What were your impressions?'

Kennedy pursed his lips. 'She was competent. A professional. A diligent worker who knew her stuff.'

'Attractive?'

'I didn't look at her in that way.'

'And with a rich daughter.'

'Semilla wasn't at the height of her career then. Money wasn't an issue.'

Lyall smiled. 'Nae at that point, perhaps.'

Kennedy folded his arms and sat back. 'Get to the point, Detective Inspector.'

'Okay. Seeing as you ask, I will. You first met Mrs Rachman over a business deal. The deal went pear-shaped. One of the parties sued the arse off ye.'

Kennedy's mouth dropped open.

'So, tell me why on God's earth you wanted to stay in touch with a woman who'd cost you a fortune? One you didn't look on as *'attractive,'* he said, looking at his notes for emphasis, 'Unless she had something you wanted. Like a daughter wi' aspirations o' greatness, perhaps?'

**

Sam Maynard returned to Danskin's interview with Trove. She held a finger to her lips as Ryan joined her.

'Any joy? He mouthed.

Maynard pointed towards Danskin and Trove and shook her head. Half-turning, she aimed her finger towards the opposite window. She shrugged and mimed, 'Could be.'

Ryan moved to the Lyall Parker window while Maynard observed Danskin.

'How many times have you been to the basement of the Customs House?' the DCI was asking.

'I could probably count them on the fingers of one hand,' Trove said.

'You expect me to believe that? You've been connected to the theatre for years yet hardly gan doon there?'

Trove nodded. His face had assumed its normal rose colour rather than the port-wine of earlier. It didn't escape Danskin's attention that Edwin Trove was calmer, more assured of his ground.

'Any reason why you stay away?'

'I've no reason to go under stage. It's got nothing to do with my role here. Mebbe you'll understand now why I forgot about the exit.'

Danskin chewed on his lip. What Trove said was plausible.

'You do realise we'll check for fingerprints doon there, don't you?'

Trove gave an assured smile. 'Be my guest. You won't find any of mine.'

Danskin believed him. 'Okay Mr Trove. You're free to leave.'

Trove was on his feet before Danskin had finished the sentence.

'You need to know, though, that we'll be watching you. You are not to contact anyone who was at the theatre that night. More importantly, you can't talk to anyone or post about this on social media. Or unsocial media, if it comes to it.'

Edwin Trove agreed. 'You have my word. And, I promise, if I think of anything else about that night, I'll let you know.'

'Reet. Now hadaway out of here – and not a word to anyone or I'll have you back in here before you can say Craig Revell-Horwood.'

**

'Look, I know it looks bad. I can see that, now. I swear it wasn't like that, though,' a flustered Keith Kennedy was saying. 'Elizabeth is a genuine friend who I care deeply about. That's why I need to be with her. To support her through her ordeal.'

'I agree with you on one o' those points. It does look bad.' Kennedy ruffled his grey hair. 'Do I need a solicitor?'

'I don't know: do you?'

Kennedy stood. 'Don't piss me about, Detective Inspector. Are you charging me or not?'

Lyall narrowed his eyes. 'I need to see all your financial accounts. Personal and business. I want you to hand over your telephone and PC. Most of all, I want you to go home, and stay there. Not Elizabeth's home – yours.'

'She needs me…'

'…about as much as I need ma toenails removed.'

'But…'

'There's nae buts about it. Not even a Kardashian-sized butt. You're to go home. You're to stay there. You're not to leave the house, speak to anyone about any of this, or send a message by pigeon-post or semaphore. We're taking your communication devices tae stop you doing any of that.'

Kennedy was about to speak again until Parker stopped him with a raised hand.

'We'll be going through your accounts, your computer, your phone records. If we find anything, anything at all, you'll be back in here and you won't be getting out. Och, and if any of this reaches the press, we'll know where it's come from. I'll make sure you sing soprano for the rest o' your natural. D'ya ken?'

Kennedy kenned.

'Just so you know, a car will take you home and its driver will be on watch outside your hoose twenty-four seven. Don't think of going outside, even for a tab. Got it?'

A uniformed officer escorted Keith Kennedy out of Forth Street into a waiting car.

**

Maynard led a debrief in her third-floor office. They agreed Trove wasn't their man but all four still harboured suspicions about Kennedy.

'So, we've counted one out but not really counted anyone else in,' Ryan observed. 'Can we widen the net?'

'We're waiting on Rick Kinnear's report on the security footage and the squad's review of Sophia Ridley's list. Really, until they come through, we're stuck in quicksand.'

Ryan looked into the squad room. The team worked diligently but the demeanour of the crew gave no signs of a breakthrough. Ryan noticed the lights in the darker reaches of the squad room had flickered on. Another twenty-four hours had passed with no sign of the missing girl.

'Ma'am, I need to get back to Elizabeth Rachman's house. If the call comes through...'

'You can't do Jack Shit,' Danskin interrupted. '*SHE* must take the call. If anyone else picks up, they'll know we're involved.'

'I didn't mean take the call, but I am a crisis negotiator, remember. I could coach her through what to say.'

'Not tonight, Ryan,' Maynard said.

'The call could come through tonight, Ma'am.'

She dipped her head. 'Indeed. Ravi is still there, though. We had a plain clothes cop dress as the plumber and take the van away. If the house is being watched, they won't know Ravi's inside.'

Ryan reluctantly agree to leave it. For now. 'First thing tomorrow, then.'

'Second thing tomorrow,' Danskin corrected. 'The first thing you do is see the Mayor.'

'Again? What for, man? We're just going over old ground, surely.'

Danskin's face held a self-satisfied smile.

'Not necessarily. We've been looking for someone with a grudge against Mrs Rachman. If we want to look wider than Kennedy, we need to see if anyone holds a grudge against the Mayor. After all, he's the one who received the note.'

THIRTEEN

The skies displayed the wispy orange and pink hues of the day's end as Ryan made his way to the door. Not his door: the door to Doris Jarrod's care home.

The staff denied him entry at first. 'Too late for visitors,' the disembodied voice had said, until the evening manager intervened, empathising with both Ryan and Doris's predicament.

A casual glance as he signed the visitor's book showed both his father and brother had visited, three hours apart. *'Good, she hasn't been alone,'* Ryan thought, even if both visits were short-lived.

Ryan was warned she'd be asleep but, if his grandmother did happen to be awake, the shift manager confirmed he could spend a little time with her.

'A little time's all we've got,' he realised.

Sure enough, when the carer quietly opened the door, Doris Jarrod was fast asleep on her back, mouth open, drool hanging from it.

Ryan tiptoed towards her and gently dried her chin with a tissue. He lay a hand on her head and stroked the old woman's hair.

Looking at her now, he realised how tiny his grandmother had become, lost in her bed like a hatchling sparrow in the nest of an albatross. He chastised himself for not noticing her decline. Or, if he had noticed it, for denying himself the truth.

He left Doris Jarrod sleeping, fearful it was the last time he'd see her.

He needed comfort. He'd spend the night at Hannah's. He might have overlooked his grandmother; he wasn't about to make the same mistake with the mother of his child.

Ryan avoided the inevitable delays over the Tyne Bridge by taking the Redheugh, from where he looped around the city centre towards Jesmond and Hannah Graves.

She opened the door to her flat and Ryan launched himself at her. 'I need a hug.'

Hannah held him until he was ready. 'What's up, love?'

'It's just me Gran, man. It chokes us up, sometimes.' He pulled away from her. Noticed her hair was wet and plastered to her head, her face glowed red. 'Are you okay?'

'Yes. I'm just so bloody hot, lugging this one around all day.' She cradled her swollen belly. 'Not for much longer, though, eh?' she smiled.

Ryan grimaced. 'I hope this case I'm on doesn't stop me being there.'

Hannah took the weight off her feet and patted the space next to her on the bluish-grey corner sofa. 'Get it off your chest. You know you want to.'

'Nah. It's okay. It's just, well, when someone's kid goes missing, it kind of puts a different complexion on things, with you being pregnant, an' all.'

She threw an arm over his shoulder. 'Nobody would dare even think of taking our son. Todd Robson would see to them.'

Ryan laughed. 'Good point. He's enough to scare the crap out of anyone.'

'Ry, I know you've just got here, but I'm really done in. Let's snuggle up for a bit, yeah?'

He made a point of looking at her abdomen. 'Not sure I'll get close enough with all that in the way but I'll give it a gan.'

She gave him a playful slap and they made for the bedroom. As she changed, Ryan noticed how the Chinese Dragon, tattooed on her bloated and distorted midriff, appeared headless, its face obscured by her enlarged breasts.

He almost laughed until Hannah stopped him with a, 'What?'

'Nowt,' he said. 'Just admiring the view.'

'Oh aye, of a beached whale, you mean? Stretchmarks like a wrinkly ballsack?'

'No,' he said, nuzzling up to her, 'Of the love of my life.'

They rolled into bed, Hannah with great difficulty. Ryan draped his arms around her neck.

'Can I feel him?' he asked.

'Of course, man. You don't have to ask.'

'It's your body,' he said.

'And he's your child.'

Ryan's arms reached around her. She sighed. 'There's something I need to say, though.'

'*Here we go*', he thought. 'Gan on,' he said.

Hannah said nothing. 'I'm waiting,' Ryan prompted as casually as he could.

'Don't take it the wrong way,' she said, immediately putting him on the defensive. 'At work, you know, you're dynamic. Strong. Decisive.'

'A-ha,' he said, feeling he'd had this conversation before.

'Sometimes, when it's just me and you…'

'Spit it oot, girl.'

'Well, you can be a bit of a wuss at times, you must admit.'

Ryan said nothing, knowing anything he did say may be used against him.

'When our laddo is born, can I ask you to be a bit more dynamic with me?'

He rolled away from her.

'There – you see what I mean? Why didn't you have a go at me instead of just accepting it, in a huff?'

'Who said I accepted it, like? Look, it's been a shit day. Shit with a capital S. Can we not do this now?'

He felt Hannah nod her head. 'Aye, I'm sorry. I shouldn't have said owt. I guess, I dunno, I'm a bit on edge. I want him here, safe and well,' she said. He sensed her pat her stomach.

Ryan rolled against her once more. 'I get that. And I promise you, once we have our baby, I'll change.'

She turned to kiss him. 'Don't change too much, though. Just a little more Superman than Clark Kent, yeah?'

They laughed and fell asleep in each other's arms.

**

Ravi Sangar wasn't asleep. There again, he was one of the rare breed who functioned perfectly fine on three hours sleep a night.

Instead, he checked his phone equipment for the third time since he'd set it up. The lid of his metal briefcase stood open. One device was tapped into Elizabeth Rachman's Wi-Fi, a lead from another unravelled over the dining room table and out into the hallway where it joined the landline circuit.

A cradle inside the case held Ravi's mobile which he'd paired with Mrs Rachman's own phone, lying on her bedside table. Ravi pictured a worse-case scenario where the kidnapper called whilst Elizabeth slept through it in a brandy-induced slumber. Whilst she'd quaffed enough of the stuff, he hoped it was sufficient to allow sleep to possess her rather than render her unconscious.

Ravi ensured the kit kept both mobiles fully charged, and he never took his eyes off four green lights glowing from a cuboid pack in his case. If any light changed, he'd know either signal was lost or an outside source – the kidnapper – had tampered with the line.

He whispered into his police radio. 'Des, where are you with the CCTV footage?'

Desmond Obyego, one of Kinnear's team reviewing the CCTV from the Customs House, came back. 'There's hours of video to get through and we don't know who we're looking for. It's impossible.'

In the stillness of the house, Obyego's voice came over like a tannoy broadcast. Ravi turned the radio sound down. 'Nothing's impossible,' he said. 'Do you know if anything's emerged on social media yet?'

'Nah. That's one thing that's easier to check on, and there's zilch.'

'Good,' Ravi said, even though he wondered if it really was good. Should news break now, just as the abductor was ready to make the call, he was certain to think it had come from the police.

'*DON'T TELL ANYONE*', the note had said.

Ravi silenced the radio and the cavernous house echoed to Elizabeth Rachman's snores from the room above.

**

Someone else had fallen asleep, but he wasn't snoring.

Micky had stretched out on the deck of the vessel moored off the South Shields coast, his head resting against his locked hands, gazing up at a starlit sky. The rhythmic movement of the boat and the soothing sound of lapping waves soon sent him into a deep sleep.

He dreamt of finding untold riches in a treasure chest buried on the shores of a desert island. In his dream, he was rich beyond his wildest imagination, yet he was castaway with nowhere to spend it.

A thunderous noise startled Micky awake. He was enveloped in a damp mist, cold and shivering. He sought out his puffer jacket and snuggled into it, not knowing if this was part of his dream or a true awakening.

The noise came again. A deep, rumbling sound; haunting, mournful, and eerie, emanating from deep within the shroud.

A foghorn or, as Micky observed, 'A *fucking* foghorn,' indicated a ship somewhere within two miles of them. Far enough to be of little concern, but close enough to deprive him of sleep.

He checked his wristwatch. Wiped away moisture from its face and saw it was barely three o'clock. Micky shivered again. He craved the dry of the cabin, where the other man kept watch over their hostage. A pointless exercise, Micky thought, because she was going nowhere. Not out here.

He checked his AirPods were safely in his pocket and approached the cabin door. He heard voices from within. Not clear enough to hear what they were saying but enough for him to know the other two weren't sleeping, either.

Micky opened the cabin door.

The voices stopped, abruptly. The man and Semilla looked towards him. Both were seated at the small table, each with a Heineken can in front of them.

'I could do with one of them myself,' Micky said, opening the small refrigerator. 'It's like sleeping next to a herd of elephants, isn't it?' he said, motioning towards the ocean with his head.

Semilla and the man remained silent.

'You two not able to sleep, either?'

'It's the fault of your herd of elephants,' the man in charge said.

Micky noticed the bed hadn't been slept in. 'The horns must have been going off longer than I thought.'

'Yes,' he said simply. 'Listen, it doesn't need two of us to watch her,' the man said.

'Aye, mebbe not, but it's bloody horrible out there now. I'd rather be inside, thanks very much.'

Semilla Rachman looked at the man, who looked back at Semilla. 'If you must,' he said to Micky.

Micky fizzed open the can and took a slug. 'Aah. Just the horses,' he said, smacking his lips.

Semilla looked puzzled.

'You don't want to know,' the man told her.

'So, what have you two been up to, then? Talking about, I mean.'

'Our little captive here has been telling me all about Russia. Or, at least, how the nobility live, like her. She's one of the privileged herself. You wouldn't know what it's like to be a peasant, would you, Miss Rachman?'

'Bednyak, not peasants,' Semilla corrected him. 'They're the poorest. And you're right: I never did get to meet any. I met the odd kulak, though.'

'What's one of them, when he's at home?' Micky asked, wiping beer froth from his lips.

'Richer peasants,' she smiled. 'Farmers, mostly. Farmers who can afford to employ the bednyak.'

'It's all Russian to me,' Micky said. 'Can I have a word?' he motioned the man outside.

Once on deck, Micky asked, 'I thought we were supposed to keep our distance? Not get ower matey with her?'

'*You're* not to get friendly with her. Me? I need her confidence. If I'm going to call her folks, I want her to comply and not kick-off when I'm on the phone, you idiot.'

Micky nodded. 'Good cop bad cop, yeah?'

'Something like that. Now, you zip your jacket up like a good boy and stay out here while I do what I have to do until The Boss gives the word. Comprendez?'

Micky tapped the side of his nose and walked away as the man re-entered the cabin.

'So?' Semilla asked, arms folded across her chest.

'Don't worry about Micky,' he smiled. 'I'll take care of him.'

FOURTEEN

Ryan rose at seven and reminded Hannah to call him if baby gave any hint he was about to make an appearance. Ryan hoped he'd said it in as un-wussy way as possible, and she didn't bite so he assumed he'd succeeded.

He drove from the 'Residents Only' bay outside the apartment building knowing his priority, today, was to brief Elizabeth Rachman on how best to manage the kidnapper's call when it came. His first visit, to Stephen Rachman, would be short and to the point.

Mercifully, the cooler night had doused the stench of the Tyne as the Peugeot stopped outside Stephen Rachman's. The Mayor answered the door himself, cup of tea in hand. He was still wearing his robe - and flip-flops with socks.

Ryan rolled his eyes. So did the Mayor. 'Not you again,' Rachman said, showing him in. 'Don't worry – I'm alone. I'm not working today so Charlotte isn't here, despite what you may think of us.'

'I'll get to the point and let you get on with your day,' Ryan said, without comment. 'First, a quick update. We've placed an officer with audio surveillance kit at your ex-wife's for when the kidnapper makes contact.' He made a submissive gesture. 'Don't worry. It was all done discretely. Anyone watching the property wouldn't suspect a thing.'

'I'm not worrying,' the Mayor said, hands wrapped around the mug. 'Elizabeth told me about it last night.'

Ryan lowered an eyebrow. 'I thought you two hated each other.'

'We do. Intensely. But Semilla's still our daughter so we have enough in common to talk about her, especially at a time like this.'

Ryan nodded. 'True enough. I shouldn't have said nowt. My apologies.'

'You're forgiven.'

'Cheers. Right, on to why I'm here. So far, our investigation has concentrated on why Semilla was targeted. Yesterday, we spoke to your ex to see if she had any enemies…'

'I guess she said me. If she did, she'd be right - but I didn't take Semilla.'

'We believe you. I'm here to ask you the same question: have you made an enemy of anyone, especially recently? Someone who might be pissed off enough to take your daughter?'

Stephen Rachman stared at the wall as he thought. 'No. I don't think I have. I mean, as Mayor and a councillor, we all pretend we're playing proper politics and that can be a bitchy business but, in all honesty, there's nothing and nobody that springs to mind.'

'You're absolutely sure?'

'I am. Wait…no, it's nothing. I'm sure.'

'What were you about to say, Mr Rachman? It might be important.'

Stephen Rachman lay back into the sofa, head resting against the cushions. 'There's plans on the table for the development of the old dry docks; the graving docks. It's a contentious issue and there's pressure from several parties on both the yay and nay side of the divide.'

Ryan watched the Mayor intently as Rachman's thought processes unfolded.

'A week or so ago, I got a phone call. They didn't say who they were. All they said was *'Make sure it's the right result.'* I assumed they were talking about the development but, as they didn't say which result was the one they wanted, I couldn't help even if I wanted to.'

'Was the caller male or female?'

'Male.'

'Old or young?'

Rachman sighed. 'Detective Sergeant, it was a seven or eight-word, one-sided conversation. I really can't tell you more.'

'I'll get one of the boys to look through all your call records…'

'No point. It came through to me at the Town Hall. They don't record incoming numbers.'

Ryan sucked air through his teeth until it whistled. 'What's the name of the company pressing for the development?'

'Dennington Investment and Holdings.'

'Any connection to Mrs Rachman's company?'

'None whatsoever.'

'Do you know who they use as accountants?'

Rachman smiled. 'Not Bloor Kennedy Smythe, for sure, if that's what you're thinking.'

Ryan puffed out his cheeks. It was what he was thinking. 'Thank you, Mr Rachman. I'll do some background checks into Dennington's, all the same. Thanks for your time.'

'My pleasure.'

As Ryan moved to leave, Rachman said, 'Find her for me, won't you? I might seem calm and collected but I assure you I'm in bits in here.' His clenched fist thumped his chest.

'I promise you we'll do everything we can.'

They said their goodbyes and Stephen Rachman watched Ryan drive off.

It was only when he'd closed the front door he remembered something which had come to him during the night.

'Shit. I forgot to tell him the name of Semilla's old boyfriend.'

**

As if the squad back in Forth Street didn't have enough to do, DCI Danskin requested ANPR details of all vehicles in and around the Customs House area on the evening of Semilla's disappearance.

Des Obyego, in charge of video surveillance in Ravi Sangar's absence, blustered and spluttered and cursed. 'We don't even know what colour vehicle we're looking for, never mind make, model, or who's driving it.'

Danskin remained adamant. 'Just run all plates through one of Sangar's programmes, man. It's bound to come up with somebody we know.'

'And what if they didn't use a car?'

Danskin spat a laugh. 'So, they beamed her up, did they?' The DCI began saying something else, then stopped. 'Bloody hell. You might be onto something.'

'Might I?' a puzzled Obyego queried.

'Aye. And you'll pleased to know you've just given yourself another job.'

'I'm not following.'

'The Shields ferry, man. It's not a kick in the arse away from the Customs House. Call Nexus and get them to send every bit of footage the transport authority has from the ferry terminal.'

Obyego groaned. 'Should I stick a brush up my backside as well?'

'Either that or my boot. Your choice.'

Danskin went in search of Sam Maynard to discuss the ferry theory, leaving a crestfallen Desmond Obyego to slink away, hands in pockets.

**

The short drive from Hebburn through South Shields and into Cleadon was just long enough for Ryan to explain to Lucy Dexter back at HQ why he wanted information on Dennington Investment Holdings, and if any of their senior officials had connections to either of the Rachman's or Bloor Kennedy Smythe.

Ryan was pleased it was Elizabeth Rachman herself who answered the door. He wasn't entirely convinced Keith Kennedy would have listened to Lyall Parler's friendly 'advice' but he had, seemingly.

Once inside, his eyes immediately drifted to the oil painting of Semilla. The girl was slight, looked younger than her years, yet her face portrayed poise and utter concentration.

Mrs Rachman saw him study the portrait. 'You'd never believe the strength she needs to hold that position.'

Ryan gave a knowing smile. 'Trust me, I do.'

Elizabeth shook her head. 'Don't do that to me.'

'Do what?'

'Lie. I need you to be truthful through all this. If I can't trust what you say, I can't trust you to find Semilla.'

'I'm not lying, Mrs Rachman.'

'So, you're a ballet aficionado, are you? I don't think so, somehow.'

'Ballet, no; gymnastics, yes. I started gymnastics when I wasn't much older than Semilla was when she began dancing. Kept at it 'til I was nearly fifteen. Arabesque is one of the moves I had to do on floor routines. Mind, I was crap at it. Rings and bars were my speciality.' He looked at the painting again. 'Yes, I do know what strength and balance it requires.'

When he looked back towards Mrs Rachman, he saw something new in her eyes. Something which showed they'd found common ground. Now was as good a time to begin coaching her, Ryan realised.

'How do you feel if Ravi and me go through what to expect when the call comes in, and how you should handle it?'

'Yes. I'm up for that.'

Ryan thought it strange she hadn't questioned or berated him over Keith Kennedy's absence. Perhaps Ravi had already explained to her. He had no time to ponder it because Elizabeth was already calling Ravi Sangar to join them.

'Everything set up?' Ryan asked.

'Aye. It's just a waiting game, now.'

Sensitive to Elizabeth Rachman's presence and fragile state of mind, Ryan added, 'Don't think it'll be long now, like.' He smiled towards Mrs Rachman. 'Any chance of a cuppa before we get cracking?'

'Of course.'

'White coffee, no sugar.'

'I'll just have a glass of water, ta,' Ravi added.

Ryan waited until she'd left the room before continuing. 'Has she said owt aboot Kennedy?'

Ravi shook his head. 'The DCI called her last night. I nearly crapped mesel' when the phone rang. I assumed it was the kidnapper. Seemingly, he explained they couldn't take any chances with Kennedy or any other bugger, what with the threats and all. She said she understood, but I think that might have been the brandy talking.'

Sangar lowered his voice. 'She'd give Todd Robson a run for his money on the drinks front. We need to keep her off the hard stuff. Can't risk any cockups when the call comes.'

Ryan ran a hand through his unwashed strawberry-blond hair. 'It'd better come soon, the call.'

'You don't think Maynard will scale back resources, surely?'

'Nah, nah. I'm more worried that the longer we're waiting, the more likely it is that summat's gone wrong. I don't want the lass to turn up dead.'

They jumped at a crashing sound behind them. Turned to see a silver tray on the floor, broken glass alongside it. Coffee stains running down the Barbara Hulanicki wallpaper. And Elizabeth Rachman striding towards them.

She slapped Ryan across the cheek. 'What aren't you telling me?' she screamed, her voice shrill.

Ryan's hand went to his cheek defensively, but he wasn't going to arrest Mrs Rachman for assault. She wasn't a criminal, just a desperate mother frightened for her child.

'You said you'd protect her. All this,' Elizabeth gestured at Ravi's kit lodging in the room, 'Is supposed to find her for me. Find her *alive*, I mean.' She broke into sobs.

'Please,' Ryan said, 'Why don't we sit down? I'll explain what I meant, and how we – all of us, that is – can ensure Semilla comes home safely.'

Ryan hoped he sounded calmer than he felt. He'd put his foot in it big style by suggesting Semilla may come to harm. From every photograph in the room, Semilla's eyes seemed to stare at him.

'I'm listening,' Elizabeth said, icily.

Ryan made eye-contact with her. 'Semilla is fine, I promise you,' hating himself for not knowing if it was a lie. 'What I meant was, we need to do everything right from hereon in so we make sure it stays that way.' He hunkered down in front of her. 'Are you with us?'

Elizabeth nodded.

'Good. So, what Ravi has done here is ensure every call coming into this house can be traced and recorded without the caller knowing, yeah?'

She nodded again.

Ryan thought about letting Ravi explain the kit but he knew it would be full of technical shite no-one except Ravi himself would understand. Besides, he had just gained a modicum of Elizabeth Rachman's trust and needed to build on it.

'These lights here let Ravi know that his kit is safely attached to all your devices, and that they hold enough charge to take the call when it comes. This little screen,' Ryan pointed to a narrow gauge alongside the lights, 'Will show a graph which reveals the caller's speech pattern. Our expert's should – will – be able to tell the mood of the caller: whether he's calm, tense, nervous, and so on, aye? That'll help us manage the caller's attitude.'

Mrs Rachman tugged at her hair. 'I wish Keith was here.' Ryan let the moment pass and waited for Elizabeth to speak again. 'Okay. What do I have to do?'

In a soft but confident voice, Ryan explained the protocols. 'First rule, don't make the caller angry. Yes, you might get upset but don't abuse the caller.'

'Like call him a twat, you mean?'

'Aye, exactly that. Even though we know he is, we don't say it. Secondly, try to keep him talking. Ask questions, nothing pushy, just enough so we can pick up the call co-ordinates and any background noises which might give away his location.'

'I think I can manage that,' Elizabeth confirmed with a less-than-convincing smile.

'Also, ask to speak to Semilla. He probably won't agree but he'll expect you to ask, so do it. It'll also keep him on the line a little longer.'

Elizabeth was staring at the oil-painting. 'God, I hope he lets me speak to my baby.'

'One other thing: don't annoy him. Never say 'no' to him. Whatever he asks, either agree to it or stay non-committal. Do you get all that?'

'Oh, I understand, alright. Not so sure I'll be able to remember it all, though. I wish Keith was here.'

Ryan looked towards Ravi who raised his eyebrows.

Jarrod spoke again. 'Waiting for the call is probably going to be the hardest thing you'll ever have to do but, when it comes, Ravi and me are going to be here with you. You're not alone, yeah? When the phone rings, pick it up at the end of the second ring. That'll give Rav time to get his gear working.

I'll help you through the call as best I can but I can't speak. The caller must think you're alone.'

Elizabeth's brow furrowed as she struggled to retain all the information.

'Why don't you get some rest?' Ryan suggested.

'I won't sleep,' she said.

'Stretch out on the sofa, then. Close your eyes. Ravi and me will just be in the next room.'

'Okay.' After a pause, she added, 'Thank you.'

In the dining room, Ryan sat opposite Sangar. After the effort of remaining calm in Mrs Rachman's presence, Ryan's jaws now clamped together. A nerve twitched in his cheek. He checked his watch twice in succession.

'We need them to call soon, while it's all fresh in Mrs Rachman's mind.'

'The instructions, you mean? Yeah, we do,' Ravi concurred. 'Why do you think they're waiting?'

Ryan looked to the ceiling in thought. 'I don't know. Perhaps they're checking stuff out, like whether the Rachman's have told anyone. Or they're counting on the Rachman's nerves getting the better of them so they'll do whatever they're told to do.' He shook his head. 'I honestly don't know.'

Neither Ryan nor Sangar voiced what they knew they were both thinking: that maybe Semilla Rachman was already dead.

Ryan nearly jumped out of his skin.

A phone was ringing.

FIFTEEN

Ryan waited until he got his breathing under control. His heart fluttered like a hummingbird's wings and his face flushed red. What a fool. Unless Elizabeth Rachman had downloaded the Blaydon Races as her ringtone, the phone that rang was his own.

'Jarrod,' he said, coughing into the speaker.

'Am I interrupting you?'

Ryan remained flustered. 'Who is this?'

'Stephen Rachman.'

Jarrod let out a breath. 'Hi Mr Rachman. It's fine. What can I do for you?'

Elizabeth Rachman, having heard a ringtone and a conversation, hurried into the dining room; her face tight and gaunt.

Ryan covered the mouthpiece and reassured her it wasn't the kidnapper. He saw her whole body relax.

'It's more what I can do for you,' the Mayor said. 'I don't know if it's going to be useful, but I've remembered the name of Semilla's old boyfriend.'

'I think that'll be very useful.'

'I remember his second name. It's Gowland.'

'Anything else you can tell me about him, sir?'

'No. Sorry. I'm surprised I even remember that much, if I'm honest.'

'Nee worries. I'll check it out. Anything else you think of…'

'I know – I'll be in touch.'

The Mayor ended the call.

'Who was that?' Elizabeth asked.

'Semilla's father,' Ryan explained.

Elizabeth's mouth curled. 'Right. What did he want?'

'Mrs Rachman, does the name Neil Gowland mean anything to you? Ryan looked out the kitchen window, out over the palatial garden to the rear. Something in what he'd just said troubled him but he didn't know what or why.

'Should it?'

Elizabeth's question brought Ryan out of his trance. 'Your ex seemed to think he might have known Semilla, in the past.'

Elizabeth thought again. Finally, she shook her head. 'Not to my knowledge. Why? Who is he?'

Jarrod shrugged. 'Probably not important but we'll see if we can find anything more about him. We don't want to overlook anything, do we?'

Ryan gave Elizabeth a reassuring smile whilst wondering why he felt uneasy doing so.

**

Under instruction, Micky had navigated the craft several miles south where it lay drifting off Seaham's Blast Beach.

He didn't know it, but the area was once so polluted its black, coal-strewn sands were once used as the backdrop of desolate planet in the Alien movie series.

After years of regeneration, it was now a wildlife hotspot and tourist attraction. Fortunately, their vessel was far enough offshore to be invisible to the naked eye.

'Why are we moving further away?' Micky had asked his associate.

'It's not a case of moving away, more a case of moving. We don't want to stay in one spot long enough to attract attention to ourselves. Another day, possibly two, and we'll move again - if The Boss hasn't given us instructions by then.'

'If he hasn't, we'll need another load of scran and booze. We're just about out of both.'

The man poked Micky in the stomach. 'You could do with losing a few pounds.'

'Fuck off,' Micky replied. 'What's the lass up to?' He motioned towards the cabin.

'Trying to find a T-shirt which doesn't look like a maternity dress on her. She's tiny, isn't she?'

Micky thought back to the time she launched her assault on him. 'Just as well, probably. Any bigger and...'

Semilla opened the cabin and joined them on deck, wearing a T-shirt which did look like exactly a maternity dress.

'Next time you go ashore, get us some proper clothes, will you?'

'It's not a fashion parade. All you need is something to keep you covered. And that's all you'll get.'

The boat rocked as the wake from a passing fishing vessel fresh out of Seaham harbour washed beneath them. Semilla stumbled and fell into Micky's arms.

With a smug smile, he said, 'See, accidents do happen out here. Remember that next time I stumble.'

'If there's a repeat of what happened last time you stumbled, I'll rip them off.'

To emphasise the point, she grabbed him and squeezed tight.

Micky jack-knifed and let out a gasp. 'Jesus, man,' he wheezed.

'He won't be here to help you,' Semilla joked, as she and the man laughed at Micky's plight.

The craft rocked again. Battleship-grey skies circled a watery sun while, on the horizon, monstrous anvil-shaped clouds amassed. Waves, flecked with white and ridged like quaffed hair, lurched against the bow.

Semilla stumbled again. She avoided Micky this time but, in steadying herself, she gashed her hand on a rusted bolt on the craft's gunnel.

'Shit! That bloody hurt.' She raised her hand and blood ran down her forearm, splattering the deck like an abstract painting.

'Let's get you down below,' the man said. He held her good arm and escorted her into the cabin, Micky following close behind. 'There'll be a first-aid box somewhere, Micky. Have a hunt around.'

Meanwhile, the man grabbed the first thing that came to hand. He pressed the material firmly against the jagged cut on Semilla's palm. Held it there for several minutes. Slowly, he eased the pad away. When blood flowed again, he repeated the action.

Micky returned with some plasters and tape. The man grabbed them from him and bound the wound until the bleeding stopped.

'Do you know how much they cost?' Semilla complained.

'Eh?' He looked at what he'd been used to douse the initial blood flow. Semilla's ballet dress. 'Oh. Never mind. You'll afford another one, assuming you get out of here in one piece.'

Semilla paled.

'We'd better get out of here soon,' Micky groaned. 'I could eat a scabby horse.'

'Tough shit,' the man retorted. 'There's no way I'm rowing ashore until the storm's passed.'

'Unless The Boss orders otherwise,' Micky muttered under his breath.

'Yes. Exactly that,' the man worried.

**

'I'm bored,' Ryan said, more to himself than to Ravi.

'You don't have to stay here. I'm sure Danskin can find you summat to do back at the station.'

'I know, man. I'm torn, to be honest. If the call comes through, I'm needed here. I'm it doesn't, I'm wasting my time.'

Elizabeth Rachman was out of earshot, so Ravi took the opportunity to confide in Ryan. 'I don't like this silence. I'd expect the kidnapper to want his money and get out of it all like a shot.'

Ryan knew he was right. Ordinarily, that's what a kidnapper does. What if it wasn't money he was after, though? Not directly, anyway. What if he was after something bigger? Like, property on a redeveloped dock?

Jarrod called Lucy Dexter. 'Owt on Dennington's yet?'

'They seem pukka so far,' Lucy lisped.

'Aye, but they aren't gonna run an advert saying they're as corrupt as fuck, are they? Keep digging.' Ryan ended the call. Began drumming his fingers on the table.

'Ry, man. You're getting on me nerves. Cool your jets, will you?'

Ryan exhaled through his nose like a bull.

'Looker, borrow me laptop for a while. I'm sure there's something you can tap into back at the station.' Ravi rotated his laptop and spun it in Ryan's direction.

With little enthusiasm, and a little guilty he'd distracted Lucy Dexter from the task he'd initially given her, he pulled up the list of names Sophia Ridley had provided; the names of those present at the theatre on the night Semilla disappeared.

None of them meant anything to him. He spotted Edwin Trove's name, thought about Danskin's interview with him, and remained unconvinced he was their man.

A few names later, he came across a couple of others Sophia had mentioned to him: Myshka Hankova – Sophia's choreographer – and Patrick Wheatley, who'd showed him around the theatre.

The next name he recognised made him gasp out loud. So loud, Ravi shot him a look.

Ryan's hand went to his pocket. He brought out his phone. Fumbled with it and saw it clatter to the table. He picked it up with trembling fingers.

Everything became clear to him. The motive, the means, the opportunity.

What's more, he knew why he'd experienced such a strange feeling when the Mayor had mentioned Semilla's boyfriend's name.

The Mayor was wrong. His name wasn't Neil.

'Sir,' Ryan said as Danskin answered. 'I think I know who's got the Rachman lass.'

'Just a minute. I'm with the Super. I'll put you on speaker.' Ryan heard him say, *'It's Jarrod. He's got a lead.'*

'What have you got for us, Ryan?' Maynard asked.

Ryan used the couple of extra seconds he'd been given to gather his thought. 'We're looking for an ex-boyfriend of Semilla Rachman's.'

'You sure?'

'Pretty much, ma'am. He was at the theatre the night Miss Rachman went missing. If she was taken out the rear fire-exit, as we believe, he knew the area back there well. He also nearly took me out with a spanner the first time I met Sophia Ridley.'

'We need a name, Jarrod,' Danskin urged.

'He was working the stage lighting for the performance.'

'Just give us the bloody name, man.'

'Noel Gowland.'

Across from Ryan, Ravi Sangar held up a flat palm. Ryan gave it a satisfying smack.

SIXTEEN

'Listen up, everyone. Stop what you're doing,' Stephen Danskin shouted to his team as he and Rick Kinnear emerged from the Super's room.

He clapped his hands. 'STOP! LISTEN, PEOPLE: WE HAVE NEW INFORMATION!' he shouted even louder.

They stopped and trained their eyes on him.

'We're scaling back the review of CCTV footage...'

'Scaling back? Why?' Lucy asked.

'How's that gannin to help us?' Todd Robson added.

An irritated Danskin said he'd told them to listen, not speak.

'We have a prime suspect. His name's Noel Gowland. He's a sparky who does work at the theatre. He's also Semilla Rachman's ex-boyfriend.'

He pulled up a second whiteboard and began scribbling details.

'DI Parker will still be co-ordinating activity here, but here's what that activity is going to be. Now we know who we're looking for, DCI Kinnear's team will use facial recognition software to scan the crowds around the exterior of the Customs House.' He noted the board accordingly. 'The Super believes there's still mileage in researching activity on and around the Shields ferry terminal. Obyego's the one charged with that.'

Danskin took the opportunity to pause for a moment. He checked his team were fully focused, which they were once Trebilcock set down a half-eaten pasty.

'I want Dexter to continue looking into the background of everyone on Sophia Ridley's list. Gowland may have an accomplice – the note said, *'we'*, remember; indicating there's others involved. We need a complete check across social media for all Gowland's posts, on-line friends, owt like that. Phone records, too. They're your jobs,' he pointed to Trebilcock and Gavin O'Hara.'

'What aboot me, guv?' Todd Robson interrupted.

'You're there to support everyone else until we get the go-ahead.'

'Go-ahead for what?'

'The warrant to search Gowland's house. The Super's on it already. Once it comes through, you're coming with me to search the place.'

A smile broke across Robson's face. He cracked his knuckles. 'Expecting a bit of trouble, guv? I'm your man for that.'

'Aye, I know you are. That's why I'm coming with you. You'll knock seven bells oot of him if I let you loose.'

'Spoilsport,' Todd mumbled.

'Okay everyone: I want us on this until we know more about Gowland than his own mother.'

**

The boat pitched and tossed amidst a frenzy of waves. Below deck, Semilla clung to the bunk with her one good hand. Micky steadied himself by flexing his knees for balance whilst hanging onto the table with both hands. The other man sat on the wooden floor, sliding back and forth at the maelstrom's whim, constantly thrown against the hard surfaces of the cabin.

'She is going to survive this, isn't she?' Micky asked. He saw Semilla's eyes widen. 'I mean the boat: not you, man.'

'You're supposed to be the seaman here,' his colleague pointed out. 'You tell me.'

'You arranged to get this boat. Surely you know its seaworthiness?' His words were almost drowned out by the creaks and groans of the vessel as it strained against the elements.

'It's my cousin's mate's boat,' the man said. 'How would I know?'

'Jesus, man. What if he fancies a day's fishing or summat and finds his boat's disappeared?'

'He won't.'

The larder door swung open at the hit of a wave. The few remaining food items clattered to the floor, tins rolling like bowling balls across the floor.

'You don't know that.'

'I do. He's backpacking in Oz. Won't be back for months.'

Semilla lost her grip on the bunk and joined the man and the foodstuff on the floor.

'Shit!' She winced as her injured hand hit the deck. She clung to the man with her good hand to give herself some protection from the motion of the sea.

The air in the cabin reeked of sweat, diesel fumes, and the metallic bite of seawater. Semilla retched but, without food in her stomach, nothing emerged from her mouth.

'What happens if The Boss gives the word now? How are you going to get to shore to make the call?' Micky fretted.

'This'll blow over soon enough.'

'It's been too long already,' he shouted above the cacophony.

The man didn't reply as he slid across the floor once more, Semilla clinging to one of his legs. With a roar, the wind blew open the cabin door. Rain and seawater poured through, pooling on the floor before another list of the craft saw it spread in rivulets across the floor.

The cabin lights flickered twice. The sound of the storm deafened them. The confined space became more claustrophobic and added to the tension.

The light flickered once more, then died.

'Bloody great,' Micky shouted above the racket.

'The emergency generator will kick in.'

Despite himself, Micky laughed. 'It won't have one. This thing is too fucking small, man.'

The man waited. The light remained lifeless. Micky was right – there was no emergency generator.

'What are we going to do?' Semilla whimpered.

The man and her slid across the floor again. They came to a halt against a grille. The man peered between the slats. Gripped it with both hands and heaved. The cover came away in his hands, exposing a vent behind.

'What are you doing?' Micky yelled above the storm.

The man reached inside the space. 'I'm fixing the bloody light before you two crap yourselves.'

'Hadaway, man. You can't fiddle with the electrics with all this water around. You'll kill yourself – and probably us with it.'

The man twisted his head to look over his shoulder. 'If I don't sort it, we're pretty much fucked anyway.'

'You said yourself, the storm will pass soon.'

'It will but, with no electrics, we can't start the engine. We'll be stuck out here until the coastguard arrives and wonders what a world-famous ballet dancer is doing with two sods like us.'

The man's head disappeared back into the hole.

'So, shut up and let me do what I'm good at.'

**

The rain had arrived at Cleadon Village.

Ryan paced back and forth in front of the enormous bay window, looking towards a widow's sky weeping giant teardrops. They heralded their arrival with loud taps on the glass which soon transformed into a percussive beat.

'Bit of a change from yesterday,' Ravi mused.

Ryan wasn't listening. 'I should have questioned him at the time.'

'Who? And what time?'

'Gowland, man. When I saw him at the theatre.'

'You weren't to know.'

'Doesn't help, Rav. I could have got to the bottom of this much sooner.'

Ravi closed his laptop and joined Ryan on his walkabout. 'From what I know, you had no reason to question him. The only person of interest at the time was the Mayor. Even Danskin wasn't sure there'd been a crime committed.'

'Only 'cos I convinced him, remember.'

Sangar put his arm around Ryan's shoulder as they prowled the room. 'Neebody thinks you should have suspected him. Besides, you saw what the note said: it referred to 'WE.' Gowland isn't in this alone.'

Ryan stopped in his tracks. 'Where's Mrs Rachman?' he said quietly.

Ravi shrugged. 'Could be anywhere in a place this size.'

'Do me a favour. Step outside the room. Keep an eye out for her. If she's anywhere near, give us a shout.'

'What you got in mind, like?'

'You've given me a thought, that's all.'

Ravi gave him a quizzical look but left the room, all the same.

Ryan called DCI Danskin as soon as Ravi closed the door behind him.

'What have we got so far, sir?' he asked.

'Early doors, Jarrod. We're working flat out, here. Nothing hugely significant yet but we've just made a start. We know Gowland rents a two-bedroom flat in Shields, somewhere between Chichester Metro and West Park. I'm waiting for the Super to get sign-off on a warrant. It'll make life easier once we have a neb around.'

'Can't you just burst in?'

'Physically, aye: of course we can. Tactically, no. If we burst in and he's not there – which is probable because I divvent think he'll be holding Rachman in his hoose – we aren't exactly keeping a low profile.'

'True enough.'

'If we get a warrant and a key off the landlord, it'll be much easier.'

'When is the warrant due?'

Danskin checked his watch. 'It's overdue. Probably an administrative cock-up with the magistrate signing it off. You know what they're like.'

Ryan sighed. 'Anything from Gowland's Socials?'

'Not yet. Lyall suggested we wait for a full dossier on 'em rather than act on drip-feed.'

A flash of lightning lit up the dining room in Cleadon Village.

'I feel a fraud hanging out here when there's so much gannin' on.'

'You're not being a fraud. The kidnapper's call is key.' Danskin waited a beat. 'I know Sangar's there as well so, if there's no call by six, get yersel' home for the night. I need you fresh and alert when the call comes.'

'And if it comes when I'm at yem?'

'On the off-chance it does, Sangar can deal with it.'

Ryan mulled it over. 'I'm not happy about it but, okay; I will do.'

'Good. Use the time to check in with Hannah or your Grandmother. Or both, if there's time. Most importantly, though, rest up.'

'Can I make a suggestion, sir?'

'Be my guest.'

'While I'm twiddling me thumbs waiting for either the abductor's call or six o'clock, I think I should check for any connection between Gowland and Kennedy. After all, we suspect there's more than one kidnapper involved, and we all think Kennedy's a bit dodgy. What if they're in it together?'

It was an angle Danskin hadn't considered. He'd ordered checks on Kennedy's relationship with others potentially involved, but not between Kennedy and Gowland. 'Good thinking, Jarrod. Feel free to have a mooch.'

'Cheers, sir.'

A doom-laden thunderclap rattled the windowpanes as the call disconnected.

SEVENTEEN

The cabin lights came back to life at the same moment the clouds parted and daylight returned.

'Bloody typical,' the man complained as he wedged the grille back in place.

'Aye, but at least we can get the motor started again,' Micky said. 'I think we should get closer to shore.'

To his surprise, the man agreed.

Micky pressed the starter motor and there was sufficient spark to ignite the fuel. The engine spluttered and coughed but eventually chugged into life.

'Head north. We'll lay-up Roker-side of the Wear,' the man instructed.

Semilla still sat in pooled water. She had her arms wrapped around her, the oversize T-shirt soaked and clinging to her in folds. Her teeth chattered. 'Can we get some heating on, please? I'm freezing.'

Neither man knew how to switch it on so they helped her up top where, now the rain had stopped, the air was warmer and less dank than below deck. They gave her a dry shirt and she peeled off the old one as soon as the men disappeared below.

'Ah shit, man,' Micky swore.

'What's up now?'

He pointed to two shell-like objects floating in the flooded cabin. 'Me bloody AirPods, man. What am I gonna do now?'

'That's the least of our worries,' the other man said, stepping over the remnants of their larder afloat in the mess. 'We need more food. We need The Boss to come good - and soon – so I can get ashore.'

He picked up a bowl. 'Get to work. We need this bailed out sharp as. I'll get whatever I can salvage down here and fasten it to the rails. Our clothes will dry off quicker up there, especially with the wind.'

While Micky scooped out stinking seawater, the man disappeared up-top.

'You okay?' he asked.

A bedraggled Semilla shook her head. 'I'm pissed off, the saltwater's killing my hand, I'm hungry, thirsty, and dressed like a bag lady. In short, no: I'm fucking not alright.'

The man considered putting his arm around her, then thought better of it.

She looked at him with tears in her eyes. 'When's this going to be over?'

It was a question he couldn't answer. It wasn't his call. 'Things can only get better,' was the only thing he could think to say.

The wind eased and a hint of warmth filled the air through the broken cloud. A single strip of blue emerged from the greyness. 'See? It's better already.'

'I don't want to go through that again,' she said. 'That was bloody scary.'

'We won't have to go through it again. Micky will get the boat moving but we'll stay closer to shore where it's more sheltered.'

Semilla raised her eyebrows in a gesture which said, '*You think?*'

She shivered again. 'I'm still cold.'

'Thought you'd be used to it. Surely it's colder in Russia?'

'I'm in a luxury hotel in Russia; not sat in a freezing cold water on a sinking ship.'

She had a point, he thought.

Sand Dancer

Semilla rubbed her thighs vigorously to get the circulation flowing. 'Anyway, how did you get the power back on?'

The man smiled. 'It doesn't take a genius to flick a switch. Fuse had blown, all circuits. I just re-set the trip switch.'

Semilla swept hair like seaweed around her neck and over one shoulder. 'I wish you'd just get on with things.'

The man looked towards the shore. 'So do I, believe me.'

Before she could speak again, Micky emerged dragging a trail of soaked bedding with him. 'I'll drape this over the benches. Doubt you'll be able to use them tonight, mind, but hopefully the night after they'll be better.'

The other man retrieved Micky's puffer jacket from a hook on the door. 'You can use this tonight.' He tossed it to her, then remembered something. 'Give me it back.'

She obliged, and the man dipped into the inside pockets. He brought out two mobiles.

'Nearly a schoolboy error,' he said. 'Here, catch.' He threw the jacket back to Semilla, the communication devices safely back in his possession.

'Can't have you getting your mitts on these, can we?'

He pocketed the phones, but not before noticing they were dangerously low on charge.

**

Six o'clock came and went with no sign of the kidnapper's call, nor a hint of a connection between Keith Kennedy and Noel Gowland. When Danskin confirmed the warrant for Gowland's property wouldn't arrive until first thing next day, and reassured Ryan he'd put a watch on the place 'just in case,' Jarrod followed orders and headed for home.

He grabbed a Big Mac from the drive-through next to the MetroCentre and munched on it on his way through Swalwell. He held his breath as he drove by Doris Jarrod's care home, then realised he and his family had to face facts.

Ryan found himself outside his father's house in Newfield Walk. He licked his fingers free of burger sauce, wiped the greasy steering wheel with a napkin, and made his way up the path.

A deep bark followed by a high-pitched mewl told Ryan his approach hadn't gone unnoticed. Kenzie was on him the moment he opened the door, the dog's tongue lolling as he set his paws against Ryan's thighs.

'Come in, son,' Norman Jarrod called. 'Kenzie told us it was you.'

Norman Jarrod lay sprawled out on the sofa, an empty dinner plate on the floor. 'Get yersel' a can oot the fridge, if you like.'

Ryan declined. They exchanged some banter, discussed their thoughts on the Toon's failure to qualify for Europe, before Ryan got to the heart of the matter.

'When the time comes, do you know what Gran's plans are? You know, funeral and such like.'

Norman's lips vibrated. 'I divvent want to think of it, man. Not yet.'

'Dad, you heard what Mrs Doyle said. We need to be prepared.'

Norman sighed. 'Aye, I suppose.'

'It's just, well, I was thinking she might like to be laid to rest where Rhianne's memorial is, in Blaydon. I'd have to check with Reverend Appleby first, of course, but...'

'Bloody hell. You have been given it some thought, haven't you?'

'We have to. I'm sorry, but that's the facts.'

Norman breathed deeply. 'Nice thought but she'll want to be with me dad, in Mountsett.'

'Right.'

Norman sat up. 'What's that supposed to mean?'

'Nothing, really.'

'Which means something. Howay son – what's up?'

Ryan stayed silent. He didn't know how to shift the bloody great elephant out the room.

'Okay,' he said. 'Granda's up at Mountsett. Gran's gonna be there an' all, from what you say. Eventually, we got a memorial stone in Blaydon for us to remember Rhianne.'

Norman guessed where Ryan was going. 'You want to know about your Mam, don't you?'

Ryan bit on his lip. 'All this with Gran has got us thinking and, aye, I do. Why's Mam not remembered somewhere?'

Norman interlocked his fingers. Ryan knew his dad didn't open up easily so he waited patiently.

'It's what she wanted. She always said, *'If I need a bit of stone for folk to remember me, I've failed in life.'* Me, you and wor James, you're lucky enough to remember her as she was. We don't need a bit of carved rock to show us we loved her. All It's all tied up in here,' he tapped his temple, 'In our heeds.'

'Is that why she didn't mark Rhianne's passing, too?'

Norman nodded. 'Exactly, son. Me and your mam's memories of your sister were with us every day.'

'But you went against her wishes when you agreed to me getting a memorial for Rhianne.'

'I did. And, you know why? Because you didn't have memories of Rhianne to rely on. She came and went before you were born. Once you asked for a remembrance stone, I had to agree. I had to because I know your Mam would have agreed.'

Ryan sat in reverential silence. Even Kenzie sensed the mood and trotted off to his bed where he lay curled up, eyes never leaving Ryan.

'Dad, I know you scattered Mam's ashes. I've never asked where because I respected your privacy, and I know you said she didn't want a memorial. Now, I'm not asking for a headstone or nowt but I'd like to go there, once-in-a-while. Where did you scatter them?'

Norman's eyes slid shut. 'Where we first met. We met at a party. Not sure who's or what the occasion was, but we were both there, separately, like. We hit it off straight away. Mam didn't drink so, after a while, we went outside. Walked a bit. Talked a lot. Laughed even more. We sat and we listened to nowt in particular, and we watched the moon and the stars. That's where her ashes were scattered, Ry.'

Ryan's mind conjured up a vivid picture of his mother and father sitting side-by-side. All that was missing was a location.

'Where was the party?'

Norman looked at Ryan. 'You know the place well.'

'I do?'

'Aye. Her ashes were scattered beside the bench we sat on that very first night. The party was in South Shields. Your mother's ashes were spread next to the Customs House.'

Ryan's jaw tightened. Semilla Rachman's case had just become personal.

EIGHTEEN

Six a.m.

A pearl-like sky shimmered over the River Tyne.

Ryan Jarrod's Peugeot was already parked up, but not on Elizbeth Rachman's drive.

It sat on the cobbled courtyard of the Customs House theatre. Directly to Ryan's left, pigeons pecked at yesterday's crumbs underneath a picnic table on a grassed area fronting the riverbank.

Nicotine-stained fingers of sunlight curled around the clouds and prised them apart. Ryan turned his head in the opposite direction, to where the Merchant Navy Memorial - a bronze of a helmsman standing on an uneven keel - kept watch over a row of three benches and the river beyond.

They were simple benches, wooden slats for seats and a wooden backrest, all held together by curved wrought iron legs and a metal frame. The sort of benches found in any park anywhere in the land. Unremarkable in every way – unremarkable to all but Ryan Jarrod.

He climbed out his car. Walked slowly towards the seats basking in the early morning light. He sat on each for a few seconds, pondering which had played its part in his fate and destiny. Ryan stroked the surface of the middle bench as a passing jogger watched him with idle curiosity.

A beat of wings and the guttural coo of a pigeon landing on an adjacent bench distracted Ryan. The pigeon cocked its head to one side, looked at him, then flew off.

A discarded feather spiralled down and landed in his lap. Ryan gave a sad smile as he pocketed the keepsake.

He toyed with his mobile phone for a moment or two before making a call.

'What time is it?' Hannah Graves said through a stifled yawn.

'Half six. Sorry if it's early.'

'It is a bit. Everything okay?' She shuffled up the bed using her elbows, grunting at the effort.

'Yeah.'

She swung her legs out of the bed with another groan. Hannah yawned again and rubbed sleep from her eyes. She yearned for the day she could get out of bed without the sound effects.

'Summat must be up for you to call at this time.'

Ryan remained silent for a while. 'It's funny. You think you know who you are, yet life never fails to chuck in a curveball or two, y'knaa what I mean?'

'Not really; no.'

'Well, it's not even a year since I discovered I had a sister neebody had told me about. Next thing you know, I learn I'm going to be a dad. Then, you find out stuff out about your mam.' His voice was quiet, flat. 'Like I say, life's funny.'

Hannah stood. Felt a twinge so sat back down. 'Are you sure you're okay?'

She heard Ryan breathe. 'Aye, man. Stop being a wuss,' he replied, echoing Hannah's comment about him.

She gave a half-laugh. 'If you're sure.'

'I'm sure. Anyhoo, what about you?'

She winced as she sensed another crampy pain. 'I'm fine, apart from being woken up at first light.'

'Sorry. 'Bye, then.'

Ryan ended the call, leaving Hannah to wonder what the hell that was all about.

**

Seven a.m.

Stephen Danskin had ordered his troop to be in early. He wanted to make as much progress as possible with the hunt for Noel Gowland before the warrant arrived. He was delighted to see the team already assembled as he arrived shortly after seven.

Although Danskin had no direct influence over DCI Kinnear's squad, he made a beeline towards Des Obyego to thank him for his prompt arrival. Obyego informed him facial recognition had drawn a blank on Gowland and, to date, he'd seen nothing of significance from the ferry terminal cameras.

'Keep at it. Something might turn up yet,' Danskin told him as he squeezed his shoulder. Returning to his own team, he asked Gavin O'Hara for an update on Gowland's phone records.

'I've run a check on his call lists. He hasn't been in touch with Semilla Rachman's number, or vice-versa. As far as I can tell, they've had no contact in the build up to her disappearance.'

'Aw hell, though I expected he wouldn't present us with an open goal.'

'There's records of him contacting a few of the folk on Sophia Ridley's list.'

Danskin scratched his jaw. 'I suppose that's feasible seeing as he was prepping for the performance. Any numbers jump out?'

'There's a few he's called more than others. This one,' O'Hara said, pointing to the call log on his screen, 'Is Ms Ridley's, this is the stage manager, Patrick Wheatley.'

'I guess he'd need regular contact with those two. Any others?'

O'Hara smiled as he pointed to a third number. 'Edwin Trove.'

'Interesting.' Danskin mulled over a thought. 'None to either of the Rachman's or Keith Kennedy?'

Gavin shook his head. 'We've seven calls to unrecognised numbers. Non-contracted phones, pay-as-you go, and such like. Only one of those numbers appears more than once.'

'And there's no way we can trace them?'

'Nope.'

'Shit.'

He looked towards the door as Sam Maynard swept in. 'I'm straight onto that warrant,' she said even before Danskin could speak. 'I'll let you know the minute I get it.'

The DCI turned his attention to Nigel Trebilcock. 'What about Gowland's on-line presence?'

'He ain't on Insta or TikTok. His X account consists exclusively of re-posts.'

'Is he following anyone? Or has followers himself?'

'Yeah. He follows hundreds, which I guess is where he gets his reposts from, so I do.'

'He's not following the Bolshoi by any chance?'

Trebilcock smiled. 'No, but that brings us to Facebook.'

'You've found summat?'

Trebilcock brought up Gowland's Facebook profile. 'The account's set to private. Without access to his own laptop or phone, oi can't do much of a check,' he said in his agricultural Cornish tone.

Lyall Parker interrupted. 'Sangar will, though. I'm already arranging for him to have the details. If anyone can break into it, Ravi can – and he's nae exactly busy sat waiting for the phone tae ring.'

Danskin agreed. He rubbed behind his ear and addressed Trebilcock again. 'In the meantime, though, you've got us something, yeah?'

'I thinks I do.' He clicked the 'Posts' tab on Gowland's profile. *'No posts to show,'* it said. He tried the 'About' tab and was greeted with:
*'No workplaces to show
No schools/universities to show
No places to show
No relationship info to show.'*

Trebilcock moved the cursor over 'Friends'.

'If this is going to say, *'No friends to show,'* divvent bother,' an irritated Danskin snapped.

Instead, Trebilcock displayed the 'Following' list. Gowland followed dozens. The Viz, random comedians, electrical wholesalers, a few bands Danskin had never come across.

Nigel quickly scrolled down until he came to *'Classical Ballet Lovers,' 'Wonderful World of Ballet,'* and *'The Bolshoi Appreciation Society.'*

'Well, well,' Danskin muttered. 'Fancy finding a sparky who's into ballet.'

'I've joined the groups myself, just for research purposes, minds you, and there's something about Semilla Rachman on all of them. Not much, oi gives you, but she gets a mention or two.'

'Brilliant work, Trebilcock. It all adds up.'

'Yous ain't seen the best bit, yet.'

Danskin held his breath. 'Go on.'

'All Gowland's photos are private – except for his past and present profile pictures. Look what we have.'

Trebilcock scrolled through them, one-by-one. There were eleven in total. And four were of a young Gowland and a teenage Semilla Rachman.

'Even more interesting, if these were taken six or seven years ago, why would Gowland use them as profile pictures as recently as the last six months?'

**

Eight a.m.

The man stepped outside the cabin. 'I'm gonna have a quick check around. Make sure there's no damage now the storm's...'

'Already done,' Micky interrupted.

'Won't do any harm to have another look.'

'Okay. I'll come look again as well.'

The man rolled his eyes. 'No, you won't. You're going to keep an eye on Rachman. I don't want her to think we trust her. She might get braver than is good for her and try something.'

Micky tisked but followed orders.

Once the cabin door closed, the man leant against the metal rail of the craft and looked out to sea. All was calm, the tide serene. Closer to shore, he felt safer though he was wary they were more visible.

He turned to face the land. Roker lighthouse stood out, proud and assertive against the flat terrain. He worried they were too exposed to dog-walkers on Roker Beach before dismissing the thought. He was becoming paranoid. To anyone watching, the vessel was any one of a number of boats which came-and-went every day.

The man sauntered back to the cabin, more relaxed. He entered to find Semilla tidying up to retro music from Micky's phone.

'Do I have to listen to that shite?' he said.

'Me AirPods are shafted, man. How else am I supposed to listen to me music?' Micky retorted.

'Silence is golden,' the man reminded him.

'Nah. Wrong era. That was sixty-seven. The Tremeloes. I was on Popmaster once, you know,' he said to Semilla, before remembering he shouldn't reveal much about himself.

'Really? How did you get on?' she asked, feigning interest.

'I was pants,' he said, downcast.

They sat in a silence interrupted by David Gahan's vocals.

'Depeche Mode. *'Personal Jesus'*. Eighty-nine,' Micky said triumphantly as he sang along to the lyrics.

'You're all alone
Flesh and bone
By the telephone
Lift up the receiver
I'll make you a believer.'

With an abruptness which surprised Micky and Semilla, the man stood. He unlocked an overhead storage unit. Brought out a canvas bag, a *'Tech Air'* logo etched onto a patch on its side.

'Where'd you get that from?' Micky asked.

'The cabinet, doh.'

'I know, man. I meant…'

'I know what you meant.'

'What is it?'

The man shook his head. 'You really think I'd use a phone to make the call? No,' he said, patting the bag, 'This'll make us impossible to trace.'

Micky smiled. 'You've had word from The Boss?'

'When I was on deck, yeah.'

'It's time?'

The man nodded. 'Yep. I'm going ashore. Time I found my land legs again.'

'Don't forget the beer,' Micky laughed.

'And can I have some clothes, please? If I'm going home soon, I'd like to look half-decent.'

The man looked at them in turn. 'I think we'll be able to drink champagne soon, not beer. As for you, princess, I didn't say anything about letting you go.'

Semilla's face blanched while Micky was already counting his money.

**

Nine a.m.

'It's here.'

Sam Maynard held aloft an embossed sheet of paper as she dashed from her office.

'Champion,' Danskin said, rubbing his palms together. 'The knock's on, lads.'

Lyall Parker was straight on the blower to arrange back-up from local plod. 'Nae blues 'n' two's,' he told them. 'Low key, two units only.' He ended one call and went straight onto another. Danskin listened in as his deputy gave a scant explanation to the landlord and instructed him to meet them outside Gowland's flat in forty minutes.

A stir-crazy Parker asked to be relieved of his admin role and the Scotsman travelled to the location with Danskin and Todd Robson, who spent the journey rolling his shoulders like a prize fighter waiting for the bell.

They met with the owner of the accommodation who held onto the keys unless they agreed he could accompany them inside.

'What do you know about the tenant?' Danskin asked.

'He never misses a payment. He's never complained or asked for repairs. A model tenant, I'd say. I wish there were more like him.'

'Neighbours?'

The landlord shook his head. 'I've had no complaints. Have you?'

'*Only that he's abducted a world-famous star,*' Danskin thought, although he said nothing.

DI Parker rapped on the wooden door. It was so flimsy he feared his fist would penetrate the door panel. He knew the knock would go unanswered but he had to go through the motions.

'Key, please.' Danskin held out a hand.

He unlocked the door, stood aside, and allowed one of the uniform patrols to enter first.

'Mr Gowland – this is the police,' Danskin shouted up to the first floor. Please step into view. We have patrols front and rear so don't go getting any ideas. We just want to ask you a few questions.'

He gave a nod and the uniform officers led the way upstairs, the landlord following Danskin and Parker, while Robson skirted the building and waited outside the back door.

At the head of the stairs, Danskin repeated the instructions. He knew no-one was there to hear. Danskin looked at the landlord and pointed to a door. 'Living room,' the man answered.

Danskin nudged open the door. The place was untidy but not overly so. No half-full teacups, no beer cans, no takeaway cartons. Not like many of the places he'd raided in the past.

The kitchen was the same. Dishes washed and put away. Pots and pans in their place.

Parker opened the fridge. It was empty. 'I'd say he knew he was going away. There's nae fresh food left to go unfresh. He's planned this.' He opened a cupboard door. No tins or jars. 'And it looks tae me like he's not planning on coming back.'

They moved onto the second bedroom, which wasn't a bedroom. Instead, it stocked tools and electrical gadgetry. A desk littered with invoices and paperwork stood beneath a sash window.

'We'll need all this inspected,' DCI Danskin said to the landlord. He jangled the keys. 'We'll keep hold of these for a while.'

'He's left some toiletries behind, anyway,' Parker called from the bathroom.

Danskin entered the main bedroom. The bed was made, the room tidy. He opened an Ikea wardrobe. Half-a-dozen shirts hung to the left, a couple of pairs of jeans to the right. And an empty space between them.

'He's taken clobber with him,' Danskin shouted towards Parker. 'Not all of it, but enough to indicate he'll be away a while.'

Lyall joined him. The DI moved to a chest of drawers. He opened the bottom-drawer first. Standard procedure to avoid having to shut one drawer before checking the contents of the one above.

'Socks and undies,' Lyall said.

He opened the one above. 'T-shirts. Not many, mind,' he continued his commentary.

The next drawer contained receipts and guarantees. 'Paperwork. We'll go through all this back at Forth Street.'

Parker pulled on the top drawer. It resisted. He tried again. 'This wee bugger's jammed,' he said. He tried lifting and pulling. It didn't budge.

He took out his credit card. Slid it back and forth. Something inside moved. He tried again. More movement inside.

'There's some loose stuff got wedged in the drawer. I cannae make out what it is.'

Parker grunted as he gave the drawer a yank.

The drawer half-opened. He didn't need it to open further.

'Will you look here?' he whispered.

Stephen Danskin hurried towards him. 'You found something, Lyall?' He looked over Parker's shoulder and gave a low whistle.

The drawer was crammed with photographs, newspaper cuttings, and magazine articles.

Each one featured Semilla Rachman.

NINETEEN

There was little warmth in the mid-day sun but, cooped up in Elizabeth Rachman's dining room, neither Ryan Jarrod nor Ravi Sangar were aware of it.

Mrs Rachman sat in her garden, a long, knitted pullover wrapped around her. Her foot tapped rhythmically.

'How's she been?' Ryan asked.

'Quiet.'

'Has she had more brandy?'

Sangar shook his head. 'Not unless she's got a stash in her bedroom.'

'Must be hard for her, like,' Ryan mused. He watched as the woman stood and walked back towards the house. 'I think the DCI should let us tell her.'

'About Gowland, you mean?'

'Yeah. Or at least let her know we've a chief suspect, even if we don't name him. It'd give her some hope that we're making progress.'

They heard the back door slam shut as the wind caught it when Elizabeth returned.

'I haven't gained access to Gowland's Facebook account, yet. I think if I manage to get in, we'll learn even more. I reckon once I'm in and we've got a bit more evidence, Danskin will…'

A mobile phone in Ravi's briefcase rang. Ryan glanced at the case. A red light pulsed.

'Mrs Rachman!' he called out.

Elizabeth rushed in. Her breaths were shallow. Ryan could tell she was in panic.

'Just remember what I told you. Pick it up. Now.'

Elizabeth almost dropped the phone as she picked it up, the wires from Ravi's kit entwining it.

'Yes?' she answered, half bent over the belt.

There was a silence of almost four seconds. She started to speak again when the reply came.

'We have your daughter.'

Elizabeth grasped her chest.

'If you want her back, have fifty-thousand pounds in unmarked notes ready.'

Ryan and Ravi stared at each other. The voice wasn't what they expected. It was calm. Melodious, even. No sign of stress or anxiety.

Most significantly, it was American.

'I don't have that sort of…' Elizabeth began saying until she saw Ryan make crossing gestures through the air. *'Don't argue with him,'* she remembered Ryan's advice.

Ryan made a pecking motion with his hands. *'Keep him talking'*, it said.

'Yes. I'll get it for you. I need to speak to my daughter…'

The voice spoke over her. 'I shall call back in two hours with instructions. If you don't answer, your daughter is a dead woman.'

The call ended.

Ryan looked at Ravi, who shook his head. 'Not long enough.'

'Shit, man.'

'What do you make of the caller?'

Ryan let out a breath. 'It's not him.'

'Not who?' Elizabeth asked.

'Please, get in touch with your bank. Arrange to get the money,' Ryan said. 'Tell them it's police business. If they doubt you, they'll ask for a codeword. The word is Pepper. They may ask for an authorising name. If they do, tell them it's Samantha Maynard. She's our Superintendent. The bank will know your call is genuine. If there are any problems, which there won't be, let me know straight away. Go make the call now, please. Try not to worry.'

Mrs Rachman didn't have the strength to argue. She left the room and made the call.

Once she'd left, Ryan resumed his conversation with Ravi. 'That wasn't Gowland. I know his voice.'

'So there is more than one kidnapper, after all.'

'Looks like it. The use of *'we'* plural isn't a distraction tactic.'

Ravi was replaying the call on silent, focusing on the screen graphs rather than the voice.

'Strange. There's no stress levels whatsoever.' He shook his head. 'There's something I'm missing, here.'

'Aye but there's no time to think of that now. He'll be calling again in a couple of hours. We might learn more from that call. I need to brief the Super and Danskin. I reckon we need a steer on how we proceed.'

Ravi thought for a long moment. 'I suggest you make sure Mrs Rachman's got the money ready, first. We're shafted if we fall at the first fence.'

**

An onshore breeze caused the man to shiver as he zipped up the Tech Air bag and walked away from the free Wi-Fi zone outside of The Balmoral and Terrace.

A quick check of his watch told him he'd got his timings right. He looked out to sea and saw the outline of the craft which hid Semilla Rachman. It was near enough to civilization to have a phone signal.

'It's on,' he told Micky. 'I need you to hang onto her for a bit longer yet.'

'It's cool. She's inside, I'm outside. The cabin door's locked and the key's in me jacket.' He patted his coat to reassure himself the key hadn't moved.

'Listen. I need you to move again. I'm abandoning the rowing boat so I need you close to shore.'

'Is this not close enough, like?' Micky protested.

'I'm not going to swim back to you, pal. No, I need you to get close to dock. Dock in the old dock where we started off.'

He heard Micky gasp.

'That's too risky, man.'

'Not if you're careful. It'll be dark before I'm done here. I'm getting the Metro to Shields and when all this is over, I'll meet you at the dock.'

'It's too shallow for…'

The man had already ended the call.

**

'The bank recognised your codeword. They're even sending the cash by courier. It'll be with us within the hour.'

'Well done, Mrs Rachman. I know how traumatic this must be,' Ryan said.

Her next words astonished him.

'Stephen should know.'

'I think that's a good shout, Mrs Rachman.'

'Will you tell him? I think he'll take it better coming from you.'

Ravi Sangar put himself forward. 'I'll talk to him, Ryan. You need to be available for the Super's directions.'

Ryan nodded his appreciation and moved to a different room to call Danskin.

'The more I think about this, the more it doesn't add up,' the DCI said. 'Fifty grand's nowt these days. Why not ask for more? And in cash – neebody does that anymore. It's all hidden electronic fund transfers to offshore accounts.'

A phone rang. One of the phone's in Ravi's kit in the next room. 'Bollocks - they're early. Got to go.'

Ryan dashed into the room just as Elizabeth Rachman grabbed for the phone.

'No. Let it ring twice, remember. Whatever he says, agree to it.' Ryan pulled on a headset as Ravi dived into the seat next to him.

Ryan counted down on his fingers. Elizabeth picked up, on cue.

'Hello?' she said, the word choking in her throat.

'Any news?' the male said.

Ryan swore under his breath. He recognised the voice. It was Keith Kennedy.

Jarrod made a cutting motion. *'Hang up,'* it said.

'No, nothing yet,' Elizabeth told Kennedy.

'I thought maybe we could…'

'I need to get off. Don't call again.'

'Don't be like…'

Elizabeth cut the call dead.

Mrs Rachman's eyes brimmed with tears. 'I can't do this,' she cried. 'It's killing me.' She paced the room. 'It's really killing me. What if the kidnapper doesn't call again?'

Ryan walked to her and held her arms to stop her pacing. 'He will call. He wants his money. He doesn't want Semilla, and he certainly doesn't want a murder charge. He just wants your money and, when he gets it, we'll be there to get him and Semilla.'

Ryan hoped he sounded more assured than he felt. This was all new territory to him. Then the phone rang again.

Adrenaline rushed through him as he and Ravi donned their headsets. 'Let it ring…'

She didn't.

'Hello?'

Silence. Four seconds of silence, then the detached voice spoke.

'I was never going to give you two hours. That gave you too much time. Have you got the money?'

Elizabeth almost said '*no*', then remembered Ryan's advice. 'It's on its way. I'll have it in less than half an hour.'

Another four seconds. Ravi screwed up his eyes, puzzlement on his face.

'Good,' the voice eventually said. 'The minute you have it, you need to take the Shields ferry. When you get off on the other side, you make your way to a restaurant. It's called '31 The Quay'. You go on foot. You go alone. No cops, no friends, no nobodies. Just you and the money.'

'Do I meet you there?'

A delay. 'Of course not. Before you get to the restaurant, you will come across a bank of lockers. They are named '*24/7 InPost.*' You will have the cash in a plastic shopping bag and you will place it in locker number eighteen.'

'What if it's full? Or locked?' the woman panicked.

After a delay, the voice said, 'It won't be.'

'When do I get my daughter?'

The wait for his response seemed interminable. When it came, it wasn't an answer.

'You will close the locker. You will walk away. You will take the ferry back across the river, and you go home without telling a soul.'

'When do I get Semilla?' The phone was shaking in Elizabeth's hands as she yelled into it.

Four seconds later, the voice said, 'You have one hour fifteen minutes.'

'My baby...'

The line was silent as a corpse.

**

'Get anything, Rav?'

'Negative,' Sangar said, shaking his head.

'Howay, man. Surely it was long enough to get a trace.'

'He's a clever shite. He didn't use a phone, as such. It was VOIP. That's Voice Over Internet...'

'...Protocol. Aye, I know what it stands for, man. Why can't you get a handle on it?'

'Because VOIP bounces data around servers all over the world. It's impossible to discover the source.'

Mrs Rachman sat sobbing on the floor. Ryan was torn between consoling her and following his duty. As always, duty won.

'Does that explain the weird delay?'

A look crossed Ravi's face. 'No, it doesn't. I've been wondering about that, an' all. VOIP happens,' he snapped his fingers, 'Like that. As instantaneous as is possible.'

They'd reached a dead-end.

'Bloody hell. I need input here. I need the DCI and the Super on this, like five minutes ago,' Ryan said, hoping not to alarm Elizabeth. He glanced towards her. She was way beyond alarm.

'What about the voice patterns?' Ryan pondered out loud. 'Any change in the inflection?'

Ravi nodded slowly, but his words contradicted the gesture. 'No. There again, the voice isn't human.'

'Hadaway, man. This is no time for winding us up about aliens.'

'Not aliens. Artificial Intelligence. That's why there was a delay. The real abductor was either dictating or typing, for AI to translate into speech. That's why there was a delay. That's why he sounded American.'

'...And that's why we've learned sod all from the last twenty minutes,' Ryan swore. 'We'll never identify the voice or the location.'

He made sure Elizabeth wasn't watching before mouthing to Ravi.
'We're fucked.'

TWENTY

The courier arrived at the same time as Stephen Danskin and Sam Maynard. Ryan brought them up to date via the radio as they drove to Cleadon Village to ensure they were ready to hit the ground running.

Elizabeth Rachman paced the floor. Golden-tinted sunlight hues, slanted and fractured by the blinds at the window, gave her the appearance of a caged tiger at a zoo.

Maynard, Danskin, and Ryan talked in hushed tones. Jarrod explained he'd released Ravi Sangar from the audio surveillance on the basis he'd achieved as much he ever would. Ryan said he believed Sangar could be better utilised back at Forth Street.

Their praise reassured him. He wasn't at all sure he'd made the right decision or, indeed, if he'd managed Gowland's call correctly.

'We need our focus to be forward-looking. Our next steps are critical,' Maynard reminded them.

'Aye, we need to manage the drop quietly. Question is, do we nab him on the spot, or let him lead us to Semilla?' Danskin pondered.

'Unless he has Miss Rachman with him, I vote we follow him,' Ryan suggested. 'If Semilla's not with the kidnapper when he picks up, it means she's with the accomplice. No money, no release.'

'I agree,' Maynard said. 'How do we follow without being seen, though?'

'We hide a tracking device in the bag,' Ryan offered.

Maynard whistled. 'It's a risky strategy, Ryan. If it's discovered, we're done for.'

'True, but if we're spotted following him, the result's the same.' Ryan lowered his voice still further. 'Plus, what guarantee do we have they'll let her go, whatever we do?'

The trio mulled over the dilemma.

'I say we use the tracker,' was Danskin's conclusion, 'While we hope the lass is brought along. If she's there, we'll have sufficient back-up hidden around the area to rescue her, catch the bastard, and get her cash back to boot,' he tilted his head in Elizabeth's direction.

Sam Maynard tossed her hair. 'Are we all agreed?'

Ryan and Danskin gave their approval.

'Right. Let's get Lyall to sort out back-up and we'll organise the drop.'

The trio separated, which was enough to catch Elizabeth's attention.

'We're going?' she said, hesitatingly.

'We are,' Maynard confirmed.

'How do you want me to handle it?' Elizabeth asked.

'You don't. We do,' Ryan told her.

'No. You can't. If they see it's not me, they'll…' she covered her mouth, 'Kill her,' she concluded between sobs.

'What size are you?' Maynard asked.

'Me? I'm a twelve. Why?'

'Height?'

'Five-six. I don't…'

'I'm size ten and an inch taller but it's close enough.'

Danskin's eyes widened. 'Ma'am, you can't…'

'Have you any other suggestions?' she cut him short. 'Lucy Dexter's way to young and small, DS Graves is out-of-commission, and it would take too long to brief the girls on Rick Kinnear's team.'

Danskin shook his head.

'It's my call, Stephen.' She turned to Elizabeth. 'Now, lead me to your wardrobe. Let's see what fits best.'

It was Semilla's mother's turn to object. 'They want me there. It's my daughter they've got.'

'Which is precisely why you shouldn't go. You'll be too emotional. It's not a criticism,' she said, holding up her hands, 'I would be, too, if I were in your shoes. Please, I know what I'm doing.' Maynard let the words settle. 'Now, are you going to help me choose some clothes and your best hairpiece, or do I do it myself?'

**

The man strode brazenly past the Customs House. Part of him wished someone would see him. What better alibi could he have than to be on the other side of the Tyne when the action kicked off?

There again, with a bit of luck there wouldn't be any action, which meant The Boss had been right all along. As usual.

It also meant Stage Two of the plan would proceed seamlessly.

He buttoned his jacket against a stiffening breeze and strolled uphill. He gave himself a little smile as he walked by the *'Now Open 24 hours'* sign at the entrance to The Word's car park - before he shivered. If the woman had seen the sign on the night, none of this would have panned out so perfectly.

The man didn't dwell on the thought as he stepped into the foyer. The building had a Tardis-effect: spacious and bright inside.

A banner announced: *'The Word – National Centre for the Written Word'*. He looked up at the dome-shaped interior and took the stairs rather than the lift, knowing there was more chance of being caught on security cameras that way. Another alibi opportunity, should one be needed.

He walked past the Exhibition Pods and ignored the library. He bought a bottle of Irn-Bru from the cafeteria and whistled as he continued upwards, bypassing the design centre and media wall.

Finally, he reached the Rooftop Viewing Terrace, a three-hundred-and-sixty degrees glass fronted platform with exterior access. The man tilted back his head and let the wind comb his hair.

He turned to look inland, took in the sight of St Hilda's Church and the Market Square, before he turned his attention to the River Tyne.

On a day as clear as this, the panorama was stunning. He stepped towards the outdoor platform's guard rail and gazed down. He had a perfect view of the South Shields ferry terminal.

A couple sauntered by, the man pointing out a storyboard containing tales of Tyne voyagers, past and present. The man exchanged pleasantries with them. Once they turned the corner, he faced the river again .

A bank of powerful telescopes were mounted on the rail to give visitors a bird's-eye view of the shipping traffic flowing in-and-out of the Tyne. The man draped one arm over a telescope. He turned to his left and spotted the dock where Micky would wait for him.

He smiled and faced forward. Directly across from him lay the North Shields ferry terminal. To its left, the restaurant he'd directed Elizabeth Rachman towards. And, just before it, a bank of storage units.

The man stroked the telescope lovingly. It was his best friend. After all, it was about to give him the greatest gift imaginable: a close-up viewing of his future wealth.

**

Sam Maynard stepped from the unmarked car a mile from the ferry terminal. She'd take the rest of the journey on foot. On foot, and alone.

The clothes Maynard selected from Rachman's wardrobe suddenly felt noticeably large on her. *'It's just imagination'*, she told herself. She carried a run-of-the-mill carrier bag, albeit a Waitrose one as befitted a woman of Elizabeth Rachman's standing. She'd tied the handles together so no-one could peer in. The last thing she needed was to be mugged for fifty grand on the streets of Shields.

As she approached the Alum Ale House, she saw the ferry already docked, its engine throbbing. She broke into a sprint and made it with moments to spare.

Maynard opted to stand on deck rather than take cover. She suspected her movements were being monitored and, if they were, she wanted it known that she was unaccompanied.

The river breeze caught the blonde wig and she felt it tug at the roots of her own hair. She freed one hand from the carrier and frantically held her hair in place with it.

The wind rippled her cheeks like a skydiver once the ferry reached the middle of the river, travelling cross-current to the Tyne's north bank. Sam wanted to look around, to check if anyone was watching her, but she feared her disguise would fail closer inspection.

She continued to stare out across the thick murky water.

The propellor began to churn the river into a ferment as the pilot thrust the engine into reverse, slowing its approach. Maynard checked her watch. By her reckoning, she had less than twenty minutes to make the drop.

She made her way to the craft's exit point, determined to be the first to exit. She wasn't. Three people were already waiting, two men and an elderly lady. Neither of the guys were Noel Gowland – but either of them could be his accomplice.

Maynard turned her head away from them, the wind stiffening her neck.

It was another five minutes before the pilot signalled disembarkation.

Fifteen minutes left.

Maynard tried to fight down rising panic, then realised panic was exactly what Elizabeth Rachman would experience, and what Gowland would expect to see.

She let herself drown in fear.

**

The telescope raked across the area on the north bank of the river. The man behind it cursed himself. The drop-off location wasn't ideal.

Although he had an unobstructed view of it, the approach to it was partly-hidden by neighbouring buildings. He had no way of ensuring Rachman wasn't under surveillance.

He scanned the surrounding area. There were vehicles parked at the ferry terminal itself, cars in the restaurant car park, vans at the nearby Pulpo Heating services HQ. All could be innocent, any could be unmarked police surveillance.

He'd been so engrossed he didn't see Sam Maynard board the ferry, and it was pure chance he saw it dock. He held his breath as he played with the zoom facility. If she wasn't on this one, she wasn't going to show.

'There's my girl,' he said to himself as he saw her, fourth in line. He checked out the three in front of her. All three walked off in the opposite direction. Of the passengers lined up behind her, most headed away from the river once off the ferry.

Four, though, followed his target. He toyed with the zoom. Managed to determine two were young teenagers. The others fell into the category of possible cops.

He watched closely until he was satisfied that they weren't keeping pace with Elizabeth Rachman as she ran towards the drop, playing peekaboo behind the onshore units.

'You're in a hurry, I see,' he mumbled to himself. 'That's good. It shows you're keen to get your girl back.'

He smiled, knowing what that meant for the rest of the plan.

**

Sam Maynard reached the restaurant.

'Shit.'

She'd overshot the location.

She backtracked. Came across an odd-looking, crescent-shaped turning circle made from pink bricks, not one hundred yards from the restaurant.

Its purpose became clear to her when she saw the bus shelters on its inner curve. And, to her relief, next to them stood a block of dirty-cream yellow lockers.

Maynard relaxed, glanced at her watch. She had less than two minutes remaining, and panicked when she couldn't find locker number eighteen.

On her hands-and-knees, she finally found it at ground level.

She flicked the catch and pulled.

To her relief, the locker swung open without the need for a code.

She looked around her, checking for anyone who looked like they didn't belong. There was no-one in sight.

Maynard examined the locker interior. Her fingers roamed the framework. They rested on something taped to the metal door. In a stylized, capital font someone had left a note. It read 'LOCK IT. DOOR CODE IS 3181.'

Maynard placed the bag inside. Began to shut the door. Remembered something.

She removed the carrier bag, untied the handles, put her hand into her pocket and slipped the tracking device between the wad of banknotes.

Maynard returned the bag to the locker. She shut the locker, typed in the code number on the touchscreen, checked the door was secured, and walked away towards the ferry dock.

'Tut, tut, tut,' the man with his forehead pressed against the rim of a telescope whispered. 'And to think you'd been doing ever so well until then.'

TWENTY-ONE

Sam Maynard made for the one place she was certain no-one would follow. She gave each door a gentle push. Satisfied she was alone, she locked the cubicle door and sat on the toilet seat.

She brought out the miniature radio and spoke to Lyall Parker who'd been monitoring operations from Forth Street. She patched in both Stephen Danskin and Ryan Jarrod.

'Have we got the girl?' was her whispered first question.

'No, ma'am. I'm following all channels here. There's nae sight of her.'

'Damn,' though it was the answer she'd expected. She kept her voice low as she asked, 'No sign of a pick-up, either?'

'Negative. No-one has approached the lockers.'

Maynard swore again.

'It's early days, ma'am,' Danskin reassured from within the house in Cleadon Village. 'Gowland, or whoever collects on his behalf, will want to be assured we don't have eyes on him.'

'What about me? Was I followed?'

'No,' Parker confirmed. 'Not as far as we can tell. Our guys are confident no-one watched you.'

Maynard ran her fingers down the blonde wig. 'Then I guess we just have to wait.'

She heard the washroom door creak open. She muted the radio and held her breath as someone took three steps inside. They stopped. Maynard calculated the intruder stood somewhere near the centre of the room, neither at the washbasins or in a cubicle.

One more step, heels clacking on the tiled floor. Maynard saw a shadow darken the space beneath the cubicle door. Her eyes closed.

The intruder moved again. Four steps. Maynard heard the washroom door open and swing shut. Still, she waited.

Satisfied she was alone, she let out the breath she'd been holding and gulped in air. It had been a long time since she'd been actively engaged on undercover work. It gave her a definite buzz although, she decided, she could do without anymore.

She switched the radio back on and heard Danskin saying, 'Ma'am – are you there? Everything okay?'

'Yes, no problem,' she said, although her head hadn't told her voice. It trembled as she spoke.

She quickly regained focus. 'Lyall, I want you to ensure the surveillance crew is changed regularly. If Gowland is watching, I don't want his suspicions aroused.'

'Already in hand, ma'am. And we've a couple of men at the bus stop next to the lockers noo, as well. They'll hop on the first bus that comes, and there's a lassie lined up to replace them at the stop once they leave.'

'Good work. Listen, I'm coming back to the house. Have the car pick me up at the museum on Salem Street. I'll be there in ten.' As an afterthought, she asked, 'How's Elizabeth coping?'

Ryan looked out the window. 'She's busying herself in the garden. I told her these things take time. She's doing aal reet, I guess. Better than I would, for sure.'

'I'll speak to her when I get back.'

'Ma'am,' Parker said, 'How long do we keep up surveillance?'

It was a good question. They couldn't keep watch indefinitely without raising suspicions. That's why they'd planted the tracker. 'Two hours from now. After that, we rely on the tracking device and CCTV in the area.'

'Understood. For what it's worth, I think that's a good call.'

'Thank you, Lyall. I appreciate it. Right, I'm signing off. Get the car ready - and, Stephen, not a word to Elizabeth until I get there.'

**

The lower the sun, the lower the temperature. Aboard the craft on open water, Micky felt a chill in his bones. And an urgent need to pee.

He unlocked the cabin door. As it opened, the first thing he noticed was the smell. A pungent mix of body odour and the cloying sourness of damp.

The second thing he noticed: the cabin was empty.

'Shit, shit, shit!' he exclaimed. 'Where the fuck's she gone?'

There was nowhere for her to hide, other than beneath the bed. He checked. Semilla wasn't there.

'How the…?'

The bathroom door opened and Semilla emerged, wrapped in a towel.

Micky felt embarrassed. Not at the sight of the half-naked waif but at his stupidity.

Where once he would have revelled at the sight, he treasured his jewels too much to stare. 'Sorry,' he mumbled.

'You're not staying there while I dress. Piss off outside.'

'That's why I'm here. For a piss, like. Not to see you get dressed.'

She fixed him with a glare.

'Okay. I'm going.' He stepped into the head, pleased to be out of reach.

When he emerged, a dark urine dribble trailing down his trouser front, Semilla sat on the bed, still in her towel.

'Sorry, I'll leave you to it.' He walked towards the cabin door.

'Don't bother,' she said, her voice softer. 'I know you wouldn't dare do owt. Not after last time.'

She didn't know how true her words were. Micky kept his gaze on the cabin floor while they sat in silence. The tension was palpable, a thick fog of unspoken words in the damp air.

Something troubled Micky. The girl was too calm.

'Can I ask you something?'

'You can ask,' Semilla said. 'You mightn't like the answer.'

He didn't smile. 'You haven't asked what's going to happen to you.'

Her mind raced. 'You're going to let me go, aren't you?'

He looked into her eyes for the first time. 'How can you be sure?'

It was Semilla who averted her eyes this time. 'What good would I be to you dead?'

'Once we have the money, it wouldn't matter a monkey's chuff if you were dead or not.'

Semilla swallowed hard. 'I don't think you'd do that. I don't think you're a murderer.'

Micky smirked. 'And you know what a murderer looks like, do you?'

'As it happens, yes.'

'What???'

The stink of mould filled their nostrils but, to Micky, the stench of fear was worse.

Semilla sighed. 'Russia's a fucking nightmare. I'm surrounded by protection. Anyone who's anybody over there always is. I don't see them, but I know they're there, watching my every move. And I know they'd kill anyone who so much as looked at me the wrong way. I've seen it happen.'

Micky's eyes widened.

Across from him, Semilla sat with brow furrowed and lips tight. She peeled off the dressing on her hand, inspected it, and covered the wound with a fresh plaster. She crossed her arms and stared blankly out the cabin window before she continued her story.

'There was a guy called Andrei. He was another dancer with the Bolshoi. Good looking, fab body, but a bit of a tosser. I partnered him a couple of times and, after one performance, we went to a bar to unwind. He got drunk. Bad-mouthed someone.'

Semilla hesitated, lost in her memory, before Micky urged her to continue.

'What Andrei didn't know was, the bloke he was winding up was Russian mafia. His protection knew, though. They took the guy out right in front of us. After that, Andrei left the ballet. No-one heard from him again.'

She quickly loosened her towel before wrapping it tighter around her, affording Micky a tantalising, split-second glimpse of what lay beneath. It was his turn to gulp and look away.

'So, to answer your question: yes, I know what a killer is. And it's not you. That's why I might seem calm. Believe me, though, I'm far from it. I want to be back home; to see my mother. So, yes: I am worried - but I know you're not going to kill me.'

She crossed her legs. This time, Micky didn't avert his eyes.

She edged closer to him. 'How do you know him?'

'Who?'

'The other one. The one in charge?'

'He's not in charge. The Boss is.'

'Aye, but he's in charge of you, isn't he?' Her fingers brushed against his leg. He jumped as if he'd been electrocuted.

Micky ignored the supposition. 'I'm a DJ. That's why I love my music so much.'

'Really?' Her interest seemed genuine. 'Have you played the clubs in Ibiza?'

Micky roared with laughter. 'Nah, man. I just do a few birthday parties and such like. I've got me own deck but once I get paid for this job, I'm gonna jack it in.'

'Why, if you enjoy it?'

He ignored the question. 'I was doing a gig at a party. He was there. It was coming up to his twenty-first and he'd been let down by a band he'd booked for it. He asked if I could do something for his party. That's how I got to know him.'

'You've been friends ever since?'

She moved closer, a sweet fragrance of shower gel and shampoo replacing the foulness of the cabin.

'I wouldn't exactly call us friends but, yeah, we've kept in touch.'

'How long ago was this?'

Micky thought. 'About three years… Hang on, why all the interest, all of a sudden?' The man's advice – *'don't get too pally'* – resounded through his head. 'You're just trying to find out stuff, aren't you?'

Micky stood and moved away from her.

He jumped at the sound of his phone ringing.

'You need to get the boat to the Shields dock,' the man ordered. 'We've got a problem.'

**

Elizabeth Rachman walked in from the garden, sliding the French windows shut behind her.

'It's getting chilly out there,' she said, her voice fragile and flat.

Ryan and Danskin told her to take a seat. Against his better judgement, Ryan suggested a brandy to warm her up.

'Just a small one,' she said, and meant it.

Sam Maynard, aka Elizabeth Rachman with the ice-blue eyes rather than the 'real' Elizabeth - the one with emerald green eyes - tapped lightly on the living room door and walked straight in.

Elizabeth immediately stood. 'Have you got her?'

Sam Maynard forced herself to maintain eye-contact as she replied. 'Not yet.'

Elizabeth's face crumpled and she looked towards the oil painting of Semilla. 'I've lost her,' she whispered.

'We said it'd be a long-haul, Mrs Rachman,' Ryan reassured her. 'I know it's hard but we have to be patient.'

'Patient? You are all fucking nuts! It's my daughter we're talking about, not a delayed Evri delivery.'

'The kidnappers haven't taken the money…'

She didn't let Maynard finish the sentence. 'I don't give a shit about the money, Superintendent. It's my daughter I need. My baby.'

Maynard walked to her and touched her elbow. Elizabeth recoiled from the contact.

'Please, listen to me, yeah?' she stared into Mrs Rachman's tears. 'We always knew this was possible, didn't we? That's why we used a tracking device. As soon as we get a signal, we have a location. We'll know where Semilla is, and we'll get her.'

'HOW will you get her? Go in all guns blazing like it's the OK Corral? Tell me that, Superintendent.' She collapsed onto the sofa, head in hands. 'Just tell me that,' she whispered again.

'Because we have experience in this sort of thing.'

Ryan heard Maynard's words but he could tell the Super wasn't convinced. They had their suspect yet didn't know where he or his hostage was. The telephone calls had given Ravi nothing to work on, there was no footage to back up their conviction that Gowland had Semilla. Evidence-wise, all they had were a bunch of photographs stuffed in a drawer.

In short, they had diddley-squat while, somewhere, a young woman was going through hell and none of them could do a thing about it.

'We won't be letting you out of our sight,' Ryan said. 'We'll be here until we get Semilla for you.'

'Is there anyone else we can get for you? Mr Kennedy, perhaps?' Danskin realised Kennedy was no longer in the frame. If he could keep Rachman calm and rational, it would help.

Elizabeth shook her head. 'No.' After a delay she turned towards Ryan. 'I think Stephen should be here.'

Confused, Ryan looked towards Danskin before he realised she wasn't referring to the DCI. 'Semilla's father, you mean?'

Elizabeth nodded.

The three detectives looked at each other. Sam Maynard nodded her assent.

'Okay, if you're sure,' Ryan said. 'Do you want to call him or should I?'

'You, please.'

Ryan reached for the phone just as it rang. He was about to pick up when the possibility hit him.

'Just in case…' Ryan said to Elizabeth, pointing at the telephone.

'Who's this?' she asked.

Even before the voice spoke, Ryan knew who it was. The delay gave it away.

'You have made a terrible mistake. One you will live to regret. You will receive a parcel tomorrow. You will know from its contents just how big a mistake it was.'

Elizabeth Rachman made no attempt to engage the voice in conversation.

She couldn't.

She was on the floor, unconscious, and mid-seizure.

TWENTY-TWO

Stephen Rachman arrived ten minutes after the paramedics left. He seemed wary; unsure of himself, and relieved to see a Detective answer the door rather than his ex-wife.

He peered over Danskin's shoulder, inspecting the corridor beyond. He hesitated when the DCI showed him inside, took a deep breath, and followed Danskin.

Ryan nodded an acknowledgement to the Mayor, who dipped his head in response.

'Sit down, Mr Rachman,' Danskin suggested.

The Mayor's eyes locked onto Sam Maynard. The Super introduced herself before Rachman decided to sit.

'What's all this about?' he asked, looking around the four walls decorated with portraits and photographs of his daughter. 'Is she okay?'

'She is, sir,' Maynard reassured him.

'Thank God.' He closed his eyes and exhaled.

'She's resting upstairs.'

'Can I see her?'

'Of course.'

The Mayor stood. 'And you've caught whoever did it?'

Ryan realised Maynard and Rachman were at cross-purposes. 'I'm sorry, Mr Rachman, we're still looking for Semilla but I'm sure we'll find her, soon.'

The Mayor looked puzzled. 'But you said she was fine. *'Resting upstairs'*, you said,' his comments addressed to Sam Maynard.

'Elizabeth. I was talking about Elizabeth, not Semilla,' she clarified.

The Mayor sat down again.

'I don't understand.'

'I'm afraid Elizabeth took ill. Don't worry; she's stable and resting upstairs. She's been under real strain – you both have – and I'm sorry to say it brought on a seizure. The paramedics are confident it was a one-off purely due to the situation, but she'll get an urgent appointment with a neurologist, just to be on the safe side. They recommended she avoid alcohol in the meantime.'

The house filled with an uneasy silence, broken only by the soft burr of the refrigerator from the kitchen.

'Don't you want to see your wife, sir?' Ryan asked.

'Not particularly, no. And she's not my wife. I'd rather know what you lot are doing to find my Semilla.'

Stephen Danskin spoke up. 'We believe we know the person responsible for Semilla's disappearance. We know where he lives, and what his motives are.'

'Who?' the Mayor demanded.

'I'm not at liberty to divulge that information yet, but we are doing everything in our power to locate him. That includes the use of tracking devices. Once we have a location for him, we'll know where he's holding Semilla. Until then, it's a waiting game.' Danskin deliberately refrained from mentioning the latest threat.

'I don't think you are doing everything,' Rachman complained. 'If you were, his face would be plastered all over the newspapers and on TV.'

Ryan stepped in. 'The kidnapper told Elizabeth there must be no publicity. At this stage, we don't want to do owt that might jeopardise your daughter's safety – but we are keeping the option open as the investigation continues.'

The Mayor's eyes searched the portrait of Semilla which dominated the wall as if he'd only just seen it. He swallowed back tears.

'Would you like to see Mrs Rachman now?' the Super asked.

He puffed out his cheeks. 'You're sure this isn't just a stunt of hers? I mean, why would she want to see me, apart from wanting to rip my eyes out?'

'I suppose the parental bond runs deep,' Ryan said, wondering where the hell the words came from.

'I'll accompany you, if you'd prefer,' Sam Maynard offered.

Rachman remained silent. They all did. A wall clock ticked away time towards what the Mayor knew would be an inevitable confrontation.

'No,' he said firmly. 'If Elizabeth really is ill, seeing me won't help. By all means let her know I'm here. I'll stay tonight in one of the spare rooms. Tell her I'll see her in the morning.' He stopped short. 'One of you will be here, I take it. I won't stop by myself.'

Ryan thought he sounded like a child scared of the dark.

'I'll be staying all night', Danskin reassured the Mayor. 'Superintendent Maynard needs to be back in the Forth Street station but she'll be available if needed.' The Super was about to protest before Danskin continued. 'It's important she gives direction on all aspects of the investigation.' Maynard raised her eyebrows but knew he was right.

'I'll be here as well,' Ryan said.

'Detective Sergeant Jarrod will be back first thing in the morning. He's been here for days now and needs some proper rest to keep on top of his game. I assure you, Mr Rachman, nothing's going to happen tonight.'

'Can I have a word, sir?' Ryan said, leading Danskin into a corner so he had no choice but to agree. Once out of earshot, Ryan whispered, 'What are you talking about?'

'You saw the note,' Danskin hissed back. 'There'll be no developments here until the so-called 'package' arrives. If there is, I'll call you. Immediately.' Ryan opened his mouth to protest. 'No buts, Jarrod. It's an order. Get some sleep. Check on Hannah. I reckon there's more chance of a *'development'* and a *'package'* at her end than here, divvent you?'

**

Ryan didn't want to admit it, but Danskin was right. He hadn't realised how much he'd been relying on adrenalin until he hit the road. He wound down the Peugeot's windows and turned the radio up high to make sure he stayed awake.

He pulled into a petrol station and grabbed a Costa from the machine inside. Along with a muffin, it proved enough to sustain him for the rest of the journey to Hannah Graves' flat.

Ryan wondered what Superman would do, in his position. He'd turn up to Lois Lane's armed with a gift, that's what. Ryan stopped at the first suitable location and called into the first shop he saw. He'd never been good at the gift thing so he chose something practical rather than go all gooey on her.

By the time Ryan pulled up outside Hannah's Jesmond residence, the sun had dipped below the horizon; the sky transformed from shades of orange and pink to a deepening blue.

The resident's bays outside the building were all occupied so he risked the double-yellows further along her street, safe in the knowledge that traffic wardens regarded evening with the same regard as a vampire viewed dawn.

He tapped on her door. 'Just me,' he announced, walking straight in.

Hannah lay spread along the sofa. Ryan's heart leapt into his mouth. Fortunately, she said, 'I'm just resting' before he could utter something wuss-like.

Ryan played it cool. 'Aal reet?'

Hannah sighed. 'Aye, I'm canny. I just wish it was all over. It's getting to us now.'

'I bet. No signs of him coming?'

'Nah. I've had a few twinges, like, but nowt like last time; you know, when I thought he was on his way. The midwife's been out today. He says all's good and it could be any day now.'

Ryan tried a laugh. 'You seem to have a longer gestation period than a giraffe.'

Hannah swung her legs to the floor. 'Howay, sit next to me.'

Once he had done, she lifted her legs again and lay them across him. 'How's the case going?'

He twisted his face. 'Meh. Fouled it up today, we did. Still, it seems nowt's happened to the lass, yet – but if we mess up again...' He shook his head.

Hannah could read him like a book. Knew he didn't want to talk about it. 'What's in the bag?' she said by way of a distraction.

'Oh this,' he said, placing the carrier onto his knee. 'It's just a little pressie for the love of my life.'

'Ah, thanks.' She manoeuvred her legs off him and shuffled upright. 'Let's see, then.'

He handed her the bag and watched as she peeped inside. He couldn't tell if her expression was one of amusement or bemusement.

'Seriously?' she said, suppressing a giggle.

'Well, I didn't know what to get you. I thought it'd come in useful, like.'

She lifted a box out of the plastic bag.

'Just what I always wanted,' she said, barely stifling a laugh. 'A breast-pump.'

Ryan felt himself smiling at his foolishness.

'Ryan, that's sooo Clark Kent,' she said, crying with tears of laughter.

**

The man scrambled down the incline like a fell runner. He hesitated momentarily before launching himself towards the craft tucked out of sight of prying eyes in the mud-filled graving yard.

Despite bracing himself for the impact, he tumbled on landing and rolled awkwardly across the deck, letting go of the Tech Air holdall. He thundered into the helm, winding himself.

He got to his feet gingerly and rubbed his ribs as he checked for damage.

When he opened the cabin door, Micky and Semilla both jumped. The man motioned Micky towards the door. 'We need a word.'

Once on deck, Micky said, 'What's up? You said there was a problem.'

'Sshh,' the man hissed. 'Keep your voice down. Sound travels, remember?'

'Just tell us, man,' Micky whispered. 'Have you got the ransom?'

'No.'

'Aw, man!'

'Listen, all's good. Yes, there was a problem but it can work to our advantage.'

'What problem, and how?'

'The bitch lied. She tried to dupe us. In fact, I don't even think it was her making the drop. I think it might have been a cop.'

Micky's eyes widened like a cartoon character realising the anvil was about to land on his head. 'How the fuck is that an advantage?'

The man remained calm. Collected. He even managed a smile. 'Firstly, she - or they - had no idea I was watching. Secondly, it means we can up the ante. We'll ask for more and, more to the point, we'll get it. I can guarantee there'll be no cops this time.'

'Does The Boss agree?'

'The Boss doesn't even know.'

'What? Are you nuts, man?'

The man ignored him. 'Be patient. I'll explain more later, when madam in there is asleep. For now, though, there's something I've got to do.'

He re-entered the cabin. A frightened Semilla asked what was going on, only to be told to shut the fuck up. She did.

The man stood on the bunk and opened another of the overhead lockers. He pulled something out, stuffed it into the bag before either Micky or Semilla saw what it was, and zipped the holdall shut.

'I'll be back,' he promised, Arnie-style, as he clambered up the dockside like the Milk Tray man.

TWENTY-THREE

Ryan overslept. Hannah, too.

It had been after two when they eventually fell asleep, joke-arguing over names for their son, chastising each other with silly comments; Ryan even threatened Hannah with the breast pump at one stage until she rightly pointed out he'd have no idea what to do with it.

Ryan fell asleep first, Hannah toying with the softness of his fair locks lying on her shoulder. She stared at the ceiling, wondering if she'd made the right decision. She'd insisted long-ago that she'd raise her son in her own home while Ryan played as full a fatherly part as he could from across the Tyne in Whickham.

Was she being fair on him? Short-term, probably not. Mid- and long-term, yes. Once he'd made it to DI, they could all settle down to a future together. Until then, she knew he'd never be entirely happy.

Hannah felt herself drift towards a hazy sleep when a sharp pain jolted her awake. Ryan snorted and turned over, never opening his eyes. She waited for something else to happen: a kick – or a contraction?

Instead, she felt nothing. At last, she fell into a restless sleep, dreaming of the child she'd lost several years ago, barely before she had known she was pregnant. Hannah thought she was long over it. Her subconscious told her otherwise.

When Ryan did wake, he did so with a start and an expletive. He dressed in his old clothes and went without a shower. There wasn't time. He had to be in Cleadon Village, for whatever awaited the Rachman's.

He kissed Hannah, left her sleeping, while he jumped into his Peugeot and set off at a speed unknown to his Captain Slow persona.

Ryan had barely travelled four miles when his phone rang. He didn't recognise the number so he took one hand off the steering wheel and cancelled the call. It immediately rang again. He reacted the same way.

When it rang a third time, he answered it with an impatient, 'Yes?'

'Detective Sergeant Jarrod?'

'Who is this?'

'Sophia Ridley.'

'Oh, hello Mrs Ridley. I'm busy right now. I've on my way to Elizabeth Rachman's and can't talk.'

Sophia's voice broke up as the signal was momentarily interrupted. Ryan filled in the missing words and guessed she was asking if Semilla was okay.

'Semilla's still missing,' he said, 'I'm sorry but I can't discuss any developments with you. I have to go.' He ended the call just as he entered the Tyne Tunnel.

When he emerged on the south side of the river, his phone rang again.

'Jeez,' he cursed. He accepted the call. 'What is it?' he snapped.

'There's something I think you need to see,' Sophia Ridley said.

'Not that bloody mural again, is it?' he said, trying sarcasm in the hope Ridley got the message.

She didn't.

'No, it's not that, although I know you love it, really.'

'Mrs Ridley, I really don't have the time...' he stamped on the brakes, realising he'd almost jumped a red light. 'I've too much on me plate, man.'

'I think I might be able to help you clear your plate, as it happens.'

'I very much doubt it,' Ryan muttered, as much to himself as Sophia.

'Please… just get here as soon as you can. I don't want to say too much over the phone.'

Ryan rolled his eyes. She'd been watching too many TV dramas.

Her next words came tinged with sadness.

'I know who did it.'

**

Micky and the man spent an uncomfortable night, too. They waited for Semilla Rachman to fall asleep. She didn't. Every time they thought she had, she'd roll over, or cough, or open her eyes.

She must have asked what the time was on half a dozen occasions. Pleaded to go home even more, and for food as many times.

It was five a.m. before the man was satisfied she was in a deep sleep, by which time Micky had his head tilted to one side, mouth open, snoring as rhythmically as the tide.

The river would be awake, soon, so he dug Micky in the ribs. When the DJ opened his eyes, he saw the man holding a finger to his lips. '*Outside*,' he mouthed.

Out on deck, they kept low in case any passing ships happened to spot them.

'What the hell happened yesterday?' Micky whispered.

'The short version: the drop was rigged. I'm fairly certain it wasn't the girl's mother. I also suspect whoever made the drop put a tracking device in the package.'

'Shit. So, aal this is for nowt,' Micky sighed.

'I don't think so. I think we can ask for at least double the cash. I think we can arrange another drop: one that won't be rigged.'

The mud sucked on the boat's keel like a baby on its bottle, a thick gurgling noise that was somehow mystical and threatening at the same time. The air hung over them, heavy with the scent of earth and decaying vegetation.

'How can you be sure this one will go smoothly? I say we just let her go, man. It's too risky.'

'And, if we do, you said it yourself: *'It's all been for nowt.'* Besides, she knows too much about us.'

'So, what do you suggest?'

He stared at Micky with eyes of flint. 'We do it my way, or you make sure the girl can't talk.'

'You mean…'

Micky knew exactly what he meant.

The sky overhead was a subdued a palette of dark blues, purples, with a hint of a grey dawn. Micky drummed his fingers on the wooden deck, worn smooth by years of salt and sun. 'Okay. Let's hear it; this masterplan of yours.'

'Listen,' the man instructed, 'We can't stay here much longer. We've been here too long already. We need to move again.'

'We'll be seen, man.'

'You'd better make sure we're not.'

Micky groaned. 'Where are we going?'

'Upriver. Closer to the city itself.'

'We're sure to be spotted.'

The man nodded. 'Possibly; ,but even if we are, no-one's looking for us. Not there. All eyes are focussed on the river mouth and on the south side. We'll layup beyond the city.'

Micky shook his head. 'No way.'

The man grabbed him by the collar of his puffer jacket. 'We need to be together on this one, okay? Are you with me, or not?'

Micky stood his ground. 'I'll hear what you've got to say, then I'll decide.'

The man's jaw was set, his eyes dark with frustration. 'Okay,' he relented, voice steady but strained.

He stopped talking as they heard noises inside the cabin. 'She's awake. I'll be quick. I know I can watch the drop unseen. The tactic worked last time and it'll work again. If I'm right and the Rachman woman makes the drop herself, there'll be no tracker this time.'

'How do you know?'

The man smiled. 'They wouldn't dare. They know the threat's real.'

'What threat?'

'No time to explain. Just trust me, okay?'

Micky no longer trusted him but kept the thought to himself. The weight of the situation pressed down, almost suffocating them both.

'We move upriver,' the man repeated. 'Slowly and openly, this time. We keep our friend locked in the cabin.'

'We've no option but to go slow. Six knots is the limit once we're beyond Herd Groyne.'

They heard the toilet flush.

'You're with me?' the man urged, his face inches from Micky's.

The thought of the reward convinced him. 'I'm with you. Do we go now?'

The man smiled.

'No, we'll wait for the post to arrive first.'

**

Sophia Ridley greeted Ryan with the thinnest of smiles.

'Come in. I'll make us some coffee.'

'I don't want to sound ungrateful but I really haven't the time.'

'There's always time for coffee,' she said, making for the kitchen. 'Make yourself at home,' she said. 'I know how much you admire the décor.'

Ryan sniffed. 'I'll wait here, ta.'

'Suit yourself but we'll have to go in there to talk.'

'Must we, really?'

'If you want to see what I've discovered more clearly, we do.'

Ryan grumbled and, despite himself, took a seat on the sofa facing *'the thing'* on the wall. The more he looked at it, the more he could appreciate the artwork, even if the subject matter was anathema to him.

Sophia Ridley brought in two mugs and set them down. 'Shame your lot didn't make Europe this year,' she smiled. 'Never mind, you could try writing a song. You might get into Europe that way.'

'Ha ha,' Ryan said, sarcastically. 'Looker, I haven't time to listen to you taking the Mick. Can we get to the point of this? It's a canny hike back to where I need to be.'

Sophia Ridley took a sip from her mug. Ryan could see she was trying to work out where to begin.

'I'm not sure whether it was you I told or your Chief Inspector, but I said I didn't have many boys in my dancing school.'

'Aye, it was me. Both of us, actually.'

She inclined her head. 'Yes, I remember now. Anyway, there weren't many. Boys, that is. There was one who lasted about, oh, three years, I reckon. He was with me at the same time as Semilla Rachman. So, whenever she needed a partner, it was always him. He couldn't dance for toffee, really,' she smiled, 'But he had the strength to lift Semilla so it helped her learn how to carry herself in lift, you know?'

He didn't but he urged her to press on.

'I want to show you something,' she said, grabbing the TV remote. 'One of the parent's thought I'd like to see a recording she took of my show. I think you'll find it interesting.'

Ryan held his breath as she cued up the recording.

'Here we go,' she said, sitting back.

The video showed a group of four dancers going through a juvenile routine. The person holding the camera shrieked encouragement.

'Excuse her,' Sophia said. 'It's the mother of one of the dancers. She's doing the recording.

Ryan watched, wondering how Ridley thought four pre-pubescent girls were the key to Semilla Rachman's disappearance.

'Mrs Ridley...'

'Ssshh,' she whispered, her voice stern. 'You'll see.'

Ryan looked away from the performers. In the darkened shadows off-stage, he could just about make out a young girl standing with her hands clenched in front of her, moving from foot-to-foot as if she needed a wee. Someone seemed to lurk in the background, behind her. Then, the shadow was gone.

'Here we go, any moment now.'

The routine finished and the camera panned to Sophia Ridley moving from the wings. As she did so, someone handed her something.

'Stop!' Ryan said. 'What's that?'

She gave a sad smile. 'That's what you're here to see, Detective Sergeant. It's the moment I was given the details of the cars which needed to be moved from The Word's car park.'

Ryan felt his heart thump against his ribs, a desperate plea for release. 'Run it back.'

Sophia Ridley did.

Ryan gasped. 'It's him!'

'I'm afraid so. He's the youngster who once partnered a very young Semilla Rachman, all those years ago. All grown up now, they both are. He's continued to work with me on some of my annual concerts – including the latest one.'

Sophia sighed.

'What's more, his next task was to give Semilla her curtain call. The curtain call she never made.'

TWENTY-FOUR

'Where the bloody hell are you, Jarrod?'

Ryan had only just put the car in gear. 'On my way, sir.'

'You should have been here yonks ago. I know I told you to get some rest, but this is ridiculous.' Danskin's voice crackled like a firework over the police radio.

'I won't be long. I'm leaving Seaham now.'

'Seaham? What are you doing there?'

'Working. I got a call from Sophia Ridley.' He hesitated. 'Are you alone?'

'Stephen Rachman's in the next room. Elizabeth's still in bed. Why?'

Conscious of being overheard, he couched his response in vague terms. 'I've received some information. In fact, more than that. Evidence, I'd call it.'

Danskin ran a hand over his shaven pate. He realised Ryan was choosing his words carefully. He responded in kind. 'What does the evidence consist of?'

'It's a video from the performance. I've downloaded it to an external hard drive and bringing it with me.' He paused for a beat. 'I think it's worth calling Ravi back in. I'm sure it's genuine but I'd appreciate his confirmation.'

'I'll get onto it.' Danskin's pulse accelerated like a rocket on take-off. 'I'm conscious of your position,' he said, acknowledging Ryan couldn't reveal too much. 'What's your ETA?'

'I've just seen a signpost for Herrington Country Park so I think I'm aboot ten or fifteen minutes away.'

Danskin listened carefully. There were no sounds coming from the kitchen, where Rachman had been. The DCI moved to the corner furthest away from the kitchen and lowered his voice.

'Is there anything you can tell me? I'm busting a gut here, man.'

Ryan sensed the tension in the DCI's voice. 'Assuming the video's kosher, I know who the accomplice is. It all makes sense.'

Jarrod avoided giving a name. Danskin understood the predicament.

'Is it someone we've considered?'

He heard Ryan rasp a breath.

'No, it's not.'

Danskin checked his watch. He had another seven minutes to wait.

**

When Sam Maynard received Danskin's text, she called Ravi Sangar and Lyall Parker into her office.

'We've a major development. Ryan believes he's discovered who Gowland's working with. He couldn't give a name in case he was overheard but Stephen says it's not someone we've considered before.'

Lyall Parker glanced towards the makeshift crime board. Mentally, he crossed off the names of Keith Kennedy, Charlotte Spencer, Madame Sophia herself, and all things Rachman.

'How long until we know who it is?' he asked.

'Ryan's on route now. I think we'll know in the next few minutes.' She turned to Sangar. 'Ravi, there's some video footage Ryan's taking with him to Cleadon. He wants you there ASAP to validate its authenticity. At this stage, we can't afford to go off piste if it's a deepfake.'

'I'm on my way, ma'am,' Ravi said, making a sprint from the room.

Parker waited for the room to stop shaking from a passing train. 'When we know who it is, do we call out the troops?'

Sam Maynard smoothed her hair. 'That's the sixty-four-thousand-dollar question, Lyall. Do we put Semilla Rachman's life at risk by going public? If we don't, can we trust the sods to let her go?'

'I say we go all oot to nab 'em, ma'am.'

She tugged her bottom lip.

'I say we wait for the package to be delivered. We'll know then how serious the threats are.'

**

Micky was below deck, tinkering with the vessel's engine in readiness for yet another short journey. Only his head was visible, protruding through the deck hatch like a coconut on a shy.

'How's it looking?' the man asked.

'Oily.'

'Is she seaworthy, though?'

'I wouldn't use it to cross the Channel, put it that way. She should just about manage a few miles down the Tyne.' He scratched his nose, leaving a black smudge on his face. 'Fuel's low, mind.'

'Low or empty?'

'If it was empty, I'd have said empty, wouldn't I?' Micky glanced at the cabin. 'If we're mooring close to the city, how do we know she won't raise the roof? One scream and we're done for.'

The man had already considered it. 'She'll be gagged.'

'What with?'

'One of your old sweaty socks. I don't know – is it important?'

Micky held his hands aloft, although they remained out of sight below deck. 'Okay. I'm only asking.'

He ducked below deck, only for his head to re-emerge seconds later. 'Once we get the cash, when do we let her go?'

The man rolled his eyes. 'What does it matter?'

'It matters a helluva lot if she identifies us before we're out of the country.'

'Don't worry, my friend. It's all covered.' He jabbed a finger against his temple.

'And does The Boss know it's…?' he tapped the side of his head, too.

The man ignored him. He checked his watch. Tried to peer upriver but saw only the opposite bank of the graving yard. 'I'll need you in the cabin, soon.'

'I thought you wanted me to check we were shipshape?'

'I do. That's why you'd better get a move on because there's something I must do before we leave here.'

'What's that, then?'

The man scowled. 'Something I have to do alone.'

A seagull circled overhead with what looked like the remains of someone's fish supper in its beak. It shipped a splat of guano inches from the man's feet.

Micky gave a wry smile. 'You're not planning on dropping me in the shit, are you?'

'Micky, do you really think I'd do that?'

Micky didn't answer. 'So, tell me how you're going to pull this heist off; how it's going to be any different to the last one?'

The man's finger tapped the side of his nose, this time. 'Let's just say my world-travelling cousin doesn't just have a boat for us to use. He has property which overlooks somewhere suitable for a drop, and a mode of transport which enables me to get away before the cops know what's hit them. That's all you need know.'

'I don't suppose he has an invisibility cloak, an' all, does he?'

The man leered at Micky. 'We won't need one. Believe me, we won't need one.'

**

Ryan's seven minutes turned out to be significantly more. Essential gas work repairs seemed to have appeared overnight on every street corner around the Rachman residence.

With the works came the obligatory temporary traffic lights. All of which were stuck on red.

No matter how he tried to avoid them, be it via Laburnum Grove, Whitburn Road, or Meadowfield Drive, traffic on the approach to West Park Road was at a standstill. For a quiet, semi-rural village, it had a helluva lot of vehicles; all trying to squeeze two ways down routes reduced to a single narrow lane.

Car horns tooted like squawking geese. The natives were restless. So, too, Ryan Jarrod.

He radioed in. 'Traffic's a mare, sir. As soon as I find somewhere I can abandon me jalopy where it won't cause outright warfare, I'll ditch it. I reckon I'm only a couple of minutes away on foot, if I can fight me way past the locals and their torches and pitchforks.'

'Don't leave the hard-drive behind.'

'I'm not stupid, man, sir,' even though his state of mind was such that he probably would have forgot without Danskin's prompt.

**

'Ah, that's good timing.'

Ryan jumped at the voice meeting him at the other side of the gates.

'It'll save us a walk doon the drive. That's the trouble with this roond. I spend more time on folks' drive than I do on the street.' The postie fumbled in his red wheelie-trolley. 'Here – parcel for you,' he said, thrusting a manilla package in Ryan's hands. 'I just need a photograph as proof of delivery…'

The postman didn't get his photograph. Ryan was already sprinting down the long driveway, package in one hand, Sophia Ridley's hard drive in the other, where the expansive Rachman residence lay in wait.

Once inside the house, Ryan faced a dilemma. Stephen and Elizabeth Rachman were in the same room, bookended on the same green Chesterfield, yet in alternative universes.

The Mayor's eyes were alert and inquisitive, Elizabeth's dull and lifeless. He was smartly dressed and groomed; his ex-wife in dressing gown with the spaghetti-like strands of her natural brown hair a tangled mess.

Stephen Rachman shot to his feet on seeing the objects in Ryan's hands. Elizabeth barely acknowledged his presence. Danskin, too, noted the objects. He knew the hard-drive contained a revelation, and he suspected he knew what the package contained: a warning, of some description.

Which to tackle first? The hard-drive was more important to the investigation, the package critical to Semilla's parents. His decision went against his natural instincts. Heart ruled Danskin's head.

'Sangar is on his way. Hopefully, he'll make quicker progress getting here than you did. Once he arrives, he'll check that out,' he said, pointing to the rectangular object in Ryan's hand. Curiosity was bursting out of him, but he couldn't ask Jarrod to name Gowland's accomplice. Not without first revealing the contents of the package to Semilla's fraught parents.

'Is that it?' Stephen Rachman said, mouth curled in distaste as if the envelope were an alien species.

'Don't touch it, sir. There may be DNA on it.' Ryan realised his words had been misunderstood when Elizabeth released the whimper of an abandoned puppy. 'The DNA of the culprit. His saliva, or fingerprints. Not Semilla's.' He shut up, knowing he was making matters worse.

Ryan placed the package on a coffee table and discreetly prepared an evidence bag. Danskin studied the parcel.

A run-of-the-mill envopak, it bulged in parts but whatever was inside was neither especially large, nor solid. The address was written in the same stylised manner as the other notes.

Stephen Rachman stood over Danskin's shoulder, Elizabeth Rachman twisted her fingers as she cowered behind her ex. The air in the room seemed to evaporate, the room around them claustrophobic and threatening.

'Get on with it,' the Mayor pleaded. 'Please, let's see what's inside.'

All four took their every breath with caution, desperate not to break the fragile atmosphere.

Danskin pulled on a pair of blue forensic gloves.

'Ready?'

'Yes, man,' Stephen Rachman urged. Elizabeth peered through the fingers covering her eyes. Whatever was inside, she knew she didn't want to see it.

Danskin slit the envelope. Slid a gloved finger inside. Then another. He gripped something between his fingers. Slowly, he brought it towards the lip of the packaging.

A tiny part of it peeked above the rim. Ryan's first thought was that it was part of an old net curtain, stained brown with age.

Elizabeth Rachman's scream told him he was wrong.

'Her dress! It's part of my baby's ballet dress!'

For the first time, the Rachman's held each other. Not an embrace of affection, more one of support.

'What's it got on it?' Elizabeth asked, not looking at it.

'It's blood, isn't it?' Stephen Rachman posed it as a question but he knew it was also the answer.

'We'll get it tested,' Ryan said, opening the evidence bag for Danskin to pop in the folds of stained fabric. The detectives shared a sad glance of compassionate understanding as Ryan sealed the bag.

'There's summat else,' Danskin said, peeping back inside the package.

He pulled out a slip of paper. Glanced at it. Gave Ryan another quick look. 'We'll send this away, as well.'

'What is it?' Semilla's father asked.

'We'll get it checked out,' Danskin said as he passed the sheet in Ryan's direction.

'Let me see!' Elizabeth Rachman demanded. She pounced on it and tore it from Ryan's hand.

'Fuck, no,' she whispered.

Stephen Rachman kept her upright as her legs buckled.

She dropped the note.

It landed face up on the coffee table.

'THIS IS WHAT HAPPENS WHEN YOU DON'T DO AS I SAY.

I HOPE YOU'VE LEARNT YOUR LESSON.

STAY BY YOUR PHONE. I SHALL BE IN TOUCH.

IF YOU DON'T OBEY ME, YOU'LL RECEIVE ANOTHER PACKAGE.

IT WILL CONTAIN A BODY PART OF YOUR CHOOSING.'

TWENTY-FIVE

'They've killed our baby, Stephen,' Elizabeth said, burying her head in Mr Rachman's chest.

'They haven't,' Ryan reassured her. 'It's a warning, that's all. The note says as much.'

'Why should we believe them? They're scummy bastards who'll do anything,' the Mayor said.

Despite his empathy, Ryan gave Stephen a stern look. 'That isn't helping, sir. We know what we're doing.'

'And what, exactly, are you doing?' Stephen Rachman said, smoothing Elizabeth's hair.

Ryan felt his throat constrict, as if iron fingers squeezed it. 'We have a full team working the case twenty-four seven. We're trawling through hours of video footage. We have a suspect.' He suddenly remembered the hard-drive. 'In fact, we have two suspects, and we're releasing their names so every police force in the land will be looking for them and your daughter.'

'We haven't had the second name authenticated by Sangar,' Danskin said – realising even he didn't know who the accomplice was.

'One name's better than none.'

'Jarrod…' Danskin cautioned, recounting the threat in the original note; the one about not involving others.

'Sir, update the Super. Ask her to release the name. To the force only; no press.'

Chastened at being told what to do by an underling, and knowing the underling was correct, Danskin updated Maynard who agreed to the request. Noel Gowland's name and face would be at the forefront of minds everywhere throughout the City and County force.

'I'll put it on the national database, too,' Maynard said, 'In case they do a runner elsewhere. They're not getting away with this. Is Sangar with you? We need verification of the footage so we can release the second name.'

'Not yet, ma'am.'

'He should have stayed.'

'With respect, ma'am, hindsight's a wonderful thing.'

Danskin heard Maynard sigh. 'Sorry, Stephen. I was out of order.'

'Nee worries. It gets to us all.'

Danskin looked up at a sound in the hallway. A door opened to reveal a dishevelled Ravi Sangar.

'The roads are a bloody disgrace,' he panted.

'Sangar's here, ma'am. I'll get him working on it straight away.

Maynard's voice noticeably relaxed. 'Good. Keep me updated.'

Ravi glanced between Ryan and Danskin.

'Have I missed much?'

**

The man observed the traffic on the Tyne. Few boats crossed the mouth of the graving yard. He wished he could see further upstream, yearning to watch activity on other vessels along the riverbank so he could assess the risk of moving.

The water around them lay thick and still, a mottled shade of brown slicked the colour of starling wings by oil. Thick green tangles of sphagnum moss flirted with both dockside and the boat's hull, the sheltered warmth of the dock a perfect habitat.

Micky stood at the stern, greasing the tiller.

'Are you nearly done?' the man asked.

'Aye. I'm just killing time, really. We probably won't need the tiller but you never know. Better safe than sorry.'

Sand Dancer

'Good. We'll be off soon.'

Micky put his arms on his hips and stretched his back. 'I could do with some of this on me own joints,' he said, holding up the grease gun. 'I'm knackered.'

'You'll get some rest soon. I'll be needing you in the cabin with the lass.'

Micky wiped his hands on a rag hooked over his belt. 'You do realise the Tyne's not dredged beyond the bridges, don't you?'

'So?'

'You don't want us grounded, do you?'

The man's brow folded. 'Is that likely?'

Micky made a sound like a motor mechanic about to break bad news. 'A motorboat might make it as far as Wylam, if it's lucky. We're bigger than that, though.'

The man's intention was for Micky to lie in wait for him west of the Utilita Arena. He didn't want Micky knowing too much so he invented a different location; a one further upriver. If it was safe for the craft there, he knew downstream would be safer again.

'What about the stathes?' he suggested, referring to the historic coal transportation structures on the Gateshead side of the river.

'Depends whereabouts. If you're talking about the tidal basin, the answer's no. Mud's thicker than this place.'

'How about on the Newcastle side?'

Micky considered it. 'Aye, that should be okay. Is that where we're headed?'

The man didn't answer. He twisted his wrist and checked the time. Noted the parcel would have been delivered by now.

'Get into the cabin, Micky. Keep her quiet. I'll join you soon.'

The moment Micky closed the door behind him, the man reached for his Tech Air bag and exposed the kit.

**

Ryan didn't need watch the recording again. He knew what it showed. He just needed reassurance it was authentic. He volunteered to stay with Semilla's parents while Danskin and Ravi watched the footage.

'What are they doing in there?' Stephen Rachman asked.

'They're reviewing evidence. I think it's going to prove crucial. We are going to get your daughter back for you.'

'I know you are,' the Mayor said. 'Just make sure when you do get her back, she's still alive.'

Elizabeth began wailing again. Ryan watched for any signs of another fit. There were none. She did, however, look twenty years older without make-up, her glamorous wig, and after countless sleepless nights.

Ryan decided conversation was the best way to engage the couple.

His first question was vacuous.

'Have you always encouraged Semilla in her dancing?'

A quick nod from Elizabeth.

'It must have cost a lot over the years.'

'Nothing I couldn't afford.'

'Mr Rachman, what about you – you must be so proud of her.'

He looked at the portrait of Semilla in arabesque. 'What do you think? I mean, look at her. She's beautiful. Graceful. And so, so strong; mentally and physically. She mightn't look it, but she is.'

'Her spirit will help her get through this,' Ryan soothed. 'It's an ordeal, for sure, but you can help her through it – both of you. Together.'

Elizabeth looked into Stephen's eyes.

'Nah,' he said. 'Too much has happened.'

Ryan noticed Elizabeth's eyes fill with tears. He moved the conversation in a different direction.

'It must have been hard for Semilla at Madame Sophia's. I mean, being the only girl an' all.' He watched for a reaction. When he saw none, he pressed on. 'How did she learn to carry herself in lifts? I mean, none of the lasses would be able to do that bit for her.'

'I guess she just knew, just like she always seemed to know. She's just such a natural, Detective Sergeant,' Elizabeth said, more calmly.

'So, there weren't any boys in the troop?' He hoped his line of questions would lead the Rachmans to a correct conclusion.

'It's not really a boy thing,' Elizabeth said.

Ryan retold his gymnastics story, hoping it would evoke empathy and jolt a memory. It didn't. 'I'm sure there must have been someone who…'

They heard pandemonium break out next door. Ravi had obviously validated the recording. And Stephen Danskin recognised the man.

The Rachman's looked at the wall as if they were about to see the whole scene pan out like it was a cinema screen. Instead, the door flung open.

Danskin strode in, Ravi Sangar trailing in his wake.

'Sangar, you get straight onto the Super. Get both the names and mugshots out in circulation.'

The Rachman's stared at him, tension in their eyes. Tension, and something else. Hope.

'You've found her, haven't you?' Elizabeth began.

'We soon will. We know who's holding Semilla, and it won't be long before we find out where.'

Stephen Rachman grabbed Danskin's shoulders and kept him at arm's length where he could look into his eyes. 'Who is the bastard?' he hissed.

The DCI nodded in Ryan's direction. Ryan took a deep breath. 'Do you remember telling me about a boy Semilla once knew?'

'What?' Elizabeth said, shocked.

'Yes. Neil Gowland.'

'Sir, his name's not Neil. It's Noel. He was working at the theatre the night Semilla disappeared. We believe he is responsible.'

Elizabeth sat, crying. Ryan couldn't tell if they were tears of relief or extra concern that her daughter had kept her boyfriend a secret.

Stephen Rachman remained calm. Focused, even. 'You said there was more than one person involved. Who's the other rat? Do you know?'

Again, it was Ryan who spoke. 'I asked you about the boys at Sophia Ridley's dance school. I asked because she did partner with someone, for a short while. Mrs Ridley said they only once performed together on stage at the annual concert.'

'Obviously after my time,' the Mayor said, throwing an accusatory stare at his ex-wife. She sat with her brow knitted, frantically searching her memory banks.

'That person still does some work for Mrs Ridley,' Ryan explained, 'And he was also at the theatre the night Semilla went missing. We have pretty strong evidence which indicates he's heavily involved.'

'Just give me the bastard's fucking name!' Stephen Rachman demanded.

It was Elizabeth who answered, quiet and mouse-like.

'It's the stage manager, isn't it? Patrick Wheatley.'

TWENTY-SIX

Superintendent Maynard and Lyall Parker set the wheels in motion. While a uniform presence was despatched to Wheatley's residence near South Tyneside College, mugshots and descriptions of the two suspects were winged to every police station in the City and County jurisdiction, as well as to the Prince Bishop force.

The instructions were to keep everything low-key, and only apprehend if both suspects were together. Maynard was determined not to leave Semilla in the hands of one suspect whilst interrogating the other. Lord knows what the consequences would be should that happen.

Parker himself entered the details on the PNC database, accessible to every force in the land, with similar instructions. Although they knew the suspects were currently in the region, that could change at any moment.

'Anything else we can do, ma'am?' Parker asked, feeling utterly helpless.

'We load Wheatley's mug into the Facial Recognition software and see if we have more luck with him than we did with Gowland.'

'Aye, good call. What about Mr and Mrs Rachman? Do they need more support?'

'No, but we should have family liaison specialists on stand-by should the worst happen.'

'I dinnae ken how I'd cope in their shoes.'

'None of us do, Lyall.' She lost herself in thought for a moment before coming back to earth with a jolt. 'Until then, it's a waiting game. Gowland and Wheatley have this all planned. The Rachmans will get another call. The only question is, 'when' - and what will be demanded of them?'

**

Stephen Rachman sat alongside Elizabeth in an awkward embrace. She needed comfort, he wanted the men responsible. She clung on to Stephen, he sat straight-backed and pinch faced.

Ryan conferred with Danskin before addressing the Mayor.

'Mr Rachman, the people who have Semilla will make another call. It's absolutely imperative we don't intervene. They will want to speak to Elizabeth. She's been briefed on how to handle the call. You haven't. I'm afraid you'll have to leave the room.'

The Mayor stood. 'No way; not an earthly. I want to hear what they have to say, and I want to tell them exactly what I think of them.'

'I'm sorry but that's the last thing you should do. We want to appear compliant, as if we're going along with their plans while finding as much oot about them as we can.'

Rachman scoffed. 'That worked well last time, didn't it?'

The two stood in the centre of the room, locked in a standoff. Ryan could see Rachman was wired, his muscles tense. At the first sign of provocation, Ryan knew the man would lose his shit.

'Sir,' Ryan continued, 'You can listen to every word. DC Sangar will provide you with a headphone set. You will hear, but you can't speak. This must be between them and Mrs Wheatley.'

'Semilla's my lass, as well. I'm sick to death of being second best all the time.' He clenched both fists by his side, the knuckles shining bone-white through the flesh of his hands. His breath came in shallow, controlled bursts, each exhale punctuated by the silence that enveloped them.

Elizabeth Rachman broke the silence. 'I think the detective is right. I think you should leave this to me.'

'No, man. You're not strong enough.'

'I am. I've done it before, remember. I know what to expect and what to do. You don't. Please, wait with Mr Sangar.'

In the silence, any sound was amplified: the rustle of clothing, a creak of the floorboard, the wind against the window. Stephen Rachman blinked. In that split-second, the fragile balance of power shifted.

'Fine. I'll do as you say. Mind, I'm warning you, Detective Sergeant, if this goes tits-up, you'll be the one to pay.'

Ryan tried a smile. 'It won't go tits-up, sir. I promise you.'

While Danskin steered Stephen Rachman in Ravi's direction, Ryan heard the wise words of Doris Jarrod in his head.

'Never make a promise you can't be sure you'll keep.'

**

Ryan and Danskin tried to remain calm, not to let their impatience spread to Elizabeth. It wouldn't have mattered. She was beyond impatient.

Although seated on the Chesterfield, she never stopped moving. She crossed and uncrossed her legs, tapped her fingers on the armrest. She stood, sat down, and stood again. She walked to the oil painting of Semilla and checked it for dust. She returned to the leather sofa.

Elizabeth took a magazine from a rack beneath the coffee table's surface, riffled the pages, and set it down. She picked up her mobile, stared at it as if she would make it ring by willpower. She turned the ring volume up. Checked the battery level.

Ryan and Danskin looked at one another, knowing nothing they said would make the wait less painful.

'Should I make us some tea,' Ryan volunteered.

'Brandy, please.'

'I'm sorry, Mrs Rachman. You know that's not wise.'

'I don't give a shit.'

A knock on the wall, followed by Stephen Rachman's voice. 'Don't you dare,' he ordered. 'I mightn't be able to take the call but I can stop you from making an arse of it.' The voice sounded distant but the message clear.

Elizabeth's fingers went to her hair. She twisted thin strands around her fingers, a worry-bead substitute. She leaned forward, elbows on her knees, head in her hands.

The phone rang.

Elizabeth's heart leapt. With shaking hands, she snatched up the phone before Ryan could finish saying, 'Remember – don't argue, and don't let on you know who he is…', but Elizabeth waved him off with a hand gesture.

'Hello.'

The delay again. 'It's pay time or playtime. You decide.'

Somehow, the placid, cultured tone of the AI voice made the words more threatening.

'I'll pay,' she whispered.

After the delay: 'I was looking forward to some fun time with your daughter. Never mind, I suppose money will do.'

'I'll get the fifty thousand again.'

After a pause: 'Sorry. The banker's withdrawn his offer. Two-hundred thousand.'

'What? I can't…'

Ryan waved an arm frantically, grabbing her attention. *'Agree,'* he mouthed.

Four seconds later: 'Deal or no deal?'

'Okay,' she said, at the same time shrugging her shoulders towards Ryan and mouthing *'How??'*

'By yourself. No funny business. No cops. Only you,' the fake voice instructed.

'I swear'

'For insurance purposes, in case you change your mind and don't come alone, which body part do you select for your next delivery?'

Elizabeth Rachman could only sob.

'In which case, it'll be a lovely surprise for you. Please don't let it come to that.'

'What do I have to do?'

After a longer delay, AI man said, 'You just have to piss yourself with worry a little longer. You have one hour until you receive your instructions, which means you also have one hour to think about what I've said.'

Elizabeth cried out. 'Please, I want to speak to my daughter.'

'Not until I know you can be trusted. Goodbye, Mrs Rachman.'

The AI voice muted itself before it drove Elizabeth Rachman to insanity.

**

Patrick Wheatley walked into the cabin to discover Micky had followed his advice to the letter. Semilla did indeed have one of his old sweaty socks bundled between her jaws.

She opened her eyes wide in a desperate plea.

'Not yet, man,' Patrick scolded Micky. 'We don't need the gag until we moor up across the river.'

'You didn't say.'

'I think I did.' Wheatley ripped the tape from Semilla's face and unplugged her mouth. 'Don't say a word,' he warned her.

She didn't say a word but she did retch and spit on the floor. 'Fucking hell, man. Don't you dare do that again. It's rancid.'

Micky, safely behind Wheatley, said, 'Okay. I'll use a pair of me old kegs next time, should I?.'

'Outside, you!' Wheatley commanded and, turning to the girl, 'Not a sound from you or I'll let him do it. Understand?'

Semilla nodded and retched again.

Wheatley led Micky to the bow of their vessel. 'We move now. Not to the mooring point but away from here. I want to be sure we won't get intercepted by the harbour master.'

'He'll want to know where we're headed. If we get past the Swing Bridge, we're out of his jurisdiction. Until then...'

The wind ruffled Wheatley's hair. He smoothed it back in place with his tapering fingers. 'Until then, nothing.'

'Unless he sends a boat to intercept us. What happens then?'

'You'll have to think on your feet, that's what. I know it's an alien concept to you.'

Micky tightened a fist. Patrick was really testing his patience, now. 'Does The Boss know what you're planning?'

'That's for me to know and you to find out. Just do as I say and get us beyond the Swing Bridge with no interruptions.'

Micky walked to the helm. Switched on the craft's radio.

'You're wasting time. Get the motor started.'

'Looker, you don't want us spotted, yeah? The only way I'll know we're not being monitored is if I tune into VTS One-Two.'

'What's that?'

'It's a track on the Station-to-Station album.' Micky sensed Patrick wasn't receptive to jokes. 'It's vessel traffic service. The Port of Tyne use radio frequency twelve to coordinate all the navigational decision-making. It'll be the first communication channel they'll contact us on. If nowt's said, we know they're not bothered.'

A strong gust of wind caused Patrick to lose his balance. He staggered but remained upright. 'Keep me informed. Now, get this thing moving.'

'Aye, aye, cap'n' Micky saluted.

He pressed the starter motor.

It wheezed but nothing more.

Micky tried again.

The engine stuttered and died like a car on a frosty morning. 'I think the props clogged with mud,' he explained.

'Shit.' Patrick went to the rear of the boat and looked down over the stern. 'Can't see a thing. Water's too murky. Try again.'

Micky pressed the starter again.

Patrick saw a faint ripple on the surface. 'I think it's starting to give. Try again.'

Micky complied. This time, the splutter was followed by a roar as the engine kicked in and the propeller freed itself.

'Job's a good 'un,' he said as he turned to face Wheatley's back.

Patrick turned towards him at the same time.

He was caked head to toe in stinking, foul filth thrown up by the revolving blades.

'Bastard,' he spat.

Micky didn't hear him over his gales of laughter. It was the first time he'd laughed for days.

He couldn't help but wonder if he'd ever laugh again.

TWENTY-SEVEN

Frantic calls back and forth to Samantha Maynard proved fruitless. It was impossible to raise two-hundred thousand pounds in such a short timescale. The bank simply refused to authorise it.

With the clock ticking, Maynard reached a decision. 'The bank won't go above a hundred grand. Stephen Rachman can supply twenty thousand but isn't able to access it until tomorrow. Is there any way we can put them off until then?'

Danskin and Ryan shook their heads. 'I don't think we're in a position to say, not until we get the next call. If we're lucky, Gowland and Wheatley will suggest tomorrow. If they don't, I can't recommend going against them.'

The radio silence told Ryan and Danskin the Super was considering the position.

'Right,' she said. 'We retrieve the fifty grand from the initial drop. If they're preparing for a second one, they won't have eyes on it. Add that to the hundred the bank will release; they mightn't realise they're short.'

'Aye, they're not ganna hang around to count it all, I reckon.'

'So, we're agreed then? One-hundred and fifty if they call it for today, with another twenty from the Mayor if we're given another twenty-four hours?'

'Sounds good to me,' Danskin said.

'Me, an' all, ma'am,' Ryan added.

'Okay. I'll leave you to rehearse tactics with Mrs Rachman while I see what manpower I can raise.'

'Surely the Crime Commissioner won't quibble, given the circumstances?'

'I'm sure not, Stephen, but what I need to calculate is how many we dare deploy without it being obvious.'

Danskin puffed out his cheeks. 'I don't envy you making that call. We divvent even know a location yet.'

'No – so make sure you get the info to me as soon as they pass on their instructions,' Maynard concluded

Ryan knew Danskin felt under pressure – he'd hit the mint imperials big-style – and there was nothing he could do relieve it.

He settled for, 'Not long now, sir. Let's get Elizabeth prepped.'

**

Patrick Wheatley was another who felt under pressure. He hadn't banked on needing a shower and change before making the second call. He took a moment to catch his breath before emerging into the cabin.

'Right, Milly...'

'Don't call me that! You know I hate it. Always have. My name is Semilla.'

Wheatley rolled his eyes. 'Is it really such a big deal?'

'Yes, *'PADDY'*, it is.'

Wheatley almost managed a smile. 'Okay, then; Semilla it is.' He looked out the cabin window. They were making slow but steady progress, with no sign of the Port Authorities sticking their oar in.

Patrick saw they were beyond Friars Wharf Apartments and The Schooner, with the Ouseburn visible ahead of them on the opposite bank. He'd order Micky to stop under the shade of trees opposite the Cycle Hub. He'd make his last demand there.

'Can I trust you to keep quiet, Milly?' he said, deliberately.

She ignored the use of the despised name. 'I have so far, haven't I? Why should anything change, now?'

Patrick shrugged. 'I don't know – the thought of Micky's shreddies might do it for you, who knows?'

She pulled a face. 'Do what you have to do. Let's just get it over with.'

He stood. 'That sounds fine to me. Not as good as all the money, mind, but good enough for now. Right, Micky will be back in here in a minute. Play the game like a good girl, okay?'

She traced a cross over her heart with her fingers.

On deck, Wheatley told Micky to pull over.

'It's shallow here, mind. Are you sure?'

'As long as you don't ground us, it'll be fine. I need you in the cabin with her.'

'Okay. I was joking about me kegs, you know.'

'Yes, I know. Now, just make sure she keeps quiet and, more importantly, don't play your shitty music. Not even quietly, right?'

**

The call was late. Five minutes, then ten. Ryan kept his eyes on the clock, Elizabeth's on the phone.

'You know what to do,' Ryan said. 'Nice and calm, just like the other times. Make sure you don't give him reason to think you know his identity. I know there's a lot to remember, but that's most important.

'I know,' she said, her head nodding like a toy dog on a dashboard.

'Ravi's with Mr Rachman. He'll be fine. Just concentrate on what you have to do.' Ryan surprised himself at how calm he was.

Until the phone rang.

'Yes?' Elizabeth said, sounding as calm as Ryan had a few moments before, though she had to stop herself talking over the four-second delay.

'I hope you're ready.'

'I am.'

'No silly games. You come alone.'

'I know. Where to?'

'Take the Metro to St. James' station.'

Ryan raised his eyebrows. This was not what he'd expected. The location was far removed from everything else in the case.

'You will head towards the stadium. On Strawberry Place, you will see some storage lockers. Same as the last ones. DO NOT use these ones. Instead, head left. You will find another set of lockers on the corner of Barrack Road. You will use locker number twenty-three. You will deposit the money there, and you leave immediately. You will not – I repeat NOT – lock the door. Do you understand?'

'Yes.'

Ryan tapped his watch and mouthed *'When.'*

'When? How long have I got?'

'Ninety minutes exactly.'

Elizabeth Rachman was trembling but her voice remained steady. 'I'll be there.'

'You better had. You, and only you.'

'I promise.'

'So you said. Oh, and if I find you've put anything in with the money, I'm sure you know exactly what I mean, I have settled on what I shall send you next. Would you like to know?'

'No. There'll be no need. I'll do as you say.'

'I'll tell you anyway. Three toes from your girl's right foot. Should just about put an end to her career, I'd say.'

The suave American voice stopped speaking; the line filled with the silence of an empty grave.

**

Wheatley ordered Micky to up the pace, keen to make his preparations before Elizabeth Rachman arrived. Despite his protestations, he went along with it.

In the cabin, Semilla rocked and rolled as the vessel increased its pace. She knew this was it. She felt sick to the stomach, her mind racing as it went through all the outcomes, and more besides.

Once past the last bridge, Micky yanked on the wheel and the boat spun, heading cross river, contrary to all navigation rules. He prayed they were out of range of the river authorities. The radio silence provided some reassurance, but he was relieved when he was able to spin the vessel again and lay up alongside a set of worn stone stairs running from the quayside and coming to a dead-end part way towards the muddy waters.

Fortunately for Wheatley, they'd caught the tide just about right. It was a stretch and his clean trousers flirted with the Tyne but he managed to reach the lowermost step and, with a heave on the rusting metal handrail, hauled himself upright.

Micky passed him the Tech Air bag and a holdall, with not an inkling of what Wheatley had planned.

'If you're not back in an hour, mind, I'm out of here.'

'Seventy-five minutes. That's the most it'll take.'

'It'd better because if I find you've fucked off with all the cash, I'll find you and feed you to the propellor blades: and I mean it.'

'Chill, man. You just concentrate on not moving an inch – and keeping our friend silent and out of sight.'

With that, Wheatley mounted the slimy staircase and disappeared onto the deserted quayside.

**

In the Forth Street station, Sam Maynard and Lyall Parker were mobilising the troops in a bout of activity as frenetic as life in a termite mound.

Todd Robson was to play the part of a homeless man huddled up on the roadside next to the Sela Stack construction site, adjacent to St James' Park. 'I won't need much of a disguise to play that role,' Robson said to guffaws.

Lucy Dexter and Nigel Trebilcock would be tourists consulting street maps and wandering as if lost, while Gavin O'Hara hunted out a black and white scarf to wear in his role as a fan sat outside Shearer's Bar.

Plain clothes units were despatched in an unmarked van to the far end of Strawberry Place ready to close off the road, while another unit pretended to be a team of heating engineers called to the Newcastle Uni Business School on nearby Pitt Street. Two more units sat in wait on Grandstand Road, ready to block access to the A167 escape route, east and west.

Maynard mobilised a helicopter which would hover at a safe distance, and, she realised, that was all she could do; all without endangering the life of Semilla Rachman.

'It's not enough, Lyall,' she said.

'It's your best, ma'am. That's what counts.'

'Why pick that location?'

'Your guess is as good as mine. It does seem off the beaten track and at odds wi' everything they've done so far.'

'There's got to be a reason. I just don't see it.'

Rick Kinnear interrupted them. 'Phone call for you, ma'am. Should I put it through?'

Maynard tisked. 'Not now, Rick.'

'I think you should take it.'

'Really?' she scolded. 'Give me one good reason.'

DCI Kinnear's eyes settled on a spot on the floor. 'We need to rethink things.'

'Bloody hell, Rick. We haven't time.'

Kinnear groaned. 'We have to. We've got the wrong suspects.'

Her mouth yawned open at the same time as her eyes closed.

'The call's from Force Anglia. They've got Noel Gowland. He's in Kings Lynn. He's touring with a theatre company. He's been with them since dismantling the lights at the Customs House.'

'Anglia can back all that up?'

'Yes, ma'am.'

Sam Maynard did something she almost never did.

She said, 'Fuck.'

**

In the house on Cleadon's West Park Road, things were equally fraught.

'Are you ready, Mrs Rachman?' Danskin asked.

'I just need a few more minutes.' She closed her eyes, toyed with the blonde wig, and took a few deep breaths. She pulled the hairpiece into position. 'Right. Let's get this over with.'

'You'll need to wear a wire. You'll have a tiny mic and an earpiece. We'll be watching you every step of the way,' Ryan promised. 'Take your jacket off, please.'

'No. I don't want one. What if they catch me?' Her eyes were intense and authoritative.

'I agree with Elizabeth,' Stephen Rachman said, taking her arm.

Danskin could see they weren't going to budge. It was his decision and he took it. 'Okay. But you follow our instructions to the letter, yeah?'

Elizabeth nodded. 'I'm not doing anything to risk our daughter's safety.'

It didn't escape Ryan's attention that Elizabeth used the word *'our'* for the first time. 'Superintendent Maynard will ensure it's all discreet at the pick-up. There won't be an obvious presence but we'll have folk around. Even you won't see them.'

'Thanks,' she said, unconvinced. She licked lips which were chapped with stress and anxiety.

'Ravi will be on the Metro with you, but at a safe distance. Neither DS Jarrod nor me can go because the suspects know us. Like Jarrod said, we won't do owt that might affect Semilla's safety.'

Ryan looked at Semilla's parents. 'You've both got your phones on, yeah? All charged?'

They did.

'You won't have far from the Metro to the locker but try to stay in public sight. Take your time with everything. The longer our guys have to scrutinise the surroundings, the more chance they have of this going our way.'

'What about Semilla? How do I get her back?'

It was a question Ryan couldn't answer. Instead, Stephen Danskin said, 'Leave that to us.'

Ryan knew that meant he had absolutely no idea.

'Okay,' Jarrod said, 'I think we're good to go. Ravi's checked the Metro and there's no delays, which is a bit of a miracle in itself, so I think the Gods are with us.'

Stephen Rachman gave a grim smile. 'You can do this,' he whispered to his ex-wife.

'I hope so.'

She kissed her fingers and pressed them lightly against the lips of their daughter's oil painting.

'I'm coming for you, darling.'

TWENTY-EIGHT

At eighteen stories high, loved or hated, the Blue Pinnacle could never be ignored. Standing near the heart of Newcastle city centre, it provided high-end student accommodation under its official name of 'The View.'

From its upper stories, what a view it presented. On a clear day, south over the Chinatown district, the Tyne and her bridges and the slug-shaped Glasshouse performance centre sat Gateshead. To the east, Leazes Park and the green expanse of the Town Moor provided a contrast to the terraced suburbs to the west end. Patrick Wheatley, though, admired none of them.

His focus was on the ground below.

Across the road and at The View's foot stood the gates to St James' Park. To the stadium's right, the stairs to and from St James' Metro station were in clear line-of-sight. More importantly, so, too was the bank of storage lockers in which Elizabeth Rachman would soon leave two-hundred-thousand pounds.

Wheatley wasn't a religious man but he praised the Lord at having been granted such a wonderful cousin. Not only did Shane Wheatley leave a boat at Patrick's disposal, but he also had the foresight to pay advance rent as a retainer on his post-grad accommodation quarters while he travelled abroad.

Patrick had raced uphill from the boat's mooring point. The climb was a steep one and he clutched his side from the exertion as he gathered himself in the sheltered lane of Heber Street, behind the Sandeman Hotel. The View stood adjacent to the hotel; so close they could have been part of the same complex.

Dusk approached but there was not yet a need for streetlights. Wheatley calculated on there being at least ninety more minutes of daylight. Time enough to pick up the goodies and disappear.

Wheatley listened for the sound of sirens above his chesty wheeze. There were none. Of course there wasn't. The woman wasn't stupid enough to risk all.

He had no doubt she'd have told the cops but he was counting on them providing a discreet and minimal presence. Plus, the timing of his call meant he'd be in position to watch any force mobilisation before it began.

At least, he would be if he got a move on.

He breezed through the sliding doors of The View like a zephyr. He glanced to his right into the games room. A couple of gangly students hunched over a pool table; their bored girlfriends sat on odd-shaped purple sofas thumbing their mobiles.

Patrick called the lift and travelled unaccompanied and without interruption to the eleventh floor which housed Shane's Platinum Apartment. At a grand a month, it wasn't cheap by any standard. Patrick realised it was grossly overpriced by the ease in which he broke in.

The interior was an open, modern space of bland pastels and a slightly musty odour which betrayed its lack of occupancy.

Patrick noticed none of those things. Instead, he went straight to the window, pulled up a chair, and put his feet on the windowsill.

'Perfect,' he said out loud. The apartment gave him a birds-eye view of the entire scene. Not through a telescope from across the river, but right on top of it.

'Absolutely perfect,' he repeated, settling down to watch the spectacle unfold.

All he lacked was a bucket of popcorn.

**

Lyall Parker recalled Danskin and Jarrod to the Forth Street station to cover for him as he volunteered himself as another pair of eyes on surveillance.

They set off for the station as soon as the Family Liaison officer arrived to babysit Stephen Rachman.

'I'm going to call Anglia meself on route,' Danskin told Ryan. 'I'm not having it. Gowland's got to be involved.'

'Even if he's not, he might know who is.'

As the DCI drove, Ryan called Force Anglia.

'Bollocks. They've released Gowland.'

'They've what? Shit the bed, man.'

'I've got a number for him.'

'What you waiting for? Dial it and put him on speaker. I want to talk to him.'

Ryan was about to give up on the call when Noel Gowland finally picked up.

'Mr Gowland, it's DCI Stephen Danskin here. We met at…'

'Aye. I know where we met. Was all this some kind of joke: dragging me in like that in front of the company?'

'Sir, I haven't time for this. If you want Semilla Rachman back alive, I need you to help us.'

Gowland remained silent. He was obviously thinking about it.

'Of course I want Semilla alive. I don't trust you, though. How do I know you're not going to trick me into saying summat?'

Danskin drummed his fingers on the steering wheel as they stood in queuing traffic on the Tyne Tunnel approach. 'Okay. I have one question I need you to answer. If I'm satisfied with what you say, I guarantee you will no longer be a person of interest.'

Ryan gave his DCI a curious look but said nothing.

'Fire away,' Noel Gowland replied, confidently.

'If you had nothing to do with Semilla Rachman's disappearance, why are you so obsessed with her you've got half your hoose stuffed with photos of her?'

The traffic started moving. They'd lose signal in the confines of the tunnel. Danskin steered off the carriageway into a police vehicle holding bay.

Gowland sighed. 'Okay. It might be a bit of a saddo thing to do; a bit stalkerish, even. The thing is…' he paused. 'The thing is, we were each other's first, y'know what I'm saying? They reckon you always remember your first time and, when Semilla became famous, I sort of became, I dunno, obsessed, I suppose. I wanted to keep the memory with me. I know it sounds creepy but…'

Danskin cut him short. 'I'm satisfied with your answer. We haven't time for waffle and juicy gossip. Now, what is Patrick Wheatley's relationship with Semilla?'

The car rocked as it was caught in the wake of a passing freight vehicle.

'Patrick? None as far…oh, right. He danced with Semilla for a couple of years but I think that's it. I always thought he batted for the other side – you're not suggesting…?'

'Is there anyone Wheatley might work with, if he did happen to be involved – which I'm not saying he was.'

Ryan tapped his watch. Danskin nodded. Gowland whistled.

'Off the top of me heed, nah. Only person the pair of them had in common was Sophia Ridley.'

'Okay. Thanks for your time, Mr Gowland. I'm sorry we put you through such an ordeal. You're free to go back to the theatre company.'

'Huh. Too late for that. They've fired me.'

Danskin ordered Ryan to end the call and they pulled into the tunnel entrance.

'Sophia Ridley's not involved, sir, I guarantee it.'

'Aye, I agree. We're completely in the dark on who Wheatley's accomplice is. On the plus side, we only have one needle to look for, now, Jarrod.'

'True, but the haystack's no smaller.'

Danskin whistled 'Always Look on the Bright Side of Life' as they emerged from the tunnel, a reddening sky overhead.

**

Elizabeth Rachman went over the final instructions in her head. *'Take my time. If the kidnapper approaches me, stay calm. If he has Semilla with him, don't cry. Follow instructions to the letter.'*

She repeated the mantra ad nauseum as the Metro train pulled into its destination station. The platforms were deserted. Usually were unless it was a match day.

Her heels clacked on the tiled surface in the cavernous space. Her fingers gripped the escalator handrail as if her hand was a vice. Ravi Sangar waited until she was out of sight before leaving the carriage.

'She's on her way up,' he whispered into a mic tucked beneath his T-shirt.

'Got that, Ravi. Keep your distance,' Maynard instructed. 'All units, be ready. Sub is on her way.'

Elizabeth emerged from the subterranean depths onto the external concourse. 'Eyes on,' Todd Robson whispered into his sleeping bag.

'Anyone else around, Todd?'

Robson's head rotated left and right, as if stretching his neck. 'Yes, ma'am.'

Maynard sucked in breath. 'Description.'

'Tall bloke. Thin. Dark hair, bit of a beard. Could be Ravi Sangar's twin.'

Maynard tutted. 'I appreciate your attempt at levity but it's not the time. Anyone else?'

'Nah. A few people heading towards the Strawberry. Three or four students heading into toon. Nowt unusual, ma'am.'

'Keep me informed.'

'I see her.' Gavin O'Hara said into his scarf. 'She's at the top of the stairs on Gallowgate.'

'How's she bearing up?'

'Looks fine, ma'am. A lot calmer than I feel, if I'm honest. Hang on, she's almost on top of me now. 'Going silent in case she's being watched.' O'Hara picked up a newspaper and a non-alcoholic pint without looking in Elizabeth's direction.

She didn't glance towards him because she had no clue who he was. He could have been the kidnapper as far as she was concerned but she wasn't going to invite attention. A few yards further on, she stopped as if to check her shoes. Stood. Opened the bag which contained the money.

'Oi see her, ma'am,' Trebilcock whispered. 'She's taking her time. Seems to be following her instructions, so she is.' He stared at a map and looked around him. Lucy tugged his elbow and pointed in the direction they'd just come from. They looked around but saw no-one acting suspiciously.

'Everything looks clear, here,' Dexter said.

They heard Maynard whistle. 'What the hell's the plan?' The question was rhetorical.

Elizabeth stood and looked around. Her eyes met those of a man outside Shearer's Bar. When he quickly looked away, she felt her pulse quicken. Was that him? She was close enough to know it wasn't Patrick Wheatley, but it could be his accomplice?

O'Hara radioed in. 'I think she's seen me. We should have a arranged a signal so she knows it's one of us.'

'We didn't have time to think of everything. Just stay where you are. I suppose it shows she's aware of her surroundings, which is good news.'

'Ma'am,' Todd Robson's voice. 'Could Wheatley's accomplice be a woman?'

The question nonplussed her. The silence hung heavy.

'Why do you ask?'

'There's a skinny wife hanging around the Sela Stack. Saw her going in the opposite direction a few moments ago. She's back now. Just loitering, like.'

'You keep eyes on her. Let me know if she moves.'

Maynard's office door flew open as Ryan and Danskin burst in.

'What's the latest, ma'am?'

They didn't get an update. Instead, they got a question.

'Could Wheatley be collaborating with a woman?'

While Danskin considered the question, Ryan considered an answer.

He looked at Danskin. 'Not Sophia Ridley, surely?'

'Why do you ask?' Danskin said.

'Todd Robson's seen a sus per.'

Ryan reached for the radio. 'Todd, it's Ryan. Describe the suspicious person.'

'White. Skinny. Blonde.'

'Age?'

'Can't tell.'

'What's she doing now, Todd?' Maynard intervened.

'She's sort of keeping against the wall.'

'Hiding?'

'Could be,' Robson said.

'Don't see what you expect to see, Robson. Now, is she hiding or not?'

'I divvent knaa, man. She's just arse-farting around.'

Todd crawled like a caterpillar in his sleeping bag until he faced the woman. 'Okay. She's wearing skinny jeans and a scruffy jumper. One of those half-dress length things.'

'Doesn't sound like Sophia, sir,' Ryan said.

'It doesn't, I agree; but same goes for us, Jarrod: Don't see...'

Sand Dancer

'I know the rest, sir.'

Todd watched a couple walk from Chinatown towards Barrack Road; a man and a woman. The woman entered a blue tower block while the man crossed the street by a Tesco Express at the foot of the building.

He walked towards the mystery woman.

'Someone's approaching her,' Robson whispered.

Ryan, Danskin, and the Super couldn't recall Todd ever speak in hushed tones. It sounded like Velcro being pulled apart very slowly.

'What's happening, Todd?'

'I've just bloody told you. A bloke's approaching her.'

'Robson, is it Wheatley?'

'Howay, man: I'd have told you if I knew that, wouldn't I?' Normal Todd voice had resumed. 'He's got a hoodie on. It wasn't pulled up before. Summat's going to happen.'

The woman stepped from behind a portacabin. She handed something to the man, who responded in kind.

'False alarm,' Todd said. 'Repeat: false alarm. It's a friggin' drugs deal.'

They breathed a collective sigh of relief.

Until Lucy Dexter spoke.

'Elizabeth Rachman's making the drop now.'

They'd all taken their eyes off the ball.

TWENTY-NINE

'I see her,' Lyall Parker chipped in from his elevated viewpoint. 'I can see the whole transaction from here. The rest of you, stay alert but it's the suspect you're looking for, now. I'll follow the drop.'

Elizabeth Rachman stood by the 24/7 In-Post locker, paralysed. She needed to see Semilla. Her baby. What if Wheatley had seen the cops and done a runner? Worse, what if he'd eyeballed the cops and killed her girl?

She'd forgotten all her instructions. Couldn't remember what to do. Couldn't even remember the locker number. Elizabeth Rachman stood like a statue.

'Ma'am, she's frozen,' Lyall said. 'She's just standing there.'

'Confirm she's made the drop.'

'Negative. She hasn't moved a muscle since she got tae the lockers.'

Gavin O'Hara's voice broke the despairing silence. 'I can get to her in less than a minute. Whisper to her as I go pass.'

'Too risky,' Ryan said.

'Not your call, Ry,' O'Hara said.

'Your instructions from the DI are to watch for the abductor,' Jarrod persisted.

'Ma'am?'

'Ryan's right. Lyall: latest position, please?'

'She's still there.'

A cyclist swung across traffic at the Barrack Road junction with Strawberry Place. He dodged the cars but those same vehicles hid a bus lane from view.

With a malevolent hiss of air-brakes and a resounding blast on the horn, the bus driver, somehow, avoided hitting the cyclist.

Even better, it brought Elizabeth Rachman out of her trance.

'Looks like she's with us again, ma'am. Drop proceeding.'

**

Unknown to Lyall Parker, Patrick Wheatley sat two-stories above him, watching and waiting. Open in front of him was the Tech Air bag, with his communication kit ready and waiting and, alongside him, a thirty-six inch bolt cutter.

Wheatley laughed as the bus almost took out the cyclist but it didn't distract his focus. He was already tapped into the student accommodation's Wi-Fi.

Beside the lockers, Elizabeth remembered her instructions. Locker number twenty-three, that was it.

She swung the bag off her shoulder. Opened the zip. Pulled out the carrier bag inside. She took one last look around. No-one approached, no-one watched.

Elizabeth held a breath. Pulled at the locker's door. It opened, just as the AI voice had promised. She ducked her head inside the locker - and saw the locker wasn't empty.

It contained a mobile phone.

It was the wrong locker.

'Shit, shit, shit, SHIT!' she swore, trembling. She'd been sure locker twenty-three was the one she'd been told.

Her head was still inside the locker when the phone rang, so loud in its metal prison, she split open her head on its frame as she jumped in shock.

**

'Something's wrong,' Lyall Parker said. 'She hasn't put anything in the locker. Looks like, I don't know, looks like she's hurt herself.'

'I need specifics, Lyall.'

'Mrs Rachman opened the locker, looked inside, and it seems like she's sustained an injury. She's holding her head.'

'Has she still got the ransom money?' Ryan asked.

'Aye. It's at her feet.'

'All personnel: any sign of suspect approaching?' She waited while all units responded in the negative. 'Okay. Keep your eyes peeled. This could be it.'

'She's reaching inside again,' Parker commentated. 'She's got something in her hand. It looks like… I think it's a mobile. The kidnappers are giving her final instructions.'

Danskin swore. 'That's out the blue. We've been bloody blindsided.'

Parker looked on as Elizabeth brought the device to her ear.

**

'What a beautiful night for us, isn't it?' the American voice said.

'Where are you?'

'Can't you see? I'm waving to you right now.'

Elizabeth spun three-hundred and sixty degrees. A man sipped his pint outside Shearer's. A homeless man lay asleep across the road. A few others hurried by without looking, let alone waving.

'Where's Semilla?'

'We'll get to that.'

'Is she with you?'

'She's safe. That's all you need know.'

'I want my baby.'

The AI voice chuckled, a surreal, other-worldly sound. 'Your baby is a big girl now. So, are you ready for your final instructions?' He didn't wait for a reply. 'Take out the money in bundles. Just so I know there's nothing inside that shouldn't be. One bundle at a time.'

'*Oh God. Please don't count i*t,' Elizabeth prayed.

'I want you to deposit it at least six bundles. Do it randomly and slowly. Don't let anyone see what you're doing.'

Elizabeth did as instructed.

'Good girl. Remember, you do not lock the door. Understood?'

'When do I get Semilla?'

'DO. YOU. UNDERSTAND?'

'Yes,' she whimpered.

'Right. You may go now. I know you have police watching your movements,' he surmised, 'And I know you'll have your own phone with you. I want you to take it out and tell them to back off. Keep this phone on so I hear exactly what you tell them.'

Elizabeth bubbled as she pulled out her mobile. 'He knows you're watching. He can see me, so I know he can see you, too. Please, if you have anyone nearby, move them.'

'Fucking hell. What a bastard,' Danskin mumbled in Forth Street.

'He's good, I give him that,' Ryan admitted.

'I'll call them off,' Maynard agreed. 'Tell him he'll see them moving as soon as he releases Semilla.'

The Super heard her pass on the message, then listened as Elizabeth let out a howl of anguish. 'He says no deal. You have to clear off. Please. He promises he'll let Semilla go once he has the ransom.'

Stephen Danskin spoke. 'Do you believe him?'

Between sobs, she replied, 'I've no choice, do I? I have to believe him.'

Maynard muted the call. 'What do you think?'

'I think she's right,' Ryan said. 'There is no option. Remember, though, we know it's Wheatley so we'll get him, regardless. He can't go far. We've got every force in the land on the lookout for him. Once we know Semilla's been released…'

'*IF* she's released,' Danskin cautioned.

'Once she's safe, Wheatley won't know what's hit him.'

Danskin gave it further consideration. 'Aye. He's a creepy bastard but, for all it's worth, I divvent think he'd kill once he's got what he wants. We don't know owt about his partner; that's the problem.'

Defeated, Maynard unmuted the call. 'Tell him we agree. But, first, at least get him to tell you HOW you'll get your daughter back.'

They heard Elizabeth Rachman pass the message to Wheatley.

After what seemed an eternity, she replied.

'He's told me I've to keep this other phone switched on. As soon as he's got the money and is far enough away, he'll tell me where I can get her. If you don't do as he says, he'll leave her to rot.'

Elizabeth held it together just long enough to finish the sentence.

**

Wheatley stretched his arms above his head before glancing at his watch. He had fifteen minutes to get back to the boat before Micky sailed off into the sunset, if he had the balls to do such a thing.

Cars had their sidelights on and some of the offices showed a patchwork quilt of fluorescents but, mostly, it remained light enough for what he had to do.

Light enough for him to see someone follow Elizabeth into the Metro station. and a bloke who'd been hanging around Shearer's bar finish a drawn-out pint and wander towards the city centre. Light enough for him to watch a lost couple miraculous find their location and march off downhill, and long enough for a healthy-looking homeless man to roll up a sleeping bag and seek pastures new.

Wheatley smiled to himself. He'd held all the aces and was about to walk away with the jackpot. He packed the communication kit into the bag, retrieved the bolt-cutter, and carefully pulled the apartment's broken door shut behind him.

The lift stopped twice on its way down, once at the seventh and again at the third. He kept the bolt-cutter behind his back as he studied the occupants. They looked like typical students off for a night on the town.

They alighted at the ground floor, leaving Wheatley to travel to the below-ground car park alone.

He only had a vague recollection of where cousin Shane kept his motorcycle but he saw it, bright yellow, chained to a rack near the front of the car park. A quick glance around reassured him no-one lurked in the shadows. He saw the CCTV cameras located at the entrance but he'd be long gone before anyone inspected the footage from it.

Patrick knelt by the bike. Applied the bolt-cutter blades where the security chain joined the shackle. And grunted as he applied pressure.

It didn't give.

'Crap.'

He tried again.

Nothing.

He gripped the cutters in both hands and stamped on the upper handle, again and again.

The chains ruptured one-by-one, falling to the concrete floor in a tinkle which chimed like church bells in the cavernous enclosure.

After another check assured him he was alone, he found the casing holding the ignition switch connector. A quick wiggle of the hands, applying pressure as he did so, and the cover came free.

His fingers trembled as he traced the path of the exposed wires to the ignition switch. He wiped his hands on his thighs and separated the ignition wire from the others.

Now came the fun bit. He parted the two ignition wires, placed one into an exposed socket and the other into a second outlet.

As soon as he did so, a green and a red light illuminated on the panel.

Bingo!

He took a deep breath and squeezed the handle.

His triumphant roar drowned out the growl of the engine as it spluttered alive.

Wheatley noticed the fuel gauge was well in the red zone. It didn't concern him. He had enough to travel the two miles required. The one thing he didn't have was a helmet. That made him vulnerable to any nosey uniformed cop who might see him.

He didn't intend to hang around long enough to be seen.

He sped towards the ramped exit, wheels leaving the ground as he emerged into fresh air, close to colliding with an oblivious Lyall Parker walking away from The View.

Wheatley spun the motorcycle on the pavement outside and applied the brakes. He gathered his bearings momentarily, turned one-hundred and eighty degrees and sped across Barack Road towards the lockers.

Locker twenty-three was at waist-height to him as he sat astride the bike. The door eased open. He grabbed the contents, stuffed them into the trusty Tech Air bag, and pulled a U-turn.

Seconds later he was snaking through the deserted pedestrianised avenues of the Helix student quarter. Within two minutes, he was on Skinnerburn Lane which ran river side of the green shell of the Arena.

Patrick jumped off the bike, restarted it, kicked it into gear and pushed the yellow motorbike towards the riverbank. The engine squealed as it left tarmac before landing in the thick waters of the Tyne with a hiss, and a gurgle as it sank from view.

'I've only bloody-well done it!' Wheatley shrieked in joy.
Premature joy.

When he looked down river, the tide had lowered. The deck of the boat was at least twelve feet below the point the stone steps ended.

THIRTY

Darkness closed in on the craft but the cabin remained unlit. Inside, Micky paced the confined space like an expectant father.

'He should be back by now,' he said.

'I told you he'd double-cross you. He'll be miles away by now. You'll never see your share. You may as well let me go. All I can do is give you my word I won't say anything. I'll book into a chavvy B&B somewhere on the quayside. Nobody will recognise me, looking and smelling like I do. It'll give you…'

'Shut your gob! I'm thinking.'

Micky began muttering to himself as he prowled the cabin. He put his face to the starboard window, cupped his hand around his eyes, and looked down.

'Bloody tide's going out fast. I'll give him five minutes then we're out of here. Both of us.'

Semilla tried to remain calm. 'What will you do with me? How do I get home?'

'I'll drop you off near the coast. You can swim, can't you?'

Her eyes widened.

'I'm taking the piss, man. I don't know what I'll do with you. Now, shut up and let me think.'

Semilla shut up but only so she could think. 'We could go together.'

'Don't be bloody stupid. They'll soon come after me. If Patrick reneges on The Boss, we're both dead meat. Probably all three of us.'

'We won't be in Russia. We'll be protected. I'll make sure you get a visa. I've got influence, you know.'

Sand Dancer

He looked at her as if she were stupid. 'I'm not gannin to Russia, man. Besides, how would I get there? Every airport in the land will be looking for you, never mind me.'

'We've a boat, haven't we?'

He shook his head. He no longer thought she was stupid, he *knew* she was stupid.

'Right. His time's up. I'm out of here before this thing is left marooned in the mud.'

His move towards the cabin door was halted by a loud thud.

'What was that?' Semilla wondered.

Micky edged towards the cabin door. Unlocked it from the inside. Eased it open. Or, tried to. The door didn't budge.

'Summat's blocked the door,' he whispered.

He put his foot against and shoved, hard. It gave a few inches. Just enough for Micky to squeeze through.

And tumble over a prostate and unconscious Patrick Wheatley.

**

Barely a mile along the riverbank, the open-plan office on the Forth Street station's third floor was filled with tension.

'We're in this for the long-haul,' Superintendent Maynard was saying. 'For your information, DI Parker is meeting Ravi Sangar and Elizabeth Rachman at Manors Metro station in an unmarked car. From there, they'll travel back to the Rachman residence to wait further news from Wheatley. The rest of us are here. All night, if needs be.'

She waited for the mutters of discontent. None came, not even from Todd Robson. The only words came from Ryan Jarrod.

'The Domino's are on me, chaps. If we're working on this all night, we need food. The more unhealthy the better. Get your orders in now.' He gave Trebilcock a handful of coins. 'Get as many coffees as you can oot of that, Nigel. I'm sure the rest of you can make up the shortfall.'

He saw Sam Maynard looking at him. 'Sorry, ma'am. I didn't mean to interrupt.'

'It's all good, Ryan. I think it's the right call. We do need sustenance before the debrief.' Maynard smiled. 'You think of everything. A proper little Superman, you are.'

Superman. Ryan thought of Hannah, alone in the apartment, waiting to bring a new life into the world. That, he thought, really was a superpower. Ordering half-a-dozen pizzas and wedges was more Clark Kent territory.

Maynard ordered a timeout until the pizza arrived. It was the only break they'd get, and it was one Ryan could have done without. All it did was remind him he should be there for Hannah, not hunched over a desk with coffee and scran.

There again, he realised she'd rather he did all he could to rescue someone's child.

He downed a double espresso in one gulp.

**

The shove on the door caused Wheatley to roll over. Rolling over caused his eyes to open. And opening his eyes meant he saw Micky dipping into the ransom money.

'No you don't,' he groaned, pushing himself into an upright sitting position.

'I'm not doing nowt,' Micky protested. 'Just making sure the mission was successful.' He pushed a wad of notes back into the bag. 'Heard from The Boss yet?'

Wheatley struggled unsteadily to his feet. 'Not yet.'

'Looker, we need to get our arses in gear and get out of here.'

'Don't worry. I got clean away. I wasn't followed or tracked.'

Micky tutted. 'I'm not talking about the cops. I'm talking about the river. We're going to be left high and dry if we're not quick.'

Wheatley rubbed the back of his neck. 'True. The level's dropped more than I reckoned.' He squinted up at the quayside above. 'That was one hell of a jump.' His eyes suddenly cleared. 'Where is she?'

Micky twisted his head in the direction of the cabin. 'In there?'

'Behaving herself?'

Micky rocked his head from side-to-side. 'So-so. Tried to convince me you'd buggered off with the dough, then thought I could sail to Russia with her in this thing.'

'Huh?'

He help up his hands. 'I know, I know. So, are we shifting or not?'

Wheatley nodded. 'No lights, though.'

'I need to see where I'm headed, man.'

'No lights!'

Micky muttered to himself as he walked around the boat's hull, releasing the mooring ropes. He walked to the helm. Depressed the starter button.

The motor fired but failed to ignite properly.

He tried again. This time, the engine chugged to the rhythm of 'Row, row, row your boat' before it died.

'What's happened?' Patrick asked.

'Bugger all, that's what.'

'Try again.'

'No point. We're grounded, near as damn it.'

'Fuck, no!'

The lights on the seven bridges spanning the Tyne shone brightly against a sapphire blue sky which seemed to amplify the traffic noise.

'Divvent lose your shit. If I clean the prop of enough crud, it should just about get enough grip to get us afloat. It worked in the graving yard, remember.'

Wheatley listened as a siren wailed. He held his breath. Concentrated on the sound. Decided it was an ambulance, not a police vehicle. 'What do I do?'

Micky looked at him. 'As little as possible. For starters, make sure no-one's approaching, yeah?'

'Uh-huh.'

Micky made his way to the stern. He tucked his feet into the underseat cargo nets and slung himself over the stern. Only his legs and lower torso were visible to Wheatley as the rest of him hung downwards, stretching down towards propeller and rudder.

'What the fuck are you doing?'

'Having a pint with the lads, what do you think I'm doing? I'm trying to get rid of the shit between the blades.'

'Hurry up, then.'

With a grunt, Micky hauled himself back onto the deck. 'No good. Can't reach enough of it.'

The wail of another distant siren.

'So?' Wheatley asked, unhelpfully.

Micky's brow wrinkled. 'Next to the starter motor, there's a lever. It works on hydraulics. If the props not stuck fast, we should be able to raise it enough for me to fix it.'

Wheatley walked to the helm. 'Is it this rusty thing with a rubber handle?'

'Aye, that'll be it.' He resumed the over-hull position. 'Give it a gan.' The last words came out muffled as he disappeared over the hull.

'Here goes nothin'' Wheatley said as he pulled back on the lever.

It gave a piston-like wheeze.

'Give it some welly, man,' Micky mumbled.

Patrick tried again. Along with the wheeze came a sucking sound.

'She's coming. One more should do it.'

Patrick pulled again. The sucking noise gave way to a series of disturbing plops.

'Reet. I can reach it. Just need to get rid of the shite off it, now.'

'You what? I can't hear you.'

'It doesn't matter. Just stay there while I clear it,' he said, louder.

The cabin door opened. Semilla poked her head out. 'What's going on?'

'Micky, man. You didn't lock the cabin door.'

Micky couldn't hear him, either.

'What're you doing?' Semilla asked the soles of Micky's feet.

'He's getting us shipshape and Bristol fashion. Now, get back inside.'

She didn't. 'I'll stay.'

Wheatley didn't have the inclination to argue.

Micky pulled at clumps of tangled seaweed, evil-smelling clumps of thick congealed sludge. He flung fistfuls of it to one side. Blood flooded to his brain, his face burned red, and his temples played a drum solo but he continued cleaning the blades, inch-by-inch, one-by-one.

Finally, he released a breath and blew out his cheeks. He'd cleared the blades. They were on the road to freedom.

'We're good to go,' an upside-down Micky shouted. 'Lower the prop again.'

Another siren sounded. Two sirens. Patrick saw flashing lights reflect in the still water. He looked towards them at the same time as reaching for the hydraulic.

He stepped back in shock at the high-pitched whirr which greeted him. There was a brief clunking sound, a roar of engine, and the prop blades shrieked from their raised position.

'Sorry, Micky. Wrong button. Am I good to try again?'

Micky didn't reply.

'Micky - should I try again?'

Micky still didn't reply. Patrick walked towards the feet and legs tucked into the cargo nets.

'Are you deaf, or what?'

He peered over the hull.

And realised Micky's feet and legs were all that remained of him. Micky. The rest floated on the surface of the Tyne like shredded, gristly-pink shark bait.

**

The foyer of the Forth Street station was empty apart from a couple of handcuffed drunks and a bloke with a bust nose and bloodied lip.

Its lights burnt bright as a beacon, attracting them to it like moths to a flame. They walked downhill; trance-like, silent, and unfeeling. The doors to the foyer slid open.

The desk sergeant was completing paperwork to release the man with the broken nose. 'I'll be with you in a moment. Just take a seat.'

He sensed they hadn't moved a muscle. He glanced up. 'Okay,' he smiled, 'You can stand if you prefer. I won't be long.' The desk sergeant impressed himself. He hadn't even done a double-take.

He turned his back to the foyer as he slid the paperwork into a drawer. He made a play of shuffling a pile of folders while he whispered into his radio.

Within a minute, five officers shot out of a side-door.

Four leapt on the man, pinning him to the floor, arm twisted to his shoulder blade, two pairs of knees digging into his back as the cops cuffed him and patted him down.

The other officer gently pulled the lady aside.

'Everything's okay. You're safe with us, now. It's all over, Miss Rachman.'

THIRTY-ONE

Interview with Patrick Alistair Wheatley

'Detective Chief Inspector Stephen Danskin, that's me, am the chief interviewing officer, and I'm assisted by Detective Sergeant Ryan Jarrod. Please introduce yourself for the benefit of the recording.'

'Patrick Alistair Wheatley.'

'Can you confirm you are attending this interview voluntarily?'

'I am.'

'And you do not wish to have legal representation?'

'No.'

'Can you tell me how you know Miss Semilla Rachman?'

'We went to the same dance school, when we were no more than kids, really.'

'Did you stay in touch?'

'DS Jarrod interrupting the recording to say Mr Wheatley has just shaken his head. Please, remember to answer the questions for the tape.'

'Okay. Sorry.'

'So, you didn't stay in touch?'

'No. Not really. I mean, we weren't really close or anything.'

'Define *'not really'* for me.'

'When she came home, she used to visit the dance school now and then. I did some work with them.'

'I see. Now, turning to the night Miss Rachman disappeared. Can you tell me, in your own words, what you remember.'

'She was due to give a performance at the Customs House Theatre, that's in South Shields, as a favour to her dance teacher, Sophia Ridley. I was working there, too. The concert concluded, and Miss Rachman didn't appear.'

'What was your role that evening?'

'I was stage manager.'

'Which involved?'

'Making sure everyone was where they should be, prompting them, overseeing their warm-up, keeping things to time, that sort of thing.'

'When you say making sure people were where they should be, does that include Miss Rachman?'

Mr Wheatley has nodded.

'But Miss Rachman wasn't there, was she? Because you'd already seen to it, hadn't you?'

'No comment.'

'We have seen a recording of the performance which shows you handing a note to Sophia Ridley. What did the note say?'

'Something about moving cars, I think.'

'Who gave you the note?'

Mr Wheatley has shrugged his shoulders.

'I think you wrote the note yourself so that Miss Rachman's mother would leave the theatre early before she had time to suspect something was wrong.'

'No. That's not how it was. Semilla *was* in her dressing room when I gave her the curtain call. Then, she asked me to take her down the backstairs leading below stage and, from there, on to the rear fire exit doors.'

'Really?'

'Yes.'

'Mr Wheatley, shortly after Miss Rachman's disappearance, you showed me around the theatre. You showed me the fire-exit. The alarm had been disabled. You disabled it, didn't you, so you could smuggle Miss Rachman out of the theatre, unseen, before anyone knew she was missing?'

'No comment.'

'Mr Wheatley, Patrick, you're doing yourself no favours by refraining from comment. You walked into our station with Miss Rachman last night and one of your first words were, 'I can't do this anymore.' *Don't you think that tells us everything?'*

'Okay. Right. I admit I was involved.'

'Involved?'

'Yes.'

'Who else was involved? Who was your accomplice?'

'Michael Thwaites.'

'Who?'

'He was a friend.'

'Was? So, he's not a friend anymore. Has that anything to do with you keeping the ransom money for yourself?'

'Of course not. It's because he's dead.'

'Sorry?'

'A boating accident. That's how we kept out of view. We used the river and the north sea to stay out of your reach.'

'How did this Mr Thwaites die?'

'May I have a glass of water, please?'

'You can - but answer the questions while someone brings you it.'

'He fell overboard as we were trying to make our getaway. He fell onto the propellers. Please, I need that water.'

'It's coming. Right, so what did you mean when you said, *'I can't do this anymore?'*

'Precisely that: Micky was dead. I had that on my conscience. I'd had enough.'

'Ah, so you do have a conscience. Pity you didn't have one when you put Miss Rachman and her parents through the mill. Or when you threatened to kill Miss Rachman.'

'I didn't want for any of that.'

'So, was anyone else involved in this scheme of yours? Or just you and Mr Thwaites?'

'Do I need answer that, Detective Sergeant? I mean, I'm admitting here and now that me and Micky were responsible. There, I've said it. Guilty, as charged. Cuff me now and just end it here.'

'No, we can't. Not until you tell us if there's a third party involved.'

'Alright, alright. Yes, there was a third party.'

'Who?'

'The Boss.'

'Divvent be a clever-arse, Wheatley. Who is The Boss?'

'Isn't it obvious?'

'I wouldn't ask if it was.'

'Okay. If you're that stupid, I'll spell it out for you. The Boss is Semilla Rachman.'

'Interview suspended.'

**

Interview with Semilla Rachman

'Detective Sergeant Ryan Jarrod is leading the interview, along with Detective Chief Inspector Stephen Danskin. Just to repeat, this is an informal, voluntary interview although you are entitled to legal representation if you wish.'

'I don't need any.'

'Good. First, I'm pleased to see you back in one piece. How are you feeling?'

'Pretty shaken up, really. Very shaken up, in fact.'

'I'm sure. Just take your time and you'll be okay. Your mother and father are on their way here. You'll be able to see them soon.'

'They're coming together?'
'Yes.'
'Wow.'
'You seem surprised.'
'They can't stand the sight of each other.'
'Perhaps all this has brought them closer.'
'No chance.'
'Is that why you planned all this: to get your parents back together?'
'…the fuck??'
'You did, didn't you? You knew you could twist Patrick Wheatley around your little finger. Use your influence on him. *'I'm the great Semilla Rachman,'* and all that bollocks.'
'Look, I don't know what you're thinking…'
'Who was Michael Thwaites?'
'I dunno. I'd never clapped eyes on him until that little worm Wheatley snatched me.'
'Why did he do that?'
'For the money, why do you think? Two-hundred grand would see him comfy for years.'
'Two-hundred grand? Who mentioned what the ransom was?'
'Umm..'
'How did you know the ransom was two-hundred thousand?'
'I heard them talking.'
'So, they kidnapped you but let you in on all their little secrets. Sounds odd to me.'
'I don't know what they were thinking, do I?'
'Two-hundred thousand pounds is a lot of money, Semilla.'
'Not to me, it's not. Do you know how much I'm worth?'
'Actually, I do. I've done a little bit of checking up and I know you're wealthy, but only in Russia. All your capital is

tied up. You can't get it until the war's over and you're recalled by the Bolshoi.'

'I'm not going back.'

'I'm sorry, I didn't quite capture what you said – could you speak up for the tape?'

'I said, *'I'm not going back,'* Detective Sergeant.'

'Right. And why would that be?'

'I hate the fucking place and I hate the fucking ballet. I hate all of it.'

'You do?'

'Aye. The rewards are great. The lifestyle superb. But, the regime – and I don't just mean the State – I mean the training routine. It's abusive, you know what I'm saying? In every sense. I'm knackered by it all. Run ragged. Pissed right-fucking-off.'

'Oh-kay. So, rather than get a nine-to-five job, you decided to rip your parents off to the tune of almost quarter-of-a-million.'

'Hah. They were nearly as bad as the Ruskies. Never giving me a normal childhood, always pushing me on, never letting it rest. My Dad was shagging everything in sight, my mother drinking like a fish to forget about it. I never had a proper childhood, Detective Sergeant, did you?'

'I think I did.'

'And your kids? What about them?'

'DCI Danskin taking up the questioning. Why didn't you get a proper job, like DS Jarrod suggested?'

'Why should I? I'm minted but I can't get my hands on it. Me folks are minted and they never gave me anything.'

'Except you wouldn't be where you are today without them, would you?'

'Wouldn't be where I am today? Like, here, in a police station dressed in shitty clothes being asked shitty questions by the likes of you, you mean?'

'Why didn't you ask the Russian authorities if you could have your money? Or even a portion of it?'

'You're Sergeant here didn't do enough homework on me and my family. If you did, you'd know.'

'Know what, Miss Rachman?'

'You'd know why I'm fucking terrified, that's why.'

'Why would you be terrified?'

'Because of Alexei Navalny, okay?'

'Miss Rachman, Navalny was a sworn enemy of Putin. I know you have a certain status but, really, I don't think Mr Putin would be interested in you.'

'Probably not but, like I said, if you'd done your homework…'

'What did I miss? Tell me.'

'My family name, that's what. It's Rachmanov. My great grandfather anglicised it when he came to Britain.'

'I see. So, your family originated in Russia.'

'They came from Otuz. It's now known as Shchebetovka. It's in the Crimea. That's Ukraine. I performed there after Russia invaded. A solo performance as a show of support to Ukraine.'

'Carry on.'

'I danced under the name of Milly Rich. I didn't think anyone would notice but the regime, it has eyes everywhere. Shortly after, I received a threat. I'd be given to the front-line troops as a toy for them to play with.'

'I'm sorry. I didn't know.'

'No, but perhaps now you realise why I staged the whole thing. If I got the ransom money, I could start a new life, incognito. If I got caught, I'd be safe in prison. I'd have preferred the former, but I think it'll be the latter.'

'Yes, Miss Rachman. I'm genuinely sorry to say I strongly suspect you will be going to jail.'

THIRTY-TWO

Seven days later

Ryan peeped round the door. Norman Jarrod was already there, so, too, Ryan's brother. James was dressed in his Lidl uniform ready to start his shift.

'How is she?' Ryan whispered.

'Nee change, son. It's a bloody horrible illness. Horrible.'

Doris Jarrod lay in bed, covers up to her chin, held there by skeletal fingers, despite the temperature in the room closing in on the surface of Mercury.

Ryan shrugged off his jacket and crouched down beside the bed.

'Hi Gran. It's me, Ryan.'

He stroked her fingers until she opened her eyes. They were glassy, vacant. In time, she lowered her eyes to her hand as if she'd only just felt Ryan's fingers against it.

She raised her head towards Ryan. One corner of her mouth twitched; the closest she could come to a smile.

'Hi Gran,' he said, again. 'How are you? Your hair's looking nice. Have you been to the hairdressers?'

Her eyes glazed over again.

'Have they said anything?' he asked.

James said, 'Only that...' he mouthed the rest in case Doris happened to understand, '*It won't be long.*'

Ryan's lips came together. Norman looked at the floor.

'Gran,' Ryan whispered. 'Wake up, please.'

The old woman's eyes flickered open. They still held the permanently perplexed look but, this time, Ryan saw a hint of recognition in them.

'Look, Dad's here as well. And wor James, too. We've all come to see you.' He lifted a sippy cup to Doris lips but she swatted it away with a weak waft of her hand.

Norman shifted uncomfortably. Ryan knew his dad had never really come to terms with his mother's condition. It was hard on him but, to his credit, he still visited her when Ryan wasn't around. More than James ever did.

'How's work gannin?' Ryan asked.

'It's humpin' stuff around the warehouse, man. What do you think it's like?'

'At least it's a job.'

'Aye. Pays for Muzzle's gaming.'

'I thought she might have come,' Ryan said, thinking an Emo with a love of all things dark might take something from such a depressing scene.

'Not today. She's been up all night playing with The Colonel.'

Ryan raised an eyebrow. 'I hope that's not a euphemism.'

'Nah. It's a bloke in Idaho. He's into Escapists.'

Ryan's other eyebrow raised.

'It's a computer game. They play on the internet.'

'Pleased I asked,' he said. Ryan heard the clunky lift lurch to a halt on the landing outside.

Doris Jarrod turned her head as far as she could.

'There's someone here to see you,' Ryan said.

The room door opened and Hannah entered, backwards. 'Sorry I'm late.'

Once inside, she turned. A tiny head and arms protruded from the sling carrier.

Ryan jumped up to meet her, beaming. He unfastened the clips and lifted his son above his head.

'Hiya, little legs. And how are you today? Are you good. Yes, you are; yes you are.'

James rolled his eyes. Ryan chose to ignore him. Instead, he approached Doris.

'Gran, meet your great-grandson. Isn't he gorgeous?'

Doris Jarrod raised a finger and gave a tentative wave towards the baby. A light came on in her eyes. She smiled. Then, something amazing happened. 'Who are you?' she said.

Ryan, Norman, and James looked at one another. Doris hadn't spoken for weeks, yet the words came out clear as a bell.

'This, Grandma', said Hannah. 'Is Daniel. He's Ryan and my little boy.'

'Divvent tell her the rest of his name, for God's sake,' James muttered.

Just for the hell of it, she did.

'Say hello to Daniel Roman Clark Jarrod.'

James chortled.

'I don't mind the Daniel bit. That's all reet, Norman said. 'I even quite like Roman. A touch of Ryan and Rhianne. Nice one. But I'll never, ever get the Clark bit.'

Ryan and Hannah shared a knowing smile. 'I don't know, Dad. We think it's a 'super' name.'

Hannah laughed. Astonishingly, Doris gave a chuckle. It might have been anything but, to Ryan, his grandmother saw the joke.

The old woman's eyes widened and she pointed at Hannah's hand.

'Aye', said Hannah, 'This is the ring you told Ryan to give to me. Your old engagement ring. Me and your Ryan, we're going to be married. Not yet, like. It'll be a few years yet but we're getting there.'

Ryan took Hannah's hand. 'I was going to tell you all but looks like Gran realised before either of you.'

'Ah, that's great news, man,' Norman said, hugging his son and kissing Hannah.'

'Aye, I suppose,' James mumbled.

They heard Doris' bedclothes rustle. She held an arm out towards Daniel.

'I don't think you can hold him, Gran,' Ryan said. 'Here.'

He took his son towards the bed. Lifted him towards her with both hands, his thumbs supporting the infant's neck.'

'He's tiny,' she slurred.

Ryan and Norman smiled and shook their heads in amazement.

Ryan let Daniel's legs rest on the blanket. As they touched the rough surface of the bedclothes, he instinctively twitched his toes and kicked out a leg.

'Is he dancing?' Doris asked.

'No,' Ryan laughed, 'He's not.'

'Here, Dad, do you want to take him for a minute.'

'Aye, son. I'd love to.'

Ryan helped Hannah off with her harness.

'All good?' he whispered.

'How would you be if you'd shat a bowling bowl?'

'Aye. You've got a point, like.'

She squeezed his backside and leant into him. 'We'll be able to have some fun again before long.'

'Shut up, man. Me Gran's here, never mind me faatha.'

'It's okay. She's asleep, man.'

Ryan looked at his father, happy as Larry cradling his first grandson. Even James had a smile on his face as he watched them together.

Ryan bent to kiss Doris on the forehead. She, too, had a smile on her face. His lips brushed his Grandmother's hairline.

Ryan stood up.

'Dad,' he said. 'I think she's gone.'

****

Colin Youngman

COMING NEXT FROM

COLIN YOUNGMAN:

METRO

A Ryan Jarrod Novel

*'The body of a young woman is discovered in the carriage of a Metro train.
She's not been murdered: she's been mutilated in the most horrific fashion.
Worse, she isn't the only one.
As the body count rises, Ryan is forced to enter the dark tunnels of a madman's mind.
Will he succeed in bringing the mayhem to an end – or is this the end for Ryan Jarrod?'*

Acknowledgement:

To you - for taking the time to read Sand Dancer. Your interest and support mean the world to me.

If you enjoyed this, the tenth Ryan Jarrod novel, please tell your family, friends, and colleagues. Word of mouth is an author's best friend so the more people who know, the greater my appreciation.

I welcome reviews of your experience, either on Amazon or Goodreads. Alternatively, you can 'Rate' the book after you finish reading on most Kindle devices, if you'd prefer.

If you'd like to be among the first to hear news about the next book in the series, or to discover release dates in advance, you can follow me by:

Clicking the 'Follow' button on my Amazon Author page
https://www.amazon.co.uk/Colin-Youngman/e/B01H9CNHQK

Liking/ following me on:
Facebook: @colin.youngman.author

Check my website:
https://colinyoungman-author.webador.co.uk/

Best of all:
Shout 'Free Beer' in the street.

Thanks again for your interest in my work.

Colin Youngman

About the Author:

Colin had his first written work published at the age of 9 when a contribution to children's comic *Sparky* brought him the rich rewards of a 10/- Postal Order and a transistor radio.

He was smitten by the writing bug and has gone on to have his work feature in publications for young adults, sports magazines, national newspapers, and travel guides before he moved to his first love: fiction.

Colin previously worked as a senior executive in the public sector. He lives in Northumberland, north-east England, and is an avid supporter of Newcastle United (don't laugh), a keen follower of Durham County Cricket Club, and has a family interest in British Gymnastics and the City of Newcastle Gymnastics Academy.

The Author's Other Work:

The Graveyard Shift (Ryan Jarrod Book Nine)
Bones of Callaley (Ryan Jarrod Book Eight
The Tower (Ryan Jarrod Book Seven)
Low Light (Ryan Jarrod Book Six)
Operation Sage (Ryan Jarrod Book Five)
High Level (Ryan Jarrod Book Four)
The Lighthouse Keeper (Ryan Jarrod Book Three)
The Girl On The Quay (Ryan Jarrod Book Two)
The Angel Falls (Ryan Jarrod Book One)

The Doom Brae Witch
Alley Rat
DEAD Heat
Twists (An anthology of novelettes)

****

Printed in Great Britain
by Amazon